ALEXA RILEY

Claimed

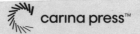

carina press™

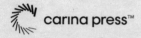

carina press™

ISBN-13: 978-1-335-28247-7

Claimed: A For Her Novel

For Heather Sage...

Diamonds are unbreakable.

Claimed

Prologue

Jordan

My breath echoes in my ears as I grip the gun in my hand. Adrenaline is pulsing through me, and it takes all of my control to focus, to turn the panic into action.

My legs burn, and my feet feel like they've got lead weights strapped to them, but I ignore it all because I can't fail. Someone has taken what belongs to me, and that was their final mistake. I'm going to rip their world apart and make them pay for daring to touch her.

I shake my head, unable to think about them putting their hands on my love. I can deal with that later. First, I have to make it to her while her heart still beats. There is no alternative.

"Stay alive," I whisper as I make it to the edge of the compound.

She owned me the moment I first saw her, and there's nothing I wouldn't go through to get her back. I close my eyes and picture Jay on her side, looking at me, the sun shining behind her. The way the light on her neck and shoulder made her look like an angel. It's the final image I hold in my heart as I step through the tree line and take back what's mine.

These guys don't know, but you can't steal what's already been claimed.

Chapter One

Jordan

"Yo, Pop!" I yell through the house as I close the front door behind me.

I can see through the kitchen out onto the back porch where he's sitting. I make my way out to him and glance around the place as I go.

This was my childhood home, so this place is more familiar to me than anywhere. Walking down the hall, I automatically kiss my fingers and touch the picture of my mom hanging on the wall as I pass, silently saying hello to her like every time I enter the house.

I grew up in Brooklyn, New York, in a small suburb on the edge of Queens. It was safe and clean, and when I was a kid I played for hours on the streets outside the house with my buddies. So many good memories surround this place, and I always feel safe when I come home.

My mom and dad were second-generation immigrants, so tradition is the most important thing. When my mom died when I was seventeen, I thought it might be the end of my dad. Hell, I'd thought it might be the end of me, too. She was the light of our lives and the center of our trio. Her death was also the reason for the scar on my face.

"There you are. Where's my scratch-off?"

My dad smiles, and the lines around his eyes crinkle. He's sitting on the back deck with the newspaper and a cup of coffee, his standard spot for Sunday afternoon. I finished up sparring with the guys and Paige, and headed out to spend the rest of my day relaxing with Dad like we do every Sunday.

I hand him his ticket, and he pulls a coin out of his pocket, kissing it before he starts scratching the ticket. I smile at him and shake my head. I guess we've both got our superstitions.

He doesn't buy the scratch-off tickets himself, so I have to do it for him. I think it's his own way of re-straining himself, and this way he's not responsible if he loses, I am. I come out to see him every Sunday, and this is always our routine. Sometimes I come home in the middle of the week, but he's so busy that most of the time he's not even home.

I'm lucky that my dad is still healthy and has a solid group of friends who keep him on the go. He's got more going on his social calendar in one week than I do in a month. It's nice not having to worry so much and to know that at least part of him is happy. I know he'll never get over losing Mom, just like I won't, but he's been able to live his life, and that's what she would've wanted.

When he's finished scratching, he's got a winner and slides it back to me. Then he puts the coin away and winks at me. "Press it for next week."

I put the winner in my pocket and nod, knowing he'll

probably hit another then, too. The old man has more luck than anybody I've ever met.

Pop leans forward and looks over the top of his bifocals. "How's our girl?"

I glance down at my watch and then roll my eyes. "That only took about five minutes this time."

His smile widens as he waits for me to answer him. I ignore him and try to change the subject. He's been on me about her for a while, knowing that I'm already in love with her. If it was up to him, we'd be married with grandbabies on the way.

"Your tomatoes are coming in."

"Oh, she's got you all twisted up today."

I grip the edges of the chair and try not to let him bait me. Pop can be like a dog with a bone when he wants.

"Already got her eyes on someone else?"

"No," I snap, and then realize I walked right into his trap. I let out a sigh and drop my head in my hands. "She's fine. Still the same."

"Ahh. You know, Jordan, I remember the first time I saw your mother."

"I know, Pop. You were at the middle school dance and spotted her on the other side of the room. She was the new girl in town, and you wanted to go over and introduce yourself. The rest was history."

He nods, then smiles and looks away, reliving the memory in his mind. There were times when he couldn't recall it without tears, but the older he gets, the more the memories stay happy ones. I wonder if it's because he thinks he's getting closer to the time when he can see her again.

Once he comes back from the stroll down memory lane, he shrugs one shoulder. "There's nothing wrong

with being friends first. It just means the first steps
will be the strongest. Take your time. But don't take
too long."

Pop picks up his crossword and goes back to it while
I sit there, silently brooding. He's right, but he doesn't
know the whole story. Or who I'm even hung up on.

I love my dad, but I don't tell him everything. He
knows me well enough to know I've got my eye on
someone. But I haven't told him her name. He also
knows me well enough to know that I haven't made a
move yet. But I haven't told him why.

How can I explain it? I guess I could come out and
say that I work with a woman so beautiful I can hardly
look her in the eyes. That before she spoke a word to
me, every cell in my body ached to reach for her. That
she's so utterly perfect, I'm not sure she even notices
me like that.

I rub my temples and think about how I've been
locked in the friend zone, with no means of escape.

Jay is the administrative assistant to Miles Osbourne,
so essentially, she's the gatekeeper for the entire company. If you need Miles, you go through her, but as the
old saying goes: though she be little, she is mighty.

She's small and perky, friendly to everyone she
meets. But there's a pit bull inside of her, and I've seen
her take a grown man down a few pegs on several oc-
casions.

The first time I saw her, I'd had to run up to the top
floor to deliver some intel to Miles. Ryan, my boss, had
asked me to run some documents upstairs because he
was on his way out. It wasn't anything above my security clearance, not that there wasn't something I couldn't
find if I wanted to, so it was an easy drop.

When I stepped off the elevator, I saw her. And that was that.

One look at her and I heard the voice of my father echoing in the back of my mind. *When you know, you know.* That first glance at Jay, and boy, did I know.

It was all a blur, but I'll never forget her chestnut-colored hair in a knot at the nape of her neck. The way her glasses slipped down her nose to reveal big, round, chocolate eyes looking at me expectantly. The way her top lip was fuller than the bottom, and how her fingers held her pen. All of that is burned into my brain, yet it feels like a dream.

Without realizing it, one second I was dropping off papers, and the next she was asking me if I wanted to eat in the cafeteria with her. I don't even think I answered her, I just followed along and got a tray of food. She was friendly and talked nonstop, but nothing beyond that. She kept her distance, and I'm pretty sure I only said about three words the whole time, but it was nice. The nicest meal I'd ever had.

"You're overthinking," my pop tuts, and I ignore him.

He's right, but it's complicated. Isn't it? I don't want to mess things up. I'd rather be in the friend zone with her than be nothing at all.

"I'm going to take a look at your computer and make sure you haven't turned that virus software off yet," I say, pushing away from the patio table and going in the house.

"The damn thing slows down my solitaire game," Pop yells from the porch, and I shake my head. That's all he thinks a computer is good for.

I spend the afternoon cleaning up his software and

then walking with him to the market and helping him bring groceries back home. We cook Sunday dinner, and some of his friends come over to eat and give me a hard time about not being married or having any kids yet.

Old men are almost as bad as the ladies. But these widowers are old softies to the core, and they all want grandkids. Some of them have their own, but apparently a lot is never enough.

When they break out the cards, I call it a night and head back into the city. I've got a place on the Upper East Side that I got for a deal when I was twenty-five. I've fixed it up, and though it's simple, it's palatial by New York standards, and it's all mine.

I take the subway back home and think about Jay the entire ride back. I always think about her this time of night. I wonder what she's doing, who she's with, and if she's thinking of me.

It's the worst part of the weekend, being away from her. And the reason why I love Mondays so much. Another chance to see her, another chance to be near her. It's the day I look forward to the most.

Chapter Two

Jay

I stare at my emails, willing Mr. Stein to respond. It's been two days and I haven't heard a peep from him on the Lannister reports he was supposed to turn in Monday. I'm starting to wonder what's really going on. This shouldn't be taking this long. I know my boss, Miles Osbourne, will ask me about the project soon, and not having a response isn't an option. This was supposed to be cleared up before he even left on his honeymoon. I hate not knowing an answer when asked a question. Picking up the phone, I call Mr. Stein's number for the third time this morning. This time it goes straight to voice mail, and I know he turned his phone off. I grit my teeth, placing the phone back down.

Normally I would go down to Mr. Stein's office and stand outside his door until I got what I needed. But he's been working from home for the last two weeks. It never fails that when I need something, there's no one to be found, but when people want Mr. Osbourne's attention, they're banging down the door. I wonder if there's a way to get his home address, but I change my mind thinking I can't just show up at his house. Can I? That might be a little too pushy, even for me.

Leaning back in my chair, I look at the clock and know my boss will be in any moment. I pull up his schedule and look at the seemingly endless list of things that need to be done. Mr. Osbourne has been out of the office for weeks on his honeymoon. I scan his agenda and debate what to go over with him first. I have a feeling it's going to be hard to get through the list. He didn't respond to any of my emails while he was gone. I wanted to keep him up to date on things, but I guess he took his honeymoon seriously.

I pull out my notebook and open it to where I'd left off. I want to enjoy the last few free moments I'll likely have today. I like coming in early and writing at my desk while it's quiet. It beats sitting at home in my tiny apartment, where my only window faces a brick wall.

My phone dings, and I see a text from Jim, one of the security guards who monitors the front entrance to the building.

Jim: Incoming.

Hopping up from my chair, I make my way to the break room on our floor and hit the start button on the coffee machine in case Mr. or Mrs. Osbourne would like something to drink. I'm guessing Mallory may not, since she's pregnant. Mr. Osborne hasn't come out and told me she's expecting, but with some of the purchases I've been making for him, she has to be.

The office has been different now that he's married. He's slowed down a lot. Things are shifting to a snail's pace, and I'm not sure how I really feel about that. Too much free time is starting to make me think about how pathetic my social life is. Or maybe it's watching my boss fall madly in love that's doing that to me. I thought men only fell head over heels like that in books.

Something is missing in my life, and I don't mean the Stein report. Stomping my foot, I head back to my desk just as Miles and Mallory exit the elevator.

"Sir," I say in greeting. "Coffee?" I ask. Mr. Osbourne reluctantly pulls his eyes away from his wife. Both of whom look like they spent most of their honeymoon in the sun. Their skin is sun-kissed, and they look pleasantly relaxed. He smiles at me, something he's been doing more and more since Mallory came around. Smiles had always been a rare thing on his face before her.

It looks good on him. The man who was always known to be ice-cold isn't so much anymore. I'm happy for him. I've been working at his side for years, and while others have thought of him as unfriendly, I knew otherwise.

"Morning, Jay, and no, thank you." He pulls his wife to him. "Maybe we should look into getting decaf," he says, making Mallory roll her eyes.

"I'm not drinking decaf. One cup of coffee in the morning isn't going to kill me."

"She's correct, Mr. Osbourne. One ten-ounce cup of coffee is permitted," I add. Mallory smiles in response.

"How do you know this shit?" he teases me.

"That's my job, sir," I remind him. Okay, maybe knowing these tidbits wasn't in my job description, but when he asked me to pick up a copy of *What to Expect When You're Expecting* a few months ago, I might have read it. I didn't know anything about babies except that they're cute and squishy and my boss was about to have one. I like to live by the motto that it's always best to be prepared.

"Can we stop with the 'sir' thing? You're making me feel old. We've been working together for over two years. Maybe you can call me Miles now?" He says it as a question, but it's not really one. Or maybe it is. He's my boss, so of course I'll call him whatever he asks me to. Though I know this isn't something he would have said months ago. I also stop myself from informing him I've been working for him for two years and nine days.

"Of course, Miles."

"I have to get to my desk. I'm sure I have a pile of things to get to, and Skyler has been blowing up my phone with ideas. I think she put us down to attend a few charity dinners," Mallory tells Miles as she tries to pull away from him. But he only holds her tighter. I make a mental note to email Skyler and get dates for any events so I can make sure there are no conflicts. Skyler and Mallory head Osbourne Corp.'s charities and share the floor with Miles and me.

"Lunch?" Miles says, pulling Mallory even closer. "I'll order from the Greek place you love."

I open my desk drawer and shuffle through the menus, looking for the right one. I grab it and set it on top of my folders. Glancing at my computer screen, I see that I'm going to have to cancel his lunch plans with the mayor. I skim my finger over my touch pad and delete the event, replacing it with a Miles-Mallory lunch. I inwardly smile at that one.

The mayor gives me the freaking creeps and doesn't know how to take no for an answer. He's pushy, and something feels off with him. I just can't seem to put my finger on what it is yet. It also means I'll be free for lunch now as I won't have to take notes during their meeting. My mind drifts to Jordan, and I wonder if he'd like to have lunch with me. I find my mind drifting there a lot.

I don't even know if he likes eating with me. He barely says three words when we have lunch together. But I like how he lets me talk. A lot of people around here don't like me. Being the boss's right hand has its perks, but it also comes with a ton of disadvantages. A lot of people don't think I've heard the whispers about me. The women always joke that I'm sleeping with the boss, and the men just say I'm a bitch. I do my best to ignore it all. I've worked hard to get this job and even harder to make sure I keep it.

Making friends at work hasn't been easy, but with Jordan, it's been really nice. Though sometimes I think they're pity lunches. He'll see me sitting alone and come sit down with me. Or I'll see him walk into the cafeteria and wave him down. What choice does he really have then? I've tried to flirt with him, but I think I'm doing it wrong. Or maybe he's just not into me like that. I'll take him as a friend if that's all I can have. I try to be honest with myself. The hot guy who can probably snap a woman in half with his muscles isn't going to go for the plain nerdy girl who should definitely lay off the bagels.

"Jay." I jump a little at Miles saying my name, realizing I got lost in my own thoughts about Jordan. Again.

"Sorry, sir. I mean, Miles," I rush to correct.

He cocks an eyebrow at me, and it's then I see Mallory is gone, and I wonder how long I was running off with my own thoughts. I pick up my folders.

"We have a million things," I tell him, getting myself

together, trying to push from my mind thoughts about a man who probably never thinks about me. My stomach does a little dip at that.

"I also have some things I need to get together as well."

"I made a folder on your computer about the best baby products," I tell him, anticipating what he was going to say.

"Am I that bad?" he asks as I follow him into his office. He is that bad, but it's sweet and endearing. It's making me wish for things I'd never thought of before. Not even in the silly little books I write when I can find the time.

"Yes, you're that bad. But I think all soon-to-be fathers are."

Chapter Three

Jordan

I turn to one of my monitors, and like every day, the first thing I do is pull up the calendar. When I see the change, my day improves. Jay is free for lunch now.

Some people might think I'm a little obsessed, and maybe I am, but having this much computer knowledge can't just go to waste. I know everything there is to know when it comes to hacking, and they've made it even easier here at Osbourne Corp. They've given me the keys to the castle, so of course I'm going to take a look around. Even more so when it comes to my obsession. I can't stop myself from checking in on her.

One of the first things I did when I met Jay was to go in and see what she was up to. Getting her calendar was the easiest way to do that. If anything, she's thorough, and her entire day is planned out to the minute on her work calendar. I know when I can bump into her. Make sure we're always running into one another. I could watch her on the cameras, but seeing her in person is so different. To be near her. To smell her and sneak small touches. It's all I have, but I soak up all I can get.

It's a little more difficult to predict her evenings as

she doesn't list her social life on her work schedule, but after a few lunches together, I realized that she doesn't seem to have one. That news shouldn't have made me as excited as it did, but I can't say I'm sorry about it.

I send her a quick email now that I know she's free to see if she wants to meet for lunch.

From: JChen@OsbourneCorp.net
Subject: Lunch?
You free today? I think they're serving potato soup.
J

I called down this morning first thing to see what they were having. The potato soup is her favorite, so this should do the trick.

From: JRose@OsbourneCorp.net
Subject: RE: Lunch
Perfect! I'm starving. Hope I can make it until noon.
Hungry like the wolf
Jay

My insides warm as I reply to her.

From: JChen@OsbourneCorp.net
Subject: RE: Lunch
Bottom left drawer. Thought you might have skipped this morning.

I wait half a second before my email pings.

From: JRose@OsbourneCorp.net
Subject: RE: Lunch

SHUUUUUTTT UUUUUUPP!!!!

Okay you've officially made my day and it's only 9 a.m. You get the biggest gold star out of everyone on my list. Pineapple muffin? It's like you're psychic.

Soups are on me at noon. Be there or be square.

I reply back with a gif of Yoda giving her a thumbs-up, then immediately regret it. I put my face in my hands and rub my eyes, wondering why I'm an idiot. No wonder she doesn't see me as anything more than a friend. I should have sent something cool and called her "babe" or "sweetheart." Something. Anything. But instead I sent an old man from *Star Wars* as a token of my love. This is why I'll remain single forever. Not that I want to be with just anyone. It's her that I want and I keep seeming to slide myself into the friend zone.

I groan, and I feel a paper clip hit the top of my head. I look up and see Paige shoot me the bird before she goes back to her computer screen.

She might know something is going on between Jay and me. She likes to know what everyone is up to, and she's spotted us in the cafeteria a time or two. Little does she know I'm solidly in the friend zone and keep reaffirming that with every email.

I was hoping today I could do something more suave. We had lunch Monday and Tuesday but I still couldn't bring myself to make a move. I know she loves the bakery down in Tribeca, so I took two subways to get her the pineapple muffin she's always talking about. It's her favorite, and she never takes the time to eat breakfast.

My plan for romancing her this morning didn't go so well, so maybe I can try again at lunch. I decide to work as much as I can before then to distract myself from the epic swing-and-a-miss.

In our security department, I run the background checks for all employees and potential employees. If you're interviewing with us, I'm the one who gets an extensive look into your past and then decides if you'd be a good fit. I also randomly research existing employees to make sure things are still copacetic. A few years ago, I found out that someone in finance had racked up a ton of debt and was slowly stealing from the company. It was only a few hundred dollars at the time, but they were well on their way to a bigger slice of pie.

Computers have always made sense to me. Women, not so much, and the problem with that is I've never tried to figure them out. Now I'm obsessed with Jay, and I have no clue how to go about it. I'm not the type of guy that sits around and talks about my feelings. Hell, I don't really talk much at all. I consider myself the strong, silent type, and it's seemed to work for me so far. I wouldn't say I'm shy, but I have no clue how to approach asking Jay out on a date.

I try to ignore my own thoughts and focus on the task at hand. I won't get anywhere brooding over how to get the woman of my dreams. Actions speak louder than words, and I'm going to try to focus on that.

By the time I go through three new employee files, I'm ready to blow up my computer. Don't people understand that social media is forever? It doesn't matter how long ago you posted it, I'll find it. Drunken college photos can be excused. But racist rants under a fake name on Twitter can't hide from me. Sorry New Hire Number Two, but you're out of here.

I check my watch and see that I have ten minutes

before I meet Jay. Pushing away from my desk, I raise my chin at Justice, letting him know I'm heading out. He's got his eyes on Paige but catches my motion and nods back. I roll my eyes at the two of them. Fresh off their honeymoon and they can't seem to stop eye-fucking one another.

I know it's jealousy on my part, so I try to shake it off. I want what they have, but with Jay.

I get on the elevator and punch the button for the caf-eteria. It was completely redone a while back, and now it's one of the best places to eat in a five-block radius. It's convenient for people who work in the building. Or people like me, who want some peace and quiet. Well, except for Jay. I'll take her noise any day of the week. I could sit and listen to her ramble for days. Sometimes I even record her without her knowing and play it back at night when I go to sleep. Just listening to her talk soothes me.

I get in line and order two soups and three grilled cheeses. Then I order two salads, yogurt, a side of chips, three chocolate chip cookies and a couple of Diet Cokes. I'll eat most of this, but I know Jay will make a sizable dent in it. She'll say she doesn't want any, but by the time lunch is over, she'll have gone through almost half. I like that she feels comfortable enough to eat around me. I hear horror stories of women who starve them-selves, but Jay doesn't look like that type of woman to me. She's all curves, and I'd love to caress every one of them.

She probably feels comfortable enough to eat most of my food because she doesn't look at me like someone she wants. My own insecurities are creeping in, and I have to fight to push them down. I made a promise to myself that today I would push outside the box and try something new. I'm going to attempt to flirt. But this may go terribly wrong.

I grab us some drinks and then pay before I sit down at our usual table. It's over in a corner by the window, and is somewhat private for a large cafeteria. As soon as I sit down, I spot her coming in the door.

She's wearing a deep purple dress that should be conservative by most standards. It's past her knees and has a high collar, so no cleavage is showing. It also has long sleeves with cuffs at the end. Nearly every inch of her is covered, but the way the material wraps around her hips and thighs ought to be illegal. I watch her move across the room, the longing I have for her pulsing through me.

I stand up and hold out her chair for her as she struts over and shakes her head at me.

"I told you lunch was on me today. You already played your royal flush with the pineapple muffin. You're going to make me feel like a jerk if you won't let me do something nice for you, too."

She says all this, but she's already sitting down and reaching for the grilled cheese and Diet Coke. I sit down next to her and pass her a napkin, hiding my smile. Her just having lunch with me is more than reward enough.

"Well, looks like everyone is back from the honeymoon. How are your love birds doing in security? God, I'm so jealous of Miles's and Mallory's tans. I'm practically a ghost next to the two of them."

"I think it's about the same so far," I say, passing her a cup of soup while I take one of the sandwiches.

"Can you imagine three weeks on a tropical island? I don't know what I'd do with myself. Probably get super sunburned because this fanny hasn't seen the light of day since *Friends* was on prime-time television."

I pause with my soup spoon halfway to my mouth as I look down Jay's body, thinking about her oiled up and lying in the sun, glistening with water droplets and smelling like coconuts. For just a moment I imagine my rough hands on her, rubbing in lotion and hearing her moan at my touch.

"Jordan?" She says my name like she's already said it a few times.

"What?" I say, grabbing the napkin and wiping away any drool that may have been on my chin.

"Are you okay? You look a little flushed." She reaches up, pressing the back of her hand to my forehead. "Hmm. You feel cool, but your cheeks are red."

"I'm fine," I say, ducking my head and taking a bite of the first thing I put my hand on. God, I've got to get the erection in my pants under control. There's no way I can stand up without putting out an eye.

"Anyway, I was saying how nice it would be to have a vacation where you just lie around practically naked for three weeks." She lets out a dreamy sigh.

I groan and try to cover it with a cough. Jesus, this woman has no idea what she's doing to me. I'm going to die from the ache in my balls. I just know it. Her not even knowing what she is doing is even more intoxicating.

"That would be nice," I manage to say without choking on my drink.

"Nice? God, that sounds like paradise. I wouldn't even need to pack. Just kidnap me and take me away. Absolute heaven."

I think about being the one to take her on that vacation, and I decide to push this time. Just a little. "I'll remember that when your birthday rolls around," I say, smiling at her.

A moment passes between us, and then a blush hits her cheek. She shrugs and gives me a playful pat on my hand. "Perfect. Just make sure you show up with a margarita."

Jay tells me about her day so far and what else she has to finish this afternoon. I love listening to her talk, so I don't say much. Just answer here and there to let her know she's got my full attention. But she always has that.

After our hour is almost up and we've both eaten all the food, she leans back in her chair and rubs her belly.

"Why do you always make me eat so much?" She gives me a wink, and my body lights up.

"You should eat more. You're too skinny." I grab her hand off her belly and wrap my fingers around her wrist. The touch is playful, but I've never done this before. "Look how skinny your wrist is."

She blushes again and sits up in her chair. But she doesn't take her hand from mine.

"Maybe you've just got bear paws for hands. Ever think of that?" Her voice is a little lower than before. She leans into me, and the smell of chocolate hits me.

I don't know where the courage comes from, but maybe it's just from months of frustration. I'm tired of being boxed in with her. I want Jay to see me as more than just a coworker she has lunch with. I want her to see me as a man. Preferably one she wants to rub up against.

"All the better to eat you with, my dear." I pull her hand closer to me and bring her knuckles up to my mouth. I brush my lips against them and then put her hand back on the table.

Her color deepens, and for a moment, she's speechless. I don't know if I went too far too fast, but I'm tired of pretending I don't want her, that I'm not a good enough man for her. I would give her anything she wanted and more. All she has to do is give me a sign. Let me know I can have her.

"That was a wolf that said that. Not a bear," she mumbles as she stands up abruptly. In her rush, her chair falls over, making a huge racket. People turn in our direction, and I can see that she's embarrassed as her face flushes even redder. "I have to go."

She practically runs out of the cafeteria before I can do anything. It all goes so fast it takes a second before I realize what happened and how she slipped through my fingers.

Once the shock wears off, I reach down and pick up her chair, straightening it. Ignoring the murmurs and the curious looks of my audience, I take the tray over to the trash. I pretend that no one witnessed what happened. And that no one saw Jay's reaction to me.

I have to tell myself this over and over as I make my way to the security floor and go into the private bathroom. Because once I'm in there, I can finally curse myself for what just happened.

Chapter Four

Jay

I shake my hand, but the tingles won't go away. All afternoon it's felt like there's a tickle right where Jordan kissed me. I can't seem to focus on anything but what happened.

Well, maybe not exactly *kissed*, but sweet lord, when that man's lips touched my skin I thought my body was going to combust right in the middle of the cafeteria. It was a simple touch, but it felt like more. It felt like something was shifting between us and I didn't know how to handle that.

"God, I'm such an idiot." I set my forehead down on the desk, and I want to crawl into a hole and disappear. I acted like a freaking spaz. He'll probably never ask me to lunch again, thinking I'm a nut like everyone else around here.

Could I have been any more dramatic in the way I ran out of there? The first time a man's ever touched me and I run like a group of angry villagers are chasing me.

"If you're going to nap on company time, you should do it in the spare office. That couch is super comfy."

I pop up and straighten in my chair to see Skyler

standing there, eating an apple with her hip against my desk. She's dressed in a white top with electric-blue trousers and pink heels. Mallory's partner on Osbourne's charity work is always dressed to wow.

"I'm not napping. I'm just dying of embarrassment," I say as I straighten papers that are already perfectly in line, like everything else on my desk.

"Let me guess. Your work bestie finally made his move?" She takes a bite of her apple and wiggles her eyebrows.

Skyler and I aren't close, but she's perceptive. We exchange friendly chat at work, and I've seen her having lunch downstairs. Apparently, she's seen me having lunch, too.

Jordan is the only one around here who talks to me about things other than work for the most part. Most seem to run when they see me coming, knowing I probably want something. Now I think I've lost my only friend here.

"I don't know what you're talking about." I pull up a document on my computer and begin typing nonsense so she thinks I'm busy.

"It's none of my business, but I've seen the way he looks at you." She shrugs and pushes off my desk, straightening up. "All I know is that Paige likes him, and she doesn't like anyone. He must be good people."

She walks away but leaves her words behind. They sit heavy on me, and I wonder if I've been reading things wrong this whole time. I know Jordan is a good guy. He's the best guy I've ever met, but that doesn't mean he wants me. He's always just been friendly with me. Sweet, even. If someone asked me who my best friend is, I'd say him.

The kiss on my hand today put me in a tailspin, and I don't like it. I'm direct, and I like to take control. Having that taken away from me is something I'm not used to, and I want it back. I'm not the kind of woman to shy away from confrontation, and I don't want to start now.

I can tackle this situation head-on and see what happens. Maybe he's into me and maybe he's not. But I don't want to sit around all day hating myself for acting like a lunatic at lunch. Giving myself a pep talk, I pull up my email and type with purpose.

From: JRose@OsbourneCorp.net
Subject: Tonight
I want to go to this wine and paint thing after work, but I don't want to go alone. Are you free?

I wait for what feels like hours but is possibly only seconds.

From: JChen@OsbourneCorp.net
Subject: RE: Tonight
Only if I can bring beer…and you promise not to laugh at my stick figures.

I feel myself smile for the first time since lunch, and I breathe a sigh of relief. Everything is okay.

From: JRose@OsbourneCorp.net
Subject: RE: Tonight
Yes, it's BYOB! And I promise.
Unless it's really terrible. Then I can't be held responsible.

Meet you downstairs after work. It's just a couple of blocks away.
PS Sorry I got weird at lunch.

I sit back and bite the edge of my thumb as I wait to see what he says back. I don't know why I'm panicking. I have a million things to do, yet this is keeping all of my attention. I just want us to be on the same page, but I have no clue what that is anymore.

When my email pings, I nearly jump out of my seat.

From: JChen@OsbourneCorp.net
Subject: RE: Tonight
I'll walk if you can keep up. Your short legs slow us down.

You weren't weird. You were beautiful. Just like every time I see you.

We'll talk more after work. You've got a meeting.
J

Just as I read the words in his email, a group of men and women come in, following Miles, and head for the boardroom. I stand up and greet them, offering coffee and drinks without missing a beat. Then I grab my notebook and follow them to take notes.

If any of them noticed that my face turned tomato red, no one said a word. And though I took eleven pages of notes, I couldn't tell you one damn thing they talked about in that meeting.

He called me beautiful.

Chapter Five

Jordan

"You know now you're just being dramatic," Jay says and lets out a little huff.

I laugh at her and nudge her with my elbow as I walk at a snail's pace for her to keep up. Her short legs are working overtime to keep up with my long strides, so I make a conscious effort to go as slow as I can.

"I can't help it if you've got mini legs," I tease.

She stomps as she walks, and huffs once more. It would be intimidating if it wasn't so damn cute. Everything she does is cute.

"You're about three seconds away from being uninvited to this," she growls, but her words carry no venom. She likes my teasing.

"But I already bought your wine." I hold up the brown bag along with my beer. "It would be a shame for this to go to waste."

She eyes the bag and then sticks her nose in the air as she continues to walk in silence.

"The Slim Jims alone are worth it. Aren't they?"

We stopped at the corner shop on the way to the art place, and I grabbed some of the jerky when I was checking out. I saw the way she looked at them, and no way was I passing up the chance to give her something I knew she wanted.

As we walk, I reach out and slip her hand into mine, and for a second she's startled, but then she tightens her hand around mine.

"Just want to make sure you don't try to run from me."

She looks down at our hands and then away just as quickly, but doesn't try to let go.

"Or maybe just so I can keep you from falling behind."

She gives me a glare, but again she doesn't try to take her hand away. I see her mouth pull at the edges as she fights a smile, so I take it as a good sign.

I was so thankful she emailed me this afternoon. I wasn't sure what to say to her, and I had composed and trashed about seventy-two emails before she finally gave me the opening I was desperate for. I had checked her schedule and then the cameras, so I knew we didn't have much time to talk. But I was happy that I was able to subtly let her know I was still very much interested in her.

"This is it," she says as we arrive at a small art studio.

We walk inside, and I look around to see rows of tables with canvases already in place. Jay walks over and talks to the lady at the desk, confirming that there are two of us here.

"Great. Looks like you two got the last spots." She looks me up and down and smiles brightly. "Oh, you're in for a treat. It's ladies' night."

It's then I realize the room is full of women, and all of them are looking our way.

Leaning down to Jay, I mumble out of the side of my mouth, "Ladies' night? Are you kidding me?"

She shrugs like she didn't know either.

Suddenly the stereo comes on, and Salt-N-Pepa's "Push It" rocks through the speakers. I hold in a groan as Jay laughs and pulls my hand to the front of the room.

We sit down, and I can feel people watching us as we settle down and pull out our drinks. Jay grabs one of the jerky sticks and leans back in her seat as the instructor begins.

As she talks about the process, I look around at our supplies and open a beer. I'm half listening when I hear the room erupt into catcalls worthy of a construction yard.

Looking up, I see a nearly naked male model walk across the room and take a seat at the stool directly in front of us. He's wearing a loose wrap around his waist, and when he spreads his legs, I hear the crowd whistle appreciatively.

"Jay?" I say, trying to avoid the direct view of another man's dick.

When she doesn't answer, I look over to see her snap the jerky stick in her mouth. Her cheeks are red and her eyes are wide. She stills, not even chewing the bite she just took.

Oh fuck no. There is no way I'm spending an hour with Jay looking at another man's junk. If she wants to draw a naked man I'll take her back to my house, give her all the art supplies she needs and she can draw me for fucking hours.

"Ma'am," I say, calling to the instructor.

She comes over, brightly bouncing on her feet and looking as helpful as an elf in Santa's workshop. "Yes, what can I help you with?" She can help me with my woman not looking at another man's junk.

I drop some bills on the table and stand up, grabbing Jay's hand. "Sorry, but the only cock either of us is looking at tonight is mine." I hear a few women give another catcall at my words. I grit my teeth a little more. Only Jay will ever be looking at my cock and I don't like the idea of them even thinking about my cock.

I hear a squeak of surprise from Jay as I pull her from the table and out of the building as the music and women behind us get louder.

When I've dragged her almost an entire block, she finally pulls on my hand to slow down. I know I'm moving too fast but I want her away from that other man as fast as possible.

"I'm um…um," she stammers, and I can see that her face is a bright shade of red. "I didn't know that was happening."

Suddenly she bursts into a fit of giggles, and I can't help but join her, some of my jealousy melting away. Not all of it but some. It's hard for me. I've wanted her from the moment I saw her and I don't like the idea of any man having her attention.

"Did you just take me to a strip club?" I ask as I pull her over to a bench near the park and we sit down close together, needing to be right next to her.

"I've never been to one. How am I supposed to know?" Her cheeks pinken even more and her sweet innocence is intoxicating. I want to lean over and feel the warmth of her blush with my lips.

"Me either," I admit and shrug.

"I thought all guys did that," she says, nudging me with her shoulder. It's playful and soft but somehow intimate but she looks over at me through her eyelashes and I can see the same spark of jealousy flash in her eyes. Clearly the idea of me seeing a woman naked is something she doesn't like. This gives me more hope that this friend zone is fast dissolving.

"Guess I missed that memo. I'm a perfect gentleman. I'd never take someone to a strip show on the first date. But you, you've got some balls, Rose," I tease, trying to making it more light.

"God, this would only happen to me." She shakes her head. "And I didn't say this was a date." I can see the shyness on her face from her words, and that's not a familiar look on her.

"You're right." I reach out and brush a strand of hair from her cheek. The need to touch her too strong to stop myself. "That was me. And I'd like a do-over."

She licks her lips, and I see how soft they are. I ache to take her in my arms and kiss her so completely that the only thought she ever has is of me.

"Another paint night?" Her voice is low, and there's more than just that question in it.

"A real date. Let me treat you like a lady." I bring her hand to my lips, but before I make contact, I look into her eyes. "No running this time."

I don't look away from her as I press my lips to her hand and then place it on my chest right over my heart, showing her this is happening. This isn't a friend thing. It's real. I'm going to make her mine. Well, make her know she's mine. To me she's been mine from the first time I saw her.

"Say yes," I tell her. Looking into her eyes.

"Yes." I feel tension leave my body at her one simple word, feeling closer to what I know my future is going to be. Her. I'm trying to be patient. To not push her too fast but it's hard. I don't want to scare my little bird with how much I feel for her. Cause if it was up to me I'd take her home with me and that's where she'd stay. Waking up every morning next to me.

We sit quietly for a long time as evening turns to night, and then I know it's time to take her home, but I don't want to. This is the first time she's shown me we can have more than friendship. I want to stay here all night, just sitting with her. Enjoying the moment for as long as I can because I know it's going to be hard to leave her at her door.

"I'll make sure you get home safe," I say, still holding her hand and hailing down a cab.

I open the door for her and slide in after her. The drive isn't too long, but she's walked far enough in her heels today, and I know her feet probably ache. I would love to offer her a foot rub, but not tonight. I think I've pushed enough for one day. I don't want to scare her off. Making her feel safe is more important than any need I have. Everything I do is for her. Her needs will always come before mine.

In the darkness of the cab, she leans over to me as we pull up outside her door. Her hand goes back to my chest, and I can feel her breath against my lips.

There's heat between us, a passion that's growing. It started as a small spark as friends, but the wind has changed, and there is a deep ember burning. I don't want to smother it too soon. When I finally take her, there will be no stopping it. I fear my control will snap and that's not something I want to push on her. I want her to want me as much as I want her but I'm not sure that will ever be possible. I don't think my need has a limit or bounds.

"Jordan?"

Her tone holds so many questions, and I understand each one.

"You're not the kind of woman that gets one night. You're worth a lifetime."

Her mouth opens a little at my words, and I lean down, brushing the softest kiss across her lips. It's not even close to what I desire, but it's enough for now. I lick my lips, wanting as much of a taste of her as I can get. Hoping it will be enough to get me through the night when I lie in bed alone thinking about her.

"Tomorrow," I whisper and place my forehead against hers. "Now get out of the cab before I change my mind." My voice is gruff and deeper than normal. I can hear my own need and have a touch of pain of having to let her go.

She smiles against my cheek as she places a soft kiss on the scar there.

As I watch her walk to her door and close it safely behind her, I touch the spot where her lips landed. She's the first person I've ever let close enough to do that. And she'll be the last.

Chapter Six

Jay

I turn from side to side, looking at myself in the mirror. I don't normally spend a lot of time on picking out clothes for work. I go with comfortable and professional. But today my eyes keep going to a pair of heels I bought on a whim last year. I've never worn them before. They've been in my closet from the moment I brought them home. They were an impulse buy one day when I was walking by a store. I saw them in the window and fell in love, even though they were way too tall for me.

They would be nice for my date tonight, though. Maybe I could try to be a little sexier. I wanted him to kiss me so bad last night. It was all I thought about after I got home and lay in bed. Could I even count what we did in the cab as a kiss? It was so soft and fast that I didn't have time to register what was happening. I run my fingers along my own lips, remembering how I kissed him on the cheek. It was bold and unlike me, but God I'd wanted my lips on him again.

I pick up the shoes and set them on the bed. They're a bold red, and I don't even know what to wear with them.

I dig through my closet and stop when I see a black halter dress I wore to a party for work a few months back. I could pair it with a blazer, and tonight, when I get off work, I can just take the blazer off to look more date-night-ready.

After putting on light makeup, I brush my hair out and pin a glossy section to the side before sliding my glasses on. I grab my bag and phone and head for the door. I see the error of my ways before I even make it to the end of my street. My shoes are already pinching my feet, and I can feel blisters forming. I have a feeling I'm also walking a little funny and making myself look awkward—not exactly what I was trying to go for today.

I hail a cab and wonder if maybe I should just go back and get different shoes, but they look so pretty. Sexy, even. I've never thought of myself as sexy before. When I get to my office building, I stop in the lobby when I see Mark, one of the security guards, staring at me with a smile pulling at his lips. I walk over to him and return the smile. Mark keeps an eye out for people I'm waiting to talk to. He lets me know when he sees them so I can cut them off and get what I need.

"You're all dolled up today," he says, and I smile at his compliment. He's never given me one before.

I eye him for a second before leaning in. "Do you think it's sexy?" I look down at my outfit, wanting a male's option. I want Jordan to like it. I want him to think I'm sexy. Not just cute. But desirable.

"Don't answer that question," I hear a deep voice growl from behind me, making me jump. I teeter in my heels, thrown off balance, and start to fall, but strong arms wrap around me in a tight hold. I look up at Jordan, who has me pressed to his body, keeping me from falling right on my face. He looks a little mad. His lips turned down in a frown.

"Hi," I whisper, and the frown on his face slowly slips away.

"You always look sexy," he says, so quietly that I know it's only for me to hear. I bite my lip as my cheeks burn. My heart does a flutter and I want to wrap my arms around his neck and have him brush his lips against mine again. I thought about it all night and want it again. Heck, I want more.

"My feet aren't on the ground," I finally say to him, becoming more and more aware of his tight grip on me. I like being in his arms. He makes me feel sexy and wanted. That he doesn't want to let me go.

Jordan lets out a deep breath, and I slide down his body until my feet touch the tile floor but his arms don't release me.

"Two o'clock, Jay," I hear Mark say, and then I realize I'd forgotten where I was for a moment. Mark's words snap me out of my daze, and I look to my right.

"Stein." My eyes narrow. I wiggle from Jordan's hold, and he reluctantly lets me go with a grunt.

"Get 'em," Mark says with a chuckle in his voice.

"She's not getting anyone."

This time, Jordan's words are loud enough for anyone around us to hear, but I don't pay them any attention. I've been trying to get ahold of this man for weeks now. He's not getting away.

"Mr. Stein!" I yell, not caring that we're on the lobby floor with people coming and going. Nope, not this time. He is going to talk to me.

He freezes at my voice, looks over at me, shakes his head, and begins to walk faster. I bet you anything he came in early to grab something off his desk, hoping to avoid running into me.

"Mr. Stein!" I yell again, chasing after him. I hear a muffled curse from behind me. I walk even faster, but these heels are slowing me down. I trip once again, almost falling over my feet, but like the last time, Jordan catches me as Mr. Stein slips from the building.

"I need that man." I point to him as if Jordan is going to chase him down for me and tackle him. I go to stomp my foot, but it seems I'm not standing on the floor again.

"I think maybe you should rephrase that."

It's then I realize what I said. "I need that man to do his job," I correct. Jordan places me on my feet, and smiles. "He's ignoring me, and it's driving me crazy. I need the Lannister report." I try to plead my case to Jordan, as if he even knows what the Lannister report is.

"I don't think anyone could ignore you." His words make all the anger and frustration I was feeling melt away so easily. He's so sweet. I don't think anyone can tell it by looking at him. He looks like he'd be rough around the edges, but he's not. At least not with me. He's the sweetest man I've ever met in my life.

"Do you think I look sexy?" I'm surprised at myself for what I just blurted out, and I drop my face into his chest, trying to hide what I'm sure is a cherry-red face.

"Do you really need me to answer that, little bird?"

"Little bird?" I ask, wondering what that means.

"You flit around from place to place. You remind me of a little blue jay. So smart and beautiful."

It takes me a moment to get myself together. Jordan just stands there, rubbing my back with a gentle hand. I thought he was going to laugh at me or something for being so crazy, but I pull back and finally get the courage to look at him. He's still wearing his soft smile, but he firms his hand on my back, pressing me further into him, and I nudge against what has to be a lead pipe in his pants. Either that or a very, very large erection.

"I'll get you your report, so don't worry about it. Why don't you think of what you want to do on our date tonight?"

"It can be anything?" I ask, feeling both nervous and excited. But maybe that has to do with the anaconda going down his leg.

"As long as the people around us aren't getting naked," he teases, and it makes me smile. I notice he didn't say *we* can't get naked, but I keep that thought to myself, having already almost died from embarrassment this morning.

He leans back a little and puts a few inches of space between us. I'm irritated by it, but then I realize he's probably got to tame that monster in his slacks or my libido is going to start salsa dancing all over him.

"I've always wanted to do one of the carriage rides in Central Park," I admit. I see people on them looking so happy and in love. I don't care if it's cheesy, I still want to do it.

"Then that's what we'll do," he replies easily.

Jordan takes my hand and leads me to the elevator, sliding his key card in. I know all the higher-security people have a fancy card that makes the elevator come directly to them, so it's nice I don't have to wait.

I eye the card for a minute. "You want one?" He holds up the little black card.

"Am I that easy to read?" I lick my lips and wonder what else he reads so easily about me. For some reason

I kind of like it. When it comes to him I can be shy at times. Something I'm not used to with people. I speak my mind but with him I care what he thinks.

"To me, yes. But I also watch you more than anyone else." He shrugs like it's normal to watch me. Then I wonder how often he does it. His security floor monitors the entire building, and they can see everything up there, even what we do on our computers, if they want to go looking.

The elevator doors open, and we both step in. He hits the button to my floor, and the doors close. I lean into him, wanting to be close. Something about him calms me. The chaos that often invades my mind, reminding me of things I need to do, people I need to talk to, slips away, and I'm left with a feeling of warmth and happiness. I think I could stand next to him and forget the rest of the world.

When the elevator dings, he puts his hand to my back and leads me to my desk.

"Have a good day, Jay," he tells me as I sit down in my chair. I look up at him, but he doesn't move, and I think maybe he's thinking about kissing me or something. He rests his hands on my desk, and leans down. I love how his big frame always makes me feel so small.

"No more asking men if you're sexy. You want someone to tell you that, you come find me." With that, he turns and leaves, heading back to the elevator, and I watch as he hits the button.

I see he left his key card on my desk. "Jordan," I say, picking it up as the elevator dings and he gets on.

"Keep it. In case you ever need to get to me faster. You know, if you need someone to tell you how sexy you look," he teases. With that, the elevator doors slide closed.

I don't know how long I sit there with butterflies dancing in my stomach, but eventually Skyler snaps her fingers in front of my face. "Earth to Jay."

"Sorry," I say, looking up at her. I take the card in my hand and slide it under my keyboard. I don't think I'll ever use the thing, but I find his giving it to me oddly sweet.

"I've never seen you sit still." She leans in a little. "Good sex will do that to you." She taps my desk before turning and leaving me alone. I've barely kissed him and I'm already this far gone. Sex could possibly put me in a coma.

I shake my head and turn on my computer, knowing I need to get to work. I glance at the clock and see Miles still hasn't made it in yet. He's prone to lateness sometimes now that he has Mallory in his life.

I fall into my work, but the time still seems to drag by. I'm usually focused at work, but this morning all I can think about is Jordan. He thinks I'm sexy. I smile thinking about it.

"Miss Rose." I look up to see Bryson standing before me with a box in his hand. He's worked in the mail room for as long as I've been around. We have an ongoing deal. He always brings me my mail first, and I always give him the special fudge I make at home once a month.

"Special delivery." He sets the box down on my desk. My name—and nothing else—is written on the top of the box.

"Thanks, Bryson." I smile at him, getting up from my chair to open the box. My mouth falls open when I see what's inside—a pair of flats with little bluebirds all over them. I pull them out and see a note at the bottom of the box. I pick it up and read it.

Wear these before you give me a heart attack. You almost tripped getting up from your desk when you went to get a drink.
-J

I slide on the flats and moan at not having on the heels anymore. They fit perfectly. Sitting back down in my chair, I pull up my emails to try to come up with what to write to him. How do I say thank you for such a great gift?

From: JRose@OsbourneCorp.net
Subject: Thank You
I love them. Our date hasn't even started and it's already wonderful. Lunch?

I hit send, and wait. A few moments later I get my reply.

From: JChen@OsbourneCorp.net
Subject: RE: Thank You
I can't today, but I promise I'll make it up to you.
J

I smile at the email and wonder if he's watching me right now.

Chapter Seven

Jordan

I sit back in my chair and mentally pat myself on the back. The smile on her face as she opened the gift was worth every penny of tracking down the shoes for her. Not that I don't have money to burn. It's not like I have much to spend it on other than myself, and it felt good to do something special for her. I'll buy her a thousand more if it keeps that smile on her face.

Hating that I have to miss lunch with her, I give myself one more minute of watching her before I get back to what's keeping me from her.

I watch as she tucks the box under her desk and straightens her paperwork. I can't sit here and watch her all day, even though I'd like to. So I close out the screen and go back to the one I really need.

"You want his files? You got it, little bird," I say to myself as I click away.

She wants a Lannister report from a Mr. Stein. That's not a lot to go on, but lucky for her, I've got plenty of ways to get what I want and what I want more than anything is to make sure she's happy. She doesn't need to be stressing about some dick not doing his job. I'm happy there's something I can handle for her.

I start by accessing her work computer and sorting through her documents with a keyword search on both. When I get the information on what Lannister is and what she needs, I set that off to the side to go through later. I don't need to know what's in there, just that Stein has something on it she needs. Then I run a file mirroring her emails so that when she receives one, I will on my end, too. The program I installed creates a carbon copy of all the information pertaining to this, which will come to her as well as my laptop. I copy all the codes to my personal drive and mark it on my desktop as Bluebird. Right now, it's not important, but if I have trouble sorting it out later, I can reference it here.

Next, I pull up the file on our employee Stein. After minimal searching, I gather all the human resource records and see that he's on an extended leave of absence due to continued medical issues. It makes me pause and wonder how Jay didn't know this. From all of our conversations, she's usually the first to know this kind of information on an employee. Especially one she's keeping close tabs on.

I scroll through several other documents and notice that his medical leave was due to his sick wife, and the file has been sealed. In my department, we have access to it all, so that may be why Jay wasn't able to find this.

It seems strange, though. Why wouldn't he just hand over the file she needs? Why all the sneaking around to avoid her? Jay can be a little bulldog when she wants, but for the most part she's harmless. Just give her what she asks for and she leaves you alone.

"Hey, Chen," McCoy says from the desk near me,

getting my attention. "You coming over to Grant's tonight to watch the Knicks?"

"He's out. He's got a hot date," Paige says, not looking up from her computer. She stuffs half a sandwich in her mouth as she keeps working, not missing a beat. I didn't know it was possible for someone to eat so much until I met her.

"A what? With who?" Sheppard pops up, and suddenly all eyes in the room are on me.

"And on that note, I've got a house call to make," I say, standing up from my desk. For some reason I don't want to talk about Jay to them. She's mine and I don't like others even thinking about her. If it was up to me they'd all believe she is a nun.

"He's going out with Jay," Paige says, with her mouth still full of food. "But he'll probably fuck it up. The friend zone is strong with that one." I grit my teeth. The friend zone might be there now but I'm going to bust though it. I don't care how hard and long it will take me but it will be happening.

"I've got a fifty that says different. Chicks love a friends-to-lovers story," McCoy says as if he knows everything about women.

"I'll take that bet," Sheppard agrees as Grant walks into the room.

"What bet?" he asks and looks around, wanting in on the gossip.

I roll my eyes as Paige chimes in again. "We're placing bets to see if Jordan can get out of the friend zone. Captain says a girl can't resist a scarred hero. I think Jay is smart enough to stay away."

Paige looks over at me and gives me the same smile a bratty sister would. We all think of her that way, so

I'm not surprised. But I can tell by the teasing smile she doesn't really mean her words.

"I've got work to do. But you gossips can sit around and talk about my love life all you want. Just let me know when to collect my winnings."

I pull out my wallet and take out the stack of cash inside, tossing it on Grant's desk as I walk out. I'll be getting my woman.

The jeers and ribbing continue even as the elevator doors close behind me. Let them think what they want. Jay has been mine from day one. Nothing is going to stop that.

The street outside the townhome is pristine. I walk up to the front door and ring the bell. It takes a moment, but I finally hear someone walking to the door. After a moment, a small elderly woman peeks through the glass then cracks the door slightly, clearly not wanting to let me in or even talk to me.

"May I help you?" Her tone is annoyed.

"Yes, I'm looking to speak with Martin Stein. It will only take a moment." I try to keep my tone easy trying to get her to open the door a little more.

"Mr. Stein is unavailable," she says, eyes narrowing.

"I apologize for the interruption, but I forgot to introduce myself. I'm Detective Chen with the homicide division of the New York Police Department. I just need him for a few questions, but if you prefer, I can come back with a uniformed officer." I press, seeing my first way of trying this isn't going to work.

Her eyes widen, and she looks around outside to see if the neighbors are watching, clearly not wanting a scene or to draw attention.

"Come in. Stand here," she says in a rush, trying to get me off her stoop.

I don't normally lie to grandmotherly types, but she seems like a mean one who wouldn't have given me cookies. So it's all fair game. Even more fair game when it comes to getting Jay something she wants.

I stand in the foyer as the little woman shuffles off. She didn't even ask for credentials. Not that it would have mattered. I could have talked my way through it. I've seen enough *CSI* shows to fake it.

The townhome is lavish. Much too expensive for the salary we're paying him. I should have dug a little deeper into his financials before getting here. I make a mental note to do that as soon as I get back. Wanting to make sure everything is on the up-and-up. Maybe he comes from money.

Looking around, I see a portrait of the guy I saw earlier this morning and a young blonde beside him. Seems like as young as she is in the painting, she should be in pristine health.

The sound of footsteps draws my attention, and I see Mr. Stein come around the corner. His face is blank, with no sign of emotion.

"What do you want?"

No greeting, no beating around the bush. I have to admit I like his style.

"I'm here on behalf of Osbourne Corporation to pick up the Lannister documents you still have."

I can see a tic in his jaw, betraying his irritation. For a fraction of a second he looks me over. I wonder if he's thinking he can take me in a fight. He must do some quick math and see that not only am I younger, stronger, and taller than him, but I'm also willing to fight. He's probably used his wallet to get out of scrapes since the time he could sign a check.

"Did that nosy little—"

"You don't want to finish that sentence," I cut him off, taking a step forward and widening my stance. "But if you'd like me to replace your tonsils with your nuts, go right ahead."

He shuts his mouth and flexes his jaw again. No one talks about Jay like that and thinks they can get away with it. "Fine. But it's not finished. I've spoken to personnel. My wife is sick, and I'm her full-time caregiver. I don't have time for this."

He walks over to a room just off the foyer, and I follow his path, not wanting him out of my sight until I get what I came for. He moves to the desk, closes an open file, and grabs the stack. He doesn't hesitate with his choice, letting me know he's looked at them recently.

"You know, as nice as this neighborhood is, I'd really hate to come back for another visit," I say, taking the stack from him. I'm not playing games with him.

I watch as his fists clench, and he goes to the other side of the desk and opens a drawer, pulling out another file folder and handing it over. I was calling his bluff, and it looks like it paid off. He doesn't know that I have no clue what this shit is, but I had a feeling a smug bastard like him would try to pull one over on Jay and that's not something I'll let happen.

"Tell that—" He stops himself and rethinks what he wants to say. "That's all of it. And if you need anything else, you can contact my lawyer. I'm speaking to the company about this kind of harassment."

"You do that," I say, smiling at him and walking out.

I have a feeling he isn't going to be with the company much longer.

I can't help feeling happy as I walk to the end of the block and flag down a cab. This stack of folders is going to make Jay's day. And seeing her happy is the only thing that matters to me.

Traffic is a fucking nightmare, so of course it takes me almost forty-five minutes to get to the other end of town. By the time I get back, lunch is long over and it's just over an hour before Jay finishes her day.

I go to the elevator, unable to wait a second more to give her the files. I reach down and scan the new pass I made for myself after giving Jay mine, and take it straight to the top.

When the doors open, I see she's not at her desk, but I can hear her voice in the distance. I place the files on her desk, neatly stacked, and wait a second to see if she's close to finishing up her conversation.

"That's very kind of you, Mr. Spencer, but I'm afraid that wouldn't be very professional."

I hear a deep voice mumble something, and then I hear Jay's voice become louder.

"Mr. Spencer, I will be sure to pass on anything you say to Mr. Osbourne, including the lewd comments."

I'm around the desk and down the hall so fast I nearly knock Jay over.

"Jordan." She says my name like I'm her walking savior come to save her soul. "Mr. Spencer, I'd like you to meet Jordan Chen. He's head of our technology department and works in security," she says proudly, and moves to stand beside me. "And he's a boxing champion and knows seventeen types of illegal punches."

I have to bite the inside of my cheek to keep from laughing, even though this scene is anything but funny.

The guy in the suit looks me over, and then his face reddens with embarrassment.

"Yes, of course. Forgive me, Miss Rose. I had a few cocktails while out with the board earlier. I think I've overstayed my welcome. If you'll excuse me…"

He ducks around me, because I refuse to move even an inch for him, and scurries to the elevator. He darts in, and I hear him hurriedly press the button several times before the doors close and he's on his way down.

"Seventeen types of illegal punches?" I ask, looking down at her and thinking she couldn't be more adorable.

She shrugs and smiles at me. "It sounded good in my head." She slips her hand into mine, and I love the feel of her soft, delicate fingers against my callused, rough ones and how easily she took my hand without a thought. "What do I owe you for coming to my rescue?"

She bats her eyelashes, and I want to pull her to me and kiss her until there's not a breath left in her lungs.

"I think I'll snowball it into the thanks you're going to give me after you see what I brought you."

"More pineapple muffins?" she asks brightly.

"Even better."

We walk around the edge of the desk, and she looks down at the files I laid there.

"Jordan Middle-Name-I-Don't-Know Chen, are you kidding me? How did you get this?"

"It's Isaiah. And it's probably better if you don't ask. But I'm pretty sure that's all of it. You can look it over and let me know if anything is missing," I tell her, because I'll go back and get anything she needs. "I'll always get you anything you need, little bird."

She's so happy I want to scoop her up in my arms and spin her around the room. But instead I play it cool and touch her cheek.

"I've got to tie up some things before the end of the day. Meet me in the lobby?" she asks.

"I'll be the one with the red rose," I say, winking at her and going over to the elevator.

"Very funny. I don't think I could miss you in a sea of people," she says, and her cheeks turn pink at her own words. Fuck I love when that happens because I know I'm getting to her. Making her fall for me.

Does she have any idea how fucking hot that is? Her soft sweetness is intoxicating.

"Later, little bird."

The elevator doors close, and I lean back against the wall. After a moment, I look up at the camera and smile, flipping it off. I hope the team got a good look at me launching out of the friend zone.

Chapter Eight

Jay

I stare down at the files with a smile pasted on my face. I can't believe he got them for me. I open them and try to look everything over but my mind keeps drifting back to Jordan daydreaming. I keep getting lost in my thoughts about him, wondering how this date will go. This isn't me. Normally I'd be focused but I can't seem to make myself with all these butterflies dancing in my stomach. I kind of like it though. This is so new to me.

I get through a few pages before I finally give up. I'll do it tomorrow when I can think straight. I don't want to miss something because my mind isn't focused and one more day isn't going to kill anything.

I dig through my desk, trying to find the dark red lipstick someone gave me last year for Christmas in the secret Santa exchange. Reaching all the way back, I lock my hands around the tube and pull it out, happy to see that it wasn't another pen. I look down at it in my hand and stare at it.

"I'm going to mess this up," I mutter to myself. Chap-Stick or gloss, I can do, but a red like this?

"Yeah, you are. That's a lip stain. Let me do it." I

look up to see Skyler standing at my desk, her bag over her shoulder, looking ready to leave.

"Really?" I ask, standing up and handing it to her. If anyone knows how to do makeup around here, it's her. Hers always looks flawless, even when she does fun things.

"Of course," she says, twisting the capsule open. "Open your mouth a little." I do as she says, parting my lips. After a couple of quick swipes, she's finished like it's the easiest thing in the world. "Color looks good on you." She closes the lipstick and hands it back to me.

"Thanks," I tell her, slipping it into my bag, then throwing my other things in with it and sliding it over my shoulder.

"You wanna walk down together?"

"Sure," I say, turning off my computer. Reaching under my keyboard, I grab the card Jordan gave me and grip it tightly. I've been playing with it all day. Or at least, I found myself slipping it through my fingers when I was working.

"Is that what I think it is?" Skyler squeaks, shaking her head. "God, women who date men in this building get the best freaking perks. Not that I haven't gotten to reap some of the benefits a few times." She laughs as we make our way to the elevator. "Swipe that thing. You don't have to wait for shit."

I laugh at how excited she is.

"I know you have plans tonight. I'm guessing from the lipstick and those heels you were trying to walk around in this morning." She smiles at me, and I wonder if office gossip is already buzzing and what they might be saying. I like the idea of people knowing Jordan is taken and mine.

"Did it really look like walking?"

She laughs. "I was trying to be nice. I'm a size seven, if you don't want them," she adds.

"Top right drawer. They're all yours."

I won't miss those things, and I know she'll wear the hell out of them. Even right now, she has on four-inch heels and can run around in them all day.

"Another perk."

The elevator dings, and we both step on. I know she's right. She and Mallory got moved up to the top floor because Mallory is my boss's obsession. Skyler got to come along, leaving their small cubicles behind.

"Anyway, some of us are going out tomorrow night. We do it most Fridays. You should come."

I turn to look at her. No one has ever invited me out from work. I know a lot of people go out at the end of the day for drinks, but not one invite has ever landed on my desk. I don't even think a lot of people like me around here. It's one of the downsides to being the wall between the boss and the rest of the world. *Annoying* is the word I hear myself being called the most. I never thought I cared, but for some reason, in this moment, a trace of wanting to fit in slips through me.

"Are you sure?" I question. Skyler hasn't been here long, so maybe she doesn't know the whispers about me being up here on the top floor. Also, I never have to bother her or Mallory for anything. They take what they do very seriously, and if I do bother them, it's only to lend a helping hand.

"Yes. It'll be fun. Maybe we can talk Mallory into coming. You know, to poke at the boss man. That's always fun to watch."

I should tell her that we shouldn't poke at him. My

job is to make sure he's poked as little as possible. But I have to admit, watching him chase Mallory around is always entertaining.

"I mean, we totally wouldn't intentionally provoke the boss man," she added, winking at me. Then her eyes go to the elevator camera before coming back to me. "Maybe you should have your new man delete this ride. Just to be safe and all."

"He's not my man," I toss back, thinking what it would be like if he were.

We get to the ground floor, and the elevator doors slide open. Straight ahead I see Jordan standing twenty feet from the elevator with a single red rose in his hand.

"You sure about that?' I hear Skyler say, but I can't take my eyes from Jordan. The elevator doors start to close, and Skyler reaches out, stopping them. "This is the part where you go to him." I hear her whispered laughter as she shakes me from my shock.

"Sorry," I mumble as I step off. I don't know why, but seeing him holding the rose makes this feel like a real date, something I've always wanted.

"Think about the drinks, and have fun," Skyler says as her goodbye and walks in the direction of the exit. Jordan moves toward me, and we meet in the middle.

"My rose." I can hear the excitement in my voice. God, I should be playing it cool, but I'm too happy.

"Your rose." He hands it to me. "I took the thorns off, so it should be fine. I would have gotten you more than one, but I know you wanted a carriage ride tonight and I didn't want you to have to carry them around and worry about them."

His words trail off, and I don't know if he's nervous or shy, but I can't focus on what he's saying. I can't stop staring at the rose. No one has ever given me flowers before. I look up at him, unsure of what to say. It's then I realize I've never been on a real date. Sure, maybe I'd grab a burger or pizza after studying with someone in college, but that was because everyone was hungry and had no choice when we had a project together.

I think back to the romance novels I love to read and write and think what would they do. Then it comes to me. I take the rose and break off the stem and try to slide it next to my ear. But the smooth move is screwed up when my glasses get in the way and it flutters to the floor, dropping a few petals along the way.

"Oh my God, I ruined it!" I try to bend down to pick it up just as Jordan does the same, and our heads knock together. I step back, feeling my face turn red, but Jordan leans down and picks up the rose. "I'm sorry, I thought..."

My words trail off when Jordan straightens and his hand comes to my breast. My eyes snap down, and I see he's putting the rose in the little pocket on my blazer.

"Wait, no—" I jump back from him once again. "I was supposed to take the blazer off!" I start to remove it, but I don't even get it halfway down my arms before Jordan stops me once again, pulling the small jacket back up my arms. "Maybe I should go back up the elevator and come down so we can start over. Or maybe I should just go. This is all a mess. Everything I—"

I'm cut off when his lips come down on mine. He softly brushes his mouth against mine but doesn't deepen the contact. I close my eyes and feel myself start to calm down as I relax into him. Letting everything else melt away as I fall into him. Just enjoying the closeness of him.

"Do me a favor, little bird. Keep the blazer on. I'm going to have a hard enough time keeping my hands off you as it is," he says against my lips.

"She's not kissing him back, so that's definitely still in the friend zone."

My cheeks warm as I remember we're in the lobby of our office building. I look over to see three men standing just a little ways away from us. I've never really met them, but I know their names are Sheppard, Grant, and McCoy. I try to know everyone who works for Miles.

Jordan growls, sending a look that could kill their way. They all chuckle, completely unfazed, before walking off.

"You growled," I tell him, as if he didn't know.

The deadly look drops from his face as he fixes his attention on me again. He finishes placing the red rose in my blazer pocket.

"I promise you, Jay. This is the best date I've ever been on and we haven't even started. Now come on." He grabs my hand and pulls me from the building.

I stop in my tracks when I see what's parked right outside. A horse-drawn carriage is there, waiting for us. I gasp at how pretty it is. I've never seen one like this in Central Park before. The whole thing is completely white, from the carriage to the horses; even the suit the driver has on is a snowy white. Both horses are wearing white feathers on the tops of their head, and I feel my face hurt from how big I'm smiling. I look back to the carriage to see thin rods radiating toward the top, forming a ball around the carriage itself. Lights are wrapped around them, creating Cinderella's perfect fairy tale.

"Oh. My. God," I whisper, stepping closer. Jordan helps me up into it, taking the seat next to me. He pulls a soft white blanket over our laps, and I see a picnic basket under it. "You're right. This is the best date ever."

I look up at him. His face is soft, and I never get why people think he looks scary. I don't see it. He always looks sweet to me. Handsome.

I drop my head to his shoulder, and he pulls me closer. "Not that I really had a lot of dates to compare this to. Have you ever done this before?"

I don't know what pushes me to ask the question, but sometimes things pop right out of my mouth when I need to know. I ask without thinking, and I'm not sure that's how you're supposed to do dating.

"Well, I've never had a girlfriend," he tells me. I glance back up at him as the carriage begins to move.

"Isn't that different? We're dating." I don't know why I want this to be clear. I know dating is more casual. I think people even date multiple people at a time. The idea of Jordan dating someone else makes my stomach turn. But if I was his girlfriend that would mean he was only mine.

He tenses a little next to me. Maybe I spoke wrong. Maybe he's thinking I'm pushing to be his girlfriend or something. Moving too fast. But Skyler's words about him being my man linger in my mind.

"I don't mean we have to label this or anything, I was wondering, you know, because—"

His mouth comes down on mine again, but this time it's not as soft as before. My body melts into his, and I moan when I feel his tongue trace the seam of my mouth. Just as I open to touch mine to his, he pulls back fast. I want to chase after his mouth and make him put it back on mine.

"I love how soft you become when I put my mouth on you," he says.

His mouth is still close enough that I can feel his breath on my lips, but not close enough that I have the courage to move in and take control. Definitely not after the whole girlfriend comment. My train of thought totally slipped my mind when he kissed me, and I got all flustered.

"There you go again," he laughs. I'm so close to him his laugh moves though my body. "Thinking too much. I don't want you to think I'm moving too fast, Jay. I'm terrified I'm going to scare you off. It's taken me a while to get you here."

"How long has it taken?" I ask, truly puzzled.

He stares at me for a moment, as if he's debating his words. "Since the moment I saw you, I wanted you to be mine. And only mine."

I smile at him and lay my head back down on his shoulder. I like the sound of that. Because I've wanted him just as long.

Chapter Nine

Jordan

I hold Jay close as the horses weave their way through the street and into the park. I've planned for us to ride down to the lake and have a picnic dinner.

But after only a short time, I start to smell it.

"Oh, that's pretty strong," Jay says, covering her nose.

I laugh it off and try not to let it bother me. "Yeah, nature of the beast, I guess. If you're going to sit behind horses, I guess you expect it to smell."

"Yeah, I'm sure the wind will change once we're closer in," she says, smiling at me.

I go to lean down and kiss her again, unable to control myself. But another waft of horse shit lands between us, and the mood is ruined.

Jay begins to cough. "God, I think I swallowed some of the smell," she sputters, her eyes watering.

"Let me see if there's a problem." I try to comfort her as I get up from the bench seat and sit forward, getting the driver's attention. "Hey, is everything okay?"

He looks back at me, and I see he's got a half mask over his mouth and nose. "Sorry, one of the horses is having a bit of a rough go of it," he says in a thick British accent. "Musta got in something."

Just then I can hear the sounds of the horse relieving himself, and I don't look down to see the aftermath.

"Just take us straight to the lake," I say as he picks up the pace.

Leaning back, I look over at Jay, who still has her hand over her nose. "I'm sorry," I say, hating that tonight isn't going perfectly. "Guess our horse has the runs."

She starts to laugh, and pretty soon I'm joining in with her. I guess sometimes that's all you can do.

We grin and bear it as we get close to the lake, and blessedly, when we get there, the smell is gone. I jump down out of the carriage and hold out my hands, taking Jay by the waist and picking her up. Slowly, I lower her to the ground, letting her rub against my body as I do.

"I couldn't resist," I say, winking at her.

"And you didn't even apologize." Her cheeks are pink, but she hasn't tried to pull away.

"I'll never apologize for what I want when it comes to you." I reach into the carriage to grab the picnic basket, and help her down to the lake.

"Thank you again for the flats," she says as we follow the path closer to the water.

"I like when you look happy. And those heels did not make you look happy."

I squeeze her hand, and the look she gives me squeezes my heart. God, this woman is going to break me in two.

When we get to the edge of the water, I take out the blanket and spread it out. The grass is soft but dry, and I help her sit down as I unpack the food and join her.

"I ordered takeout from the deli you like. I thought

finger foods might be best," I say, opening the containers and spreading them out around us.

She reaches for one of the cherry tomatoes and hums as she eats it. "They have the best food."

We eat while we laugh and talk, just being our normal selves. Time goes by, and the sun begins to set, but it feels like we've only been here for a few minutes. I wonder if being friends first didn't help ease us into this. I never wanted to only be her friend, but it was the best way to get her to know me. And to see that I'm not as scary as some people act.

"How'd you get your scar?" she asks, nodding at my cheek. "It's not something we've ever talked about, but you seem to try to hide it sometimes."

I didn't realize that was a conscious maneuver, but if she noticed it then I must be doing it. I pause, thinking about how to tell her, and she takes my hesitation as something more.

"I'm sorry. That was rude. I'm sure it's personal and—"

"No, I was just trying to think of a way to tell you without making you feel sad." I shrug and let out a breath. "But there's no way to do that. I've told you about my parents and how my mom died when I was in high school. She was hit by a drunk driver, and I was in the car with her. My face hit the passenger side window, and that's how I got it."

"Oh, Jordan, I'm so sorry." She puts her hands on her mouth like she can take the question back. Then she puts her hand on my face like she can take the hurt away.

Maybe she can.

"Thank you. It was a long time ago. I miss her, but we've had to learn to heal. She would have wanted that."

"And you still go see your father every week?" She smiles now, remembering the stories I've told her about Pop.

"Every week. The man loves his scratch-off tickets." I place her hand in mine and bring it to my mouth, kissing the palm. "Come visit him with me on Sunday."

Her eyes widen in surprise, but then she nods excitedly. "Yeah, that sounds like fun."

"I'll just have to warn him to keep his hands to himself." I trace my finger along her jaw, and she leans into my touch. "I have a hard enough time as it is."

Unable to stand it any longer, I take her face in both my hands and press my lips to hers. Almost immediately, she's opening for me, allowing me to take control and taste all of her sweetness. I moan around her lips when I feel her tongue touch mine.

Before I know what's happening, I've pulled her onto my lap, cradling her, her legs to one side. I've got both arms wrapped around her back as I hold her close to me, and she dips her hands in my hair.

I run my fingers down her side and to her hip, squeezing her there. Then I move them lower, brushing against the warm, exposed skin just below the hem of her dress. I ache to move my hand under it, to touch between her legs and see how wet she is. Wet for me.

She moans my name as my mouth moves to her neck, and I kiss her soft skin there.

"You drive me crazy, little bird," I growl, sucking the skin under her ear, praying I leave a mark.

"Are people going to see us?" she whispers, but she

doesn't stop. She's holding on to me just as fiercely as I'm holding on to her.

"Would it bother you if they did?" I bite her earlobe and feel her shiver. "If someone saw you being kissed like they could only dream of? If someone watched me hold the most beautiful woman in the world and make love to her with my lips?"

I kiss a trail down her neck to the center of her chest.

"When you put it like that…" she says, but she doesn't finish her sentence.

Kissing my way back up, I take her lips again, and this time it's even more intense. We are becoming crazed for one another, and now it might not be such a good idea to be in public.

"Take me home," she moans, echoing my own thoughts.

I stand up, holding her in my arms, and she laughs. The sound is music to my ears, and it's all I ever want to hear.

Just as I take a step, the edge of the blanket catches on my shoes. Jay thinks I'm going to drop her, so she tries to put her feet down at the same time I try to turn with her. The entire thing happens so fast I don't have time to tell her no before she's out of my arms and kneeing me in the balls as I fall backwards.

I hear a scream before I stumble back and hit the water, and as I'm submerged in the lake, I don't know if the sound came from her or from me.

"Are you sure you won't come up?" Jay asks with a disappointed look on her face.

"I honestly wish I could, but I'm afraid I might give your apartment E. coli. That lake isn't exactly sanitary."

A smile tugs at her lips, and she leans up to kiss me. As much as I hate it, I have to take a step back. I can smell the fishy stench on me, and I couldn't allow myself to do that to her.

The climb out of the lake was a mess, and even more so because my balls ached so bad. I think she apologized a hundred times, but no matter what I said, she still felt bad.

"This only half counts as a date. Tomorrow, we get a do-over."

That seems to brighten her up a little, and she nods. "Why don't you come over and let me cook for you?" I like the idea. We could end up spending the whole weekend together if I'm lucky.

"Do you own a fire extinguisher and have the fire department number handy? I'm not saying you're a bad cook, I just want to cover my bases."

"We could always order in, if it makes you feel better. But I'm pretty good in the kitchen." She winks at me and then turns, walking up the steps and into her building.

"Goddamn, woman, you are something special."

Just then I hear the horses behind me and roll my eyes. The carriage driver gives me a thumbs-up, and I bury my head in my hands. After a second, I climb into the Cinderella carriage and lean back in the seat.

"Let's go," I say, and take the ride to my place next.

Chapter Ten

Jay

"You're in early. Even for you." I look up, taking my head out of my hands to see Skyler standing there, coffee in one hand and her bag in the other. It's not even seven a.m. and she looks all done up and ready to go. "Oh no." She drops her bag on the floor and sets her coffee on my desk before leaning up against it. "Did the date go that bad?"

I run my hand through my hair, trying to make sure it's all in place. "Is it that noticeable?"

I didn't put in much effort this morning, just grabbed the first thing I found in my closet, which was a black flowy skirt that comes to my knees, and a simple light pink button-up shirt. I push my glasses back up my nose, frustrated that I'm so easy to read.

"No, you look great. Your eyes are just sad."

I let out a deep breath and give in. I tell her about the date and every horrible, sweet detail of it. That date was terrible, but it was wonderful, too. When I left Jordan, I was excited and happy, even with everything that had happened. He's asked me out on another date, but the more I sat and thought on it last night, I think he was trying to be nice. I almost killed the man. Well, *killed him* might be an exaggeration, but still. He'd backed away from my kiss at the end of the night. I tried to play it cool like it didn't bother me, making a joke and smiling, but it kept replaying over and over in my head as I tossed and turned last night.

"Yeah, that's pretty bad."

"I know." I drop my head back into my hands and cringe.

I feel Skyler's hand on my shoulder in a reassuring hold.

"It would almost be outrageously funny if I didn't like him so much. The worst part is, what if he slowly starts to back away from me? I'll lose the only friend I have around here."

"Hey, you've got me. And we're having drinks tonight," she reminds me.

I remember I told Jordan I would cook for him tonight. Maybe this is a way I can get out of that. Give myself some time to clear my head and not feel so sorry for myself.

"You still want me to come?" I ask, thinking maybe she might have told someone she invited me and other coworkers gave her crap about it.

"Hell yeah." She gives my shoulder another squeeze.

We both look over as the elevator dings, and Mallory and Miles exit together, holding hands. A small smile pulls at my lips. That always happens when I see them together. They're so in love. He chased after her for years and would do anything for Mallory. She is his everything. I want a love like that. Jordan flutters through my mind.

"Hey, lovebirds," Skyler says, getting up from my desk and grabbing her bag and coffee.

"Hey." Mallory smiles back while Miles gives a nod.

"Mal, drinks tonight."

"She can't drink, she's pregnant," Miles throws out instantly, as if we don't know she's pregnant. From the way he is with her, to the small bump that is already showing, we've got the picture.

"They have small plates there, too. Paige and Mal love small plates." I bite the inside of my cheek to keep from smiling as a scowl forms on Miles's face. He clearly didn't want her to go. If it was up to him she'd be trapped away in their condo, where they'd never leave.

"I do love small plates," Mallory says dreamily.

"Sir," I say, standing as they get closer to my desk.

"Give me ten, Jay."

I nod and sit back down in my chair as he starts to pull Mallory into his office. As she's being pulled away, she shouts over her shoulder that she's in, and then we hear the office door lock.

I put my hand over my mouth to keep from laughing out loud. I know he's in there trying to convince her to not go but in the end Mallory will win because Miles can't help but give her what she wants even if he doesn't want her doing it.

"More like thirty minutes," Skyler says, wiggling her eyebrows and making me giggle harder behind my hand. "Tonight." She taps my desk in farewell and walks away.

There was no question in her statement. She said I'm going, and truth be told, it will probably be good for me. All the other ladies are in relationships, so maybe I can pick their brains. I'm terrible at relationship stuff. One would think someone who reads and writes romance as much as I do would be better at it.

I can't even go off my own parents' relationship. They're still happily married to this day. While I love them both, I'm not into the free love they both espouse with their hippie lifestyle, but my sister seems totally okay with it. I never wanted to be the oddball in the family, but I always felt like a prude compared to them. I was the one who didn't know how to relax and have a good time.

Maybe that's why I kept messing everything up with Jordan. I worry too much, like I do with everything, but I can't turn it off. Except when he's kissing me. I can't work through a single thought when his lips are on mine.

Before I let my mind wander down that daydream path, I click on my keyboard, deciding to email Jordan. I texted him last night, but he didn't respond, which wasn't like him. That was when all my worrying about our date started.

From: JRose@OsbourneCorp.net
Subject: Cooking
Sorry, but I have to cancel tonight. I forgot I told Skyler I'd go out for a drink with her and some people from work when we get off.
    Hope you have a pleasant day.
Jay

Blah. God, that sounds terrible. I hit Send and wish I could snatch the email back. *Hope you have a pleasant day.* What is wrong with me? I shake my head at myself. I stare at my computer for minutes, but no response comes. I don't know how long I've sat there when the door to Miles's office opens and Mallory comes out.

"Small plates are on." She winks at me as she walks by, her hair a little ruffled.

I shake my head and smile.

Grabbing my notepad, I give a knock before entering Miles's office and get back to work. We go over what needs to be done today and other projects in the works. I've been noticing our workload is getting less and less with him handing off more projects to different department heads. It gives me more free time, but I'm not sure how I feel about that. I like staying busy.

Everyone he entrusts seems competent, and I haven't had to chase them down. Except one. I roll my eyes thinking about what Jordan had to do to get that file—the file that still isn't adding up.

I go back to my desk and get to work on the items Miles has flagged as urgent. Setting up some meetings and drafting some emails, I keep busy with what I know. I can do this all day every day, and it keeps my mind from drifting places I don't want it to go.

When I look at the clock and see the time, I call in lunch for Miles, Mallory, and Skyler, and then order something for myself, too. I don't want to run into Jordan in the cafeteria. I can't even bring myself to check to see if he's emailed me back. It's easier to get lost in my work than to have to deal with the embarrassment I'm still feeling.

When the food comes, I take Miles's and Mallory's into Miles's office and drop Skyler's off, too. She normally eats at her desk while she works. If she doesn't eat at her desk, it means she's using her lunchtime to shop.

I set mine on my desk next to me, but I don't really

feel hungry. I head to the small break room to grab a drink from the fridge but stop still when I turn around and see Jordan standing in the doorway. The room isn't big as we don't need a giant room with so few of us on this floor.

He walks toward me without uttering a word. He takes the drink from my hand and places it on the counter. He looks just as handsome today as he does every day. But today there's an edge to him. Or maybe he's on the edge. Something about it—him—makes my breathing heavier, and not because I'm scared. It's because I'm instantly turned on by the look he's giving me. Like he's a predator and I'm his prey.

I take a step away, and he follows until my back hits the wall. Everything we did in the park on our picnic comes flooding back, the wonderful things he made me feel, how he got me to lose control and not care about anything but the two of us.

"You've been ignoring me, little bird," he says. His voice sounds deeper than normal. I tilt my head back so I can look him in the eyes.

"I have not. I texted you three times last night and you didn't respond. Then I sent you an email. In fact, I think I might even be pestering you." I try to say the words in a stern voice, like the one I use at the office when I have to scold people.

"Hmm," he says, leaning down, his nose coming to my neck and traveling up. Then I feel his lips on me as he places small kisses up and down my neck. My eyes fall closed, and I turn my head to the side, giving him more of me.

"That tone won't work on me, babe," he informs me

as he presses into me, and I feel his hard erection between my legs. His mouth moves to my ear.

"I had to get a new phone this morning. Mine didn't survive the water last night."

"Oh?" I only half hear his words. I lean into his lips, wanting him to go back to kissing my neck. He chuckles, and his mouth goes back to it. I reach up, wanting to have my hands on him. I run my fingers through his hair as I try to rock against him.

"Fuck. You're lucky I turned off the cameras in here," he growls, and I feel us moving, but I don't open my eyes. My back lands against another wall. "Take what you want, little bird. I came up here to give you what you need."

I don't really understand his words, but I keep moving against him. The thick ridge of his cock hits me perfectly between my legs as I wrap my thighs around his waist. My lips go to his, and suddenly I'm hungry for him. My orgasm climbs closer to the surface as I rub my center over the hard line of his stiff length. Everything about him is so perfect against me, and I moan for more.

He grips my hips hard, and I start to come undone. He consumes my pleasure with his mouth as my body can't hold back any longer.

My orgasm explodes through me, and he kisses my cries of satisfaction, trying to quiet them. As I pulse, and as warmth floods my body, his body jerks against me, and he groans.

I pull my mouth from his, burying my face in his neck and trying to catch my breath. I'm wrapped around him, up against the wall of the break room, and I've just been given the most intense orgasm of my life.

I hold on to him, breathing in his scent and marking it on my skin. My eyes are still closed. I don't want to leave this moment and go back to all the thoughts I was having before.

"You feel better now, little bird?" I hear him ask, and finally I get the energy to lean back and look him in the eyes.

"I, well, I—"

"I know. You got caught up in your head, probably thinking something that isn't true."

"Maybe," I admit.

"My phone crapped out on me last night, so I went to get a new one this morning first thing. Otherwise, you would've had me walking you to work while you ate one of your muffins."

"I'm sorry."

"I don't care about the phone. I only care that you thought I was ignoring you. I would never ignore you. It's impossible for me to do that."

I smile at his admission. I lean in, brushing my lips against his. I should have known better. *My Jordan would never do that.*

"No, I wouldn't."

"Crap. I said that out loud." Heat hits my cheeks.

"I liked it. So keep on saying it. I told you that you've been mine for as long as I've known you. Even if we weren't together like this then. So trust me, I've been yours before you ever knew it."

God, I love that. "Did you get my email?" I ask.

"Yes, and I responded, but you haven't checked your emails in a while." I'm not going to ask how he knows that, because I have a pretty good idea it has to do with breaking security rules. "Then I watched you drown yourself in work, getting lost in your head, so I waited for my moment."

"You waited?"

"Yeah. I've been trying to get a chance to get you alone. Because we both know when I get my hands on you, your mind calms."

I melt even more into him. "I do, don't I?"

"I like it. It means you need me, and I fucking love the idea of you needing me." He leans in, kissing me again. This time it's soft and sweet, but he pulls back before I want it to end.

"I better let you get back to your desk before someone comes looking for you."

"Oh crap! I forgot where I was." I look around like my surroundings are new. My gaze darts to the camera in the corner.

"I turned it off. No one saw anything," he tells me, putting me back down on my feet.

"About tonight…"

"You'll make it up to me. I get you all day tomorrow."

"You can come, too, if you want. Meet us there. I think the girls and I are walking over together. I'm not sure where we're going. Skyler didn't say, but she said work people are coming, and you work here, too."

"You want me to be there?"

"Yes," I say instantly.

"I'll be there." He leans in, placing another kiss on my lips. "Until then, little bird." He walks over, picks up the drink I'd forgotten about, and hands it to me. He opens the door for me and follows me back to my desk before giving me another quick kiss and exiting onto the elevator. I can't help but watch him go, thinking how silly I was being and how I let myself get so worked up over nothing. I'm actually mad at myself for thinking he would do something like that. I've known Jordan for a while now, and he's not that kind of guy.

I shake my head and eat my lunch while clicking the email Jordan sent me this morning. It was sent long after I went into Miles's office for our morning meeting.

From: JChen@OsbourneCorp.net
Subject: RE: Cooking
No worries, little bird. You can make it up to me by giving me your whole Saturday, and maybe even your lunch break today.

I wanted to let you know I had to get a new phone this morning. If you texted me last night, there's a chance I didn't get it.

I miss you, and I'll be coming for the goodnight kiss I didn't get last night as soon as I can.
J

I look down at my lunch, feeling guilty. If I had read that email this morning, I could be having lunch with him right now. But then I wouldn't have gotten him in the break room just now. Something about him seemed a little different in there. That was a side of him I'd never seen before.

My email pings again, and I see it's a new email from Jordan.

From: JChen@OsbourneCorp.net
Subject: Smile
Smile, little bird. I had the best tasting lunch a man could ask for in your break room.

I glance up at the camera and smile. Then I end up blushing, which is what I seem to do a lot around him anyway.

I click out of my emails and get back to work. I'm glad that I have a stack of things to do today. It will keep me busy so time won't pass so slowly until I see Jordan again. When the time nears five o'clock, I start packing up my desk. I go over my last emails to try to clear them out, answering the ones I can and forwarding the ones I'm unsure of directly to Miles.

As I'm working, one pops up.

From: anonymous3640@gmail.com
Subject: none
Watch your step, you little bitch. Or you won't be smiling much longer.

I read the email and roll my eyes. For half a second, I think maybe I should send it to Jordan, but then I decide not to. I've been called worse and threatened before. Most of our corporate mergers piss someone off, and my email address is on our website. Disgruntled employees create fake accounts and send me hate mail at least once a week. This doesn't even make the top fifty.

"You ready?"

I look up to see Mallory and Skyler standing in front of my desk, looking excited, with a brooding Miles standing behind them. His eyes never leave Mallory, and I shake my head. I delete the email and grab my bag.

"Yep! Where we going? I want to text my boyfriend and let him know the place."

Both Mallory and Skyler make "ahh!" sounds, and

Skyler grabs me by the arm, locking mine with hers. "So you and the big scary man are back on? I want the details before he shows up and becomes your shadow." She looks over at Miles, whom she's clearly taking a dig at. She's trying to poke at him, but I like the idea of having a shadow of my own.

Chapter Eleven

Jordan

When I get to the place Jay texted me, I see there's a crowd already forming near the bar.

"I'm going to the bar," McCoy says, walking around me and making a beeline for it.

"Grab me one," I say and he throws his hand up and signals he heard me.

I scan the place, and it takes only a second before I spot my chestnut beauty toward the back. She's surrounded by several people I know by face, but not because I've met them. I probably know more about their lives than any of them would like, but it's the nature of the beast.

"Hey." She pops up from her seat, all smiles and red cheeks. "This is everybody. Everybody, this is Jordan." She waves around to the group of women, who all look at me with knowing smiles.

I wonder for a second what she's been telling them, but then the one to her right fills me in. "Yes, we know all about you. I'm Skyler." She holds up her drink in toast before she smiles at me.

"Nice to meet you," I say, walking around and taking Jay's hand. I've seen Skyler a few times, and I appreciate that she's direct. She gives off a cold vibe, but that's definitely not a bad thing.

"Mallory," I say, nodding to her as she sips her water.

"Hey, Jordan. Is he outside?" she asks, looking over her shoulder.

"Right by the door. Don't worry. Paige and Captain are keeping him company."

I got to know Mallory a little when I was assigned to her security detail. But I'm not normally her protection and am usually a last resort. The whole team is trained in combat, and we all know how to use a gun, but I'm usually the one behind the computer when it comes down to it.

"It's fine. I think I'm ready to go." She winks at Skyler before placing her empty plates on the table and standing up. She tells everyone bye, and before she can make it halfway to the exit, Miles is by her side. She shakes her head, but I see the look they give one another.

"They're kind of cute in a gross way," Skyler says and then leans over to talk to the woman on the other side of her.

"I think they're sweet," Jay says, and I lean over to be closer to her.

"I think you're sweeter." I kiss her below her ear and savor her shiver under my lips.

"Guess I'll take this empty seat," McCoy says, and hands me my beer.

He plops down between two women who work in marketing and starts chatting them up. The redhead on his left is Lori. She's recently divorced, and her supervisor is waiting to make his move. He's over by the bar, pretending not to stare at her as she flirts with McCoy. The woman on the right is Corey. She works weekends at a strip club to help support her younger brother and sick mom.

"What are you thinking about?" Jay asks me as she holds my hand and sips her wine.

"Just how I know so much about these people, but none of them know me."

She frowns. "Do you think I know you?"

"Better than anyone. Probably as much as my pop."

"Are we still going to see him on Sunday?" She brightens when she asks, like she's genuinely excited.

"There's no way you're getting out of it. I called him this morning and he's beside himself."

I called him on the way to work, and he sounded like he'd been waiting for this call. He told me he'd make a special dinner and not to be late. I knew he was excited because he didn't remind me to bring his scratch-off.

"Maybe I'll make something to bring. Does he like cake?" she asks, leaning into my side.

I wrap my arm around her, and for anyone looking at us, it's clear we're together. There's no hiding the look on her face and the one I'm pretty sure is on mine.

"Little bird, every man likes cake made by a beautiful woman."

She beams at my compliment, and I vow to give her more of them.

I look over to see the redhead McCoy is talking to flipping her hair and touching his arm. He doesn't look to be enjoying it, but she doesn't stop. In the distance, I see the supervisor getting worked up at the blatant flirtation. For a second I think she might not notice, but then I see her glance ever so slightly out of the corner of her eye at her boss.

"Maybe we should get out of here," I whisper to Jay.

"Why?" A look of disappointment crosses her face, but before I have a chance to explain, all hell breaks loose.

The boss must have had one too many drinks in him, because he clearly doesn't see the size difference between him and McCoy as he lunges for him. McCoy reacts instinctively and blocks him, tossing him into the middle of our group, sending him crashing down on the table.

Drinks and food go flying, and Skyler is on her feet, cursing a streak that would make a sailor blush. Lori covers her mouth, but I can see her shoulders shaking. She's trying to cover her laugh as she goes to help the poor guy who just got laid out with an arm drag. McCoy always did love wrestling.

Corey shakes her head and pulls out some bills for the drinks when McCoy stops her. They exchange some words, and she takes off, leaving him there with his mouth open.

I look down and see Jay is in my lap and I've got her turned away from the wreckage. Without even thinking, I wrapped her up and protected her, and she came straight into my arms.

"Ready to go?" I ask, tucking her closer to me.

"I am now."

I stand her up on her feet as people from the restaurant come over and help clean up the mess. Lori and her boss are arguing in hushed voices, while McCoy has his eyes glued on the door Corey exited.

"You okay to handle this?" I look around at the mess, and he finally snaps out of his trance.

"Yeah, yeah. We're good."

I nod to him as I tug Jay's hand behind me, helping her out of the bar. I hear her say her goodbyes over her shoulder to a steamed Skyler and the group she was with.

"I just don't get it," she says. "Why didn't she just tell that guy how she felt instead of creating a scene?"

"You caught all that?" I ask, feeling pride at how she paid attention to her surroundings.

"Oh, I see more than most people give me credit for. It's the reason I'm so good at my job. I can sit in a meeting and afterwards tell Miles about a hundred things he didn't catch. And it's how I'm able to get what I want from most people."

"And what do I want?" I bring our joined hands up to my mouth and kiss hers.

She bites her lip as she takes her hand from mine and waves for a taxi. "I think you want to come back to my place."

"I think you're on to something."

As soon as we're in the back of the cab, she's on me. She climbs on my lap, straddling my legs, and I give her the kiss she's after. It's burning hot, and when she tastes my tongue, I grip her hips tighter.

"Fuck," I grit against her lips, rubbing my hands over every part of her.

Her hands are in my hair, and she moans just as the cab driver is beating on the glass and yelling at us to sit in our seats.

I pull her off of me—I don't want an audience for this—and sit her beside me, not touching.

"You stay on your side and behave," I say, trying to catch my breath.

Jesus, that was like a tornado. One second I was sitting in a cab and the next I was about to fuck Jay to within an inch of her life in the middle of Times Square.

"I'll be good if you stop being hot." Her smile turns into a laugh, and I reach out, touching her cheek. "Hey. No touching," she chides, pointing a finger at me.

"Fine." I cross my arms, and she glares at me.

"Okay. Maybe a little touching." She places her hand on the seat, palm up, ready for me to hold it.

I'm not strong enough to deny her, and so I place my hand in hers. Then after a moment of hesitation, I bring it to my mouth and start to kiss her knuckles.

"I can't help it," I say when she gives me a look. "I like having my mouth on you." I run the tip of my tongue between two of her fingers, and I feel the pulse on her wrist quicken. "I can't wait to see what you taste like everywhere."

The cab comes to a stop right outside Jay's apartment, and I throw some money at him as we jump out.

"Quick, let's get inside," she says, nearly running into her building.

"What's wrong?" I'm confused, looking around for potential danger.

"Are you kidding me? I'm just waiting for something to go wrong. Hurry up!"

I scoop her up in my arms, and she squeals with laughter. I carry her to the elevator, and she puts in her key and enters a code to go to her floor.

"I like the safety you've got here."

"I thought you might. Too bad there's not a doorman twenty-four/seven. He's only here from lunchtime until ten. Anything after and we've got to trust the automatic locks."

"Hmm," I say, wondering if I can look into that for her. I'm already thinking about the next time I'll be here. Or better yet, I could just get her to come to my place. And stay. Forever.

Chapter Twelve

Jay

Jordan puts me down on my feet as we enter my little apartment. I don't want to be out of his arms. I like when he carries me because it makes me feel small and precious to him. He closes the door, and I melt into his body, placing my head on his chest. He rubs firm hands along my back, and I love how he's always wanting to touch me. It's like he can't get enough, and I want to roll around in that kind of attention.

"It's cute," he says, glancing around my living room.

It's then I realize I've never had a man in my home before. I turn in his arms and glance around the room, trying to see what he sees. My walls are a soft lavender—an attempt to make the place appear more spacious. But there isn't much space. It's Manhattan, so I guess that's kind of expected. A white sofa sits up against one wall, with a couple of windows behind it. If there was a blank wall anywhere in the house, I've put some sort of shelving or bookcases on it. All the notebooks that I'm constantly writing in are piled on them, along with some of my favorite books. Off to the right is my tiny eat-in kitchen, where I spend most of my Saturdays baking.

Making sweet things has always calmed me and helped clear my mind. Well, that was until Jordan. When he's near me, I'm always calm, and even baking couldn't do that for me the way he does.

I can picture him sitting at the breakfast bar on his computer while I move around the kitchen, making us both treats and having him test them. The thought makes butterflies dance in my stomach.

The short hallway leads to a bathroom and my small bedroom. My place is simple, and everything is always tidy, because at this size the tiniest mess makes the place seem cluttered. I don't like needless things lying around either. It drives me crazy keeping things I don't need. It's a habit I picked up after living in a home that was always in disarray and overrun. I like order. It brings focus to my busy mind. When things start to get messy, I get uneasy.

"It's small." He glances down at me, still rubbing my back.

"You make it seem even smaller," I add.

Normally it's just me. I don't need a lot of space, but now with Jordan standing in my living room, the space is definitely tight.

His movements stop, and he tightens his hold on me. "Guess we'll just have to cuddle."

"You're a cuddler?" I tease.

"I think I could be." He leans down, taking my mouth in a soft kiss. It's slow, but it only takes a second before it turns into something more. Jordan deepens the kiss, and I taste his flavor as his tongue touches mine. I moan, wanting more. God, I didn't know kissing could be like this, that you could feel so connected to someone and so easily get lost.

"God, I love when you do that." My eyes flutter open to see him looking down at me.

I don't want to talk. I want to kiss. I grab the back of his neck and pull his mouth back against mine, wanting that connection.

His strong arms pick me up and carry me a short distance before my back hits the mattress. I'm so far gone that even through that, I don't break the kiss. He's on top of me, and the heavy feel of his body on mine is making my body crave more. I know that kissing alone isn't going to be enough.

He leans back, and my mouth goes to his neck, loving the rough stubble against my lips. It makes goose bumps spread across my skin, and I wonder what this would feel like in other places. I hear him moan my name, and the sound pushes me to do more. I love that I'm turning him on. It makes me feel sexy and powerful. It's intoxicating to know I can give him the kind of pleasure he can give me.

"I love how you're Miss Always In Control, but with me it's not that way," I hear him say as my eyes flutter open. "You make me feel like your whole world. You let everything go and fall into me."

I touch his cheek and stare into his dark eyes. I want so much with him, and it's all happening so fast. Every thought I have about him flies through my mind, and suddenly I'm feeling a little shy and unsure of what to do next.

"God, you're beautiful," he mutters, making my face heat. I don't think anyone has ever called me that before. Cute, maybe, but never beautiful.

"Do you have any idea how long I dreamed about this moment? Having you under me? You clinging to me?

Your lips red and swollen from me?" It's not a question, because his mouth comes back down on mine before I can answer.

His mouth leaves mine and goes to my neck, where he grazes my skin with his teeth, then soothes it with gentle licks. I let my eyes fall closed, trying to take everything in. My whole body feels like it's ready to burst. My legs are shaking, and I feel so hot and sweaty.

"Jordan," I moan, rolling my head to the side, wanting him everywhere.

"I got you, baby. Lie back and let me love you," he whispers in my ear.

Cool air greets my body as he unbuttons my shirt. He runs his hands up my stomach and to my breasts, popping the center clasp of my bra and slowly pushing the fabric to the side. My breasts spill free, my hard nipples exposed to him.

I watch his intense gaze on them right as he licks his lips and leans down. He sucks one of my nipples into his mouth, making my back bow off the bed. The sensation goes straight to my clit, and I have the urge to scream. He grips my hips, locking me into place. He switches his attention to my other nipple, giving it a little bite. God, I didn't know this could feel like this.

Just when I think I've had enough, he trails kisses down my stomach to the edge of my skirt. Slowly he pulls it down my legs, and I blink my eyes open to watch.

Once my skirt is gone, he stares down at my simple blue underwear. I suddenly feel really shy about my choice of panties. I don't own anything sexy when it comes to lingerie. I always go with function instead of sexiness. I never had to worry about anyone seeing them before, but now I wish I had on a thong or some lace. Anything to make me look prettier.

I part my legs a little, and his eyes come to mine. There's a look there I've never seen on his face before. I bite my lip, watching him. It's then I realize I'm almost naked and he still has on all his clothes.

"Take your shirt off," I blurt out, wanting to see him, too.

In one fluid motion, he grabs the back of his shirt with one hand, pulling it from his body and tossing it away.

My eyes run over him, and I moan in appreciation. I didn't think Jordan could get any hotter, but I was wrong. He might spend most of his day sitting behind a computer, but it's clear as day he hits the gym as well. Hard. His slacks hang low on his hips, and I see a trail of dark hair running down to his— My thoughts stutter when I see the outline of a very big erection.

"Eyes," I hear him say, and I look back up to his face. "That's not coming out tonight."

He gives me a cocky smirk that I've never seen before, and a small dimple shows in his cheek.

"Why—" My question is interrupted when he reaches for my underwear and rips them from my body like some sort of Viking. I audibly gasp as he tosses them aside like he just conquered a new land. "Wow, that was so hot. I didn't know that was a real thing."

The smirk on his face turns to a full-blown smile now. I didn't think men could really rip underwear off of a woman.

"Show me," he says, his eyes on my thighs.

It's clear what he wants me to show him, so I slowly part my legs. But it's not fast enough for his liking, so he grabs them and pushes them open. His need is turning me on even more. He's so close to the edge he can't even wait for me to give him what he wants.

He stares at my pussy, and I don't know how long we stay like that. My desire is skyrocketing with every breath, and I can feel myself start to throb. I want him to do something. Anything.

"Jordan." His name comes out as a cross between a cry and a moan. My hips rise off the bed, trying to get closer to him, trying to entice him into a reaction.

His eyes are darker than I have ever seen them before. He releases my thighs, and he slides his fingers through my sex. I arch, wanting more, but he grabs my hips once again, holding me in place.

I moan his name again, trying to move, but he has me pinned down to the bed.

"I want to hear you say it. You have no idea how long I've wanted this, and I want to hear you say it. I need to hear you say it. Ask me to kiss your pussy."

I know I'm blushing. I didn't know Jordan would talk like that, but I like it. No, I love it. Normally I might be shy, but I'm so turned on right now I'd say almost anything to get some relief.

"Please, Jordan, I need you. Please kiss my pussy."

Before I get the last word out, his mouth is on me. He grasps my hips as his mouth devours me. He licks and sucks my clit, taking it into his mouth, and I come undone instantly. The orgasm hits me so unexpectedly, I scream as pleasure floods my veins. The heat of it pounds in my ears, and it goes on forever.

I was too worked up. There was no time for me to brace myself for it, and I jerk against him, screaming his name over and over. But he doesn't stop as the pleasure pulses through my body.

He frees my hips and locks his hands with mine. Our fingers tangle together, holding tight to one another as his mouth keeps working over me.

This time it's slower, as if he's savoring me. It's sweet and soft, and I've never felt more connected to someone in my life. There is a deep intimacy in this act, and I feel bound to him in a way I never truly imagined.

My pleasure starts growing again, and it's not long before he's sending me over the edge once more. The orgasm is just as intense as the first one, but I felt this one build. A sheen of sweat gathers on my body as I try to catch my breath. But he still doesn't stop.

I call out his name, but his fingers only tighten in mine.

His mouth is relentless, and though I don't think I can handle any more, I'm once again sent over the edge. His intensity, his attention, his ministrations, it's all too much. I feel like I'm on a roller coaster and I can't control my body.

This time, the peak is too high, and after I've come crashing back down, it's to a wave of sleep unlike anything I've ever felt. I have no choice but to close my eyes and give in to the darkness that's calling me.

I wake with arms wrapped tightly around me, my legs tangled with his. I never dreamed of having Jordan stay the night with me. I feel warmth all over as I let myself sink deeper. Turning a little, I kiss the arm that's wrapped around me, and I hear him whisper my name in his sleep.

But instead of drifting off to sleep again, I feel his

whole body go rock-solid. Before I know what's happening, he's jumping out of bed.

I sit up, not sure what's happening and not sure I really care, because now I see he's only in a pair of boxer briefs with his thighs on full display. I never thought thighs could be sexy but with the morning light flooding in the windows I can see every inch of them. Heck, I don't think I ever really thought about thighs at all until this moment. Right now, though, I'd like to sink my teeth into his.

I watch as he picks up a gun I didn't even know he had, making my eyes almost pop out of my head. "What the hell, Jordan?" I say as my bedroom door flies open. "Summer?"

I see my sister standing in the doorway to my bedroom with a surprised look on her face. I haven't heard from her in months, but I'm not surprised to see her here. That's how Summer works. She floats around from place to place and will pop up out of nowhere. She says it's because she's a free spirit, but I think it's just an excuse to not get a job.

"Oh my!" she says, her eyes trained on Jordan.

I look over at him, not liking that she's seeing him like this. I don't want anyone seeing him like this. Plus, my sister is pretty. She's actually more than pretty, and like always, she isn't wearing much in the clothes department. If it was up to her, she'd always be naked.

"Sister" is all Jordan says, and I nod.

I pull the sheet up more, realizing I am, in fact, completely naked. Jordan walks toward Summer, and she takes a step back.

"She'll be out in a minute," he tells her, before slamming the door in her face.

Chapter Thirteen

Jordan

I see the lines of tension around Jay's mouth, and I have to use all my strength to keep from saying something.

Summer has been floating around the apartment for the past hour, moving things and leaving a trail of clutter as she goes.

"I think the energy of the space would feel so much more open with a water feature in the corner," she says, assessing the layout.

"If there's a water feature over there, it means the toilet is leaking from upstairs," Jay says in return as she sets down a book a little too firmly.

Summer gives Jay a patronizing look, and again I have to bite the inside of my cheek to keep from telling Summer to pick another face.

"How long are you planning on staying here for?" Jay asks in a straightforward tone that anyone could pick up on. Summer, however, isn't just anyone.

"Didn't you get my postcard from Sedona?" she says airily, laying out a blanket in the middle of the floor in the living room and crisscrossing her legs. She sits like she's about to meditate with her hands on her knees and her back straight.

"No. I haven't heard a word from you in months." Jay twists a towel from the kitchen in her hands until I think it may rip in half.

"I'm sure you just misplaced it." Summer makes a waving motion around the pristine apartment, where everything is in order except for what she's moved. "Anyway, I'm coming to stay with you for a while. I've finished my recent healing journey, and I'm going to live here with you in New York until I find my next guide."

"Your next what?" I can't help the question that pops out of my mouth. I look over and see Jay shake her head and roll her eyes.

"My next spiritual guide," Summer answers, like I'm the idiot.

Jay is steaming. I can almost see it coming out of her ears. Not only has her sister come in and disrupted her order and peace, she's made a statement to move in without a single question asked. I might be an only child, but that seems like a pretty dick move from a sibling.

"Jay, can I talk to you in the bedroom?" I ask, seeing her hands clenched in fists as her face gets red.

"Summer, are you serious right now? I don't hear from you for months, and then you show up saying you're going to live with me?" Her voice is getting higher, and though I should stop this, I think she kind of needs her moment. "The last time you did this, you took over my place for almost a year without paying me a dime for rent or groceries or anything. I'm not doing it again. You're my sister, and I will help you in any way I can, but I can't enable you to act like this. I'm not a last resort. If you need help, I'm sure there's room at the farm with Mom and Dad."

Summer sits back on her hands and shakes her head. "They're full right now. I already checked. Come on, you can't kick me out on the streets."

When I see the tremors go down Jay's back, I grab her arm and half drag her to the bedroom. When we get there, I close the door behind us and sit her on the bed as I go to the closet. I grab two big suitcases and put them out on the bed beside her, flinging them open.

I grab the contents of her dresser, scooping up everything in both my arms and dumping them into the bag. For a woman, she really doesn't have a ton of clothes. Next, I go to the closet, lifting the clothes—still attached to the hangers—and fold the pile in half. I stuff the clothes down in the other suitcase. Then I see a large gym bag in the bottom of her closet and decide to use that for her shoes. I'm almost finished filling it up when I hear Jay finally speak.

"Jordan, what are you—"

"This is really simple, little bird. Summer can stay here and you can stay with me until you get this worked out. It's perfect."

"What? I've never even been to your place. I can't just move in with you." She stands up and holds her arms out like this whole thing is too much.

"There's plenty of room. You'll love it." I toss the bag of shoes beside the suitcases and hold out another bag for her to get her bathroom stuff. "Unless you want me to put your lady business in here, I'll let you handle that."

"My lady business? Seriously? Has everyone lost

their damn mind today?" She drops her head in her hands, and I walk over to her, sitting down on the bed and pulling her into my lap.

"Shhh. I'm here. Hey," I say, making her look up at me. "Do you trust me?"

Her dark eyes shine with unshed tears, but she smiles and nods. "You know I do."

"Then trust that no matter what happens today, tomorrow, or fifty years from now, I've got you. I'll take care of anything that comes our way, and you don't have to worry. You let me do that for you. Okay?"

"Is it really that simple?" There's so much hope in her voice, and it makes me proud that I'm able to answer that for her.

"It is. When it comes to me and you and the way I feel about you, nothing could be simpler." I reach out and cup her cheek. "Jay, I—"

"Jay, is this garlic free-range gluten-free?" Summer shouts as she busts open the door without knocking.

I hold back the growl that's forming in my chest, because I don't want to say something to Summer I can't take back. No matter how aggravated Jay is, this is still her family. And to be honest, this probably wasn't the best time for that conversation. I want to be able to make that special.

Without answering Summer, Jay turns to me and a look of finality passes over her face. "Do you need me to carry one of these bags?"

"I think I can manage," I answer winking at her.

Chapter Fourteen

Jay

"So this is what you call 'plenty of room'?" I say, my voice echoing off the marble walls.

"I like having a big bathroom. Are you really complaining? You'll be the first woman ever to use that tub."

I raise an eyebrow and lean against the bathroom counter. "First woman? Have you had many men in here?"

"Hey, there's nothing wrong with a little self-care. So I like bubble baths. You want to make fun of me or join me?"

I watch as he walks over and turns on the taps, grabbing a ball of something from the side and dropping it in. When I give him a quizzical look, he smiles.

"Bath bombs."

"My bathtub is so tiny I've never bothered to take a bath. God, I can't remember the last time I soaked in a hot tub."

He comes back to where I am, and I see the hungry look in his eyes. I expect him to be aggressive, so when his touch is gentle, it surprises me.

He lifts off my T-shirt and then reaches down, unbuttoning my jean shorts. He pushes them off my hips and then slowly runs his hands up my waist and to my bra. I smile shyly as he unclasps it and drops it to the floor.

"So beautiful," he says, looking straight into my eyes.

He doesn't break contact as he pushes my panties off my hips and I step out of them. When he reaches for the bottom of his shirt, I stop him.

"Let me." I help him take his off. Because he's so much taller than me, he has to bend down. My hands go to his pants, and he has to help me unbutton them because my hands are shaking. So much for being super seductive right now.

Seeing my own insecurities, he brings my hands to his mouth and kisses each palm. Then he puts them on his hips and helps me push his boxer briefs off.

I try to keep eye contact like he did, but I'm a total perv and check out his junk. His hard cock is long and pointing up. It's thick, with a smooth head, and my mouth pops open at the size of it.

He takes my hand in his and leads me over to the tub, shaking me out of my shock.

"It's not polite to stare," he says as he steps into the bath and then helps me over the edge.

He sits down in the bubbles and leans back as I sit between his legs and put my back against his front. His legs rest on either side of mine, and he wraps his arms around me. I sigh as the hot water relaxes me instantly.

"God, this is nice."

"See? Already some benefits of coming to my place."

When we first got to Jordan's building, I thought it was nice. It looked like a normal building in a great neighborhood, but once I got inside, I was shocked.

He told me that computer hackers tend to make good investments and he'd made a lot of money in the stock market when he was younger. He used it to buy this place and then fixed it up himself.

He would have to be loaded to be able to afford a place this size, but I kind of like that you wouldn't know that about him unless you really knew him. It's not overly lavish or obnoxious. It's actually pretty simple and very much his personality.

The place is big, but it feels cozy. There are couches and overstuffed pillows everywhere, and it makes me want to walk in and kick back. There's no stuffy furniture or weird art. It's a place I feel welcome and happy. He seems to have a way of doing that to me.

He brings his hands to my shoulders and starts to rub.

"I'll give you an hour to quit that," I moan, closing my eyes and letting my head fall back.

He laughs and kisses my neck. "Make it two and you've got a deal."

There are three bedrooms here, yet he put all my things in his room. One side of the closet is completely empty, and since he brought all my hangers, he went on and on about how easy it was for me to move in.

I corrected him a few times, but he still keeps saying that I moved in with him. Finally, I just let it go and let him have it. For now.

When he showed me the kitchen, I swear I almost said I loved him. The space is huge—a cook's dream. Although he says he dabbles, he's not very good. I don't know if that's possible with every tool right in front of you. I ended up making us some sandwiches out of what he had in his fridge, but he promised we could go to the market and stock up so that I could cook to my heart's content. I'm already dreaming about the things I can make in there, stuff that I never had the space for at my place.

Thinking about my place reminds me of my sister and the burgeoning mess that I left at my apartment.

"I can feel you tense. You're supposed to be relaxing. Would you like me to distract you?" He rubs lower down my front and moves to my breasts.

All annoyances over my sister's surprise visit vanish, just like all my problems do in his arms.

"See. Much better." His lips are on my neck, and he traces kisses up and down.

One of his hands stays on my breast as the other moves down between my legs. I can't see through the bubbles, but I can feel his fingers as they find my clit. The sensation brings all the memories from last night flooding back, and I want more of what we shared. Only this time, I want Jordan to feel it, too.

I feel the length of his cock against my back, and I reach around between us to touch him.

He hisses in my ear when my hand makes contact, and his movements on my pussy still. "Go slow," he whispers and goes back to petting me.

I touch him gently like he's touching me. Neither of us is in a hurry for this to be over, so we take our time.

I love the feel of him in my hand. His length is bigger than anything I've seen, but it's not as if I have a ton of experience with penises. But even from the limited porn I've watched, I can tell Jordan has been blessed. He pulses against my palm, heavy with need.

"You feel so perfect in my arms. Better than I ever

dreamed of all those nights I sat in this tub alone, stroking my cock and thinking of you."

It's incredibly hard to concentrate on giving someone pleasure when you're getting it, but that doesn't seem to stop Jordan. The hand he has between my legs is tormenting me, while the one on my breast is nearly as maddening. I'm climbing close to an orgasm, and I don't know how much longer I can hold it back.

"Every time you walked away from me, I would stare at your ass so I could imagine it later when I was coming, thinking about having my hands on it and gripping it as I made love to you."

He circles my clit, and it's the steady, even rhythm that I love to use when I get myself off. But with him, it's so much better. I gasp as the orgasm hits and my body tenses. I scrabble at the sides of the tub and hold on as I ride out the wave of pleasure.

"That's it, little bird. Let it all out," Jordan says against my ear, and I have no choice but to do what he says.

My body turns into a puddle as I come down, and he holds me close. After a few moments pass, I feel a warm cloth wash over me, and then he's rinsing me off and telling me to stand up.

"It's over?" I pout, not wanting to leave the bath.

"I don't want you drowning because you pass out in here," he says, helping me out and wrapping me in a warm, fluffy towel.

He takes a second to dry me off before taking a towel for himself and doing the same. When he's finished, he wraps it around his waist, and I see his cock is just as hard as it was before we got in the tub. It's then I realize he never got off.

"I'm sorry, I got distracted," I say, trying to explain.

He smiles and shakes his head. "You're so selfish. Always so greedy to get off." I blush at his teasing, but he takes me into the bedroom and pulls back the covers on the bed. "You need to eat. Why don't you rest for a little while and I'll order us some food? You haven't eaten since the bar last night."

Exhaustion hits me as I climb into the bed naked and snuggle in. These orgasms seem to make me sleepy. The sheets smell like Jordan, and I instantly feel safe and secure. There's no other bed in the world I'd rather be in.

He says something else, but I don't catch it. By the time my head has burrowed into the pillow, I'm already asleep.

Chapter Fifteen

Jay

When I wake up, I roll over and reach for Jordan. The place I expect him to be is cool, and I open my eyes to find him. Sitting up, I see he's nowhere in the master bedroom, so I go to the bathroom to see if he's in there. I take a few steps, and I hear the shower running. I feel like being naughty.

I'm already naked, having gone straight to bed last night after taking a second bath with Jordan. I think I could live in that tub with him. I must have needed the sleep, because at one point I remember Jordan waking me up to eat dinner. I told him I wasn't hungry after the massive lunch he'd fed me. Then at some point later, I felt his warm arms around me as I drifted even deeper under. God, I must have slept twelve hours.

When I sneak into the bathroom, I see the steam coming from the shower, but the glass is clear. I can see Jordan under the spray with his eyes closed, the rivers of water washing down his back and over his firm ass. I lick my lips thinking about wanting to bite him there, and then his hips turn.

I gasp when I see his hand on his cock, stroking up

and down in long pulls. His hand is soaped up and he's fisting himself harder than I would have imagined he liked.

"Jay," he moans, and I look up to lock eyes with him. "Fuck." He grunts and scans my naked body, up and down.

I take a step forward, and he slams his hand against the glass.

"No. Don't come in. Just stand right there," he says, pain in his voice.

I reach up and put my hand against his, the glass separating us as he goes back to stroking his cock. He's on edge, I can see that. His body is tense and tight. If I were to step in that shower with him, he might lose control. And as much as I want him to do that, I know that Jordan is a good guy. He wouldn't want me to do something in the heat of the moment that I would regret. But what he doesn't know is that there isn't anything I'd ever regret when it comes to him.

"Touch yourself," he says, his voice deep and filled with need.

I slip my free hand between my legs and through my wet folds. I moan at the sensation, loving the feeling but wishing it was him.

"Faster." His voice is demanding as he runs his tight fist up and down his length, the round head of his cock almost red with need.

I do as he commands and circle my clit. I speed up to his rhythm, and suddenly we're both moving at the same speed. I've never been this bold in my life, and I realize that I don't feel any embarrassment. I'm not shy or ashamed. Instead, I'm a goddess pleasuring myself in front of my man so that he can enjoy it as much as I enjoy watching him. It's powerful, and I want to use it to my advantage.

Taking my other hand away from the glass, I use it to pinch my nipples and rub my breasts. I lean back on the counter of the sink and spread my legs so that he can see everything he wants. His grunts and moans are ringing approvals of how much he loves watching me. He moves both hands to his cock, rubbing his balls and his shaft, all while staring at me.

"I can't last much longer," he says, and there is a pleading note in his voice.

"Come with me." I pinch my nipple and rub my clit in just the right spot to send myself over the edge.

The pulses in my pussy are intense, but the sight of him coming undone sends a throb through me unlike anything I've ever felt.

A thick stream of cum shoots out of his cock and rolls down his shaft. His deep sound of pleasure sends a chill down my spine, and God, how I wish I could feel it on me. Inside me.

"Fuck," I whisper and close my eyes. The vision and the desire are too intense, and it sends me into another orgasm.

I hear the shower door open, and then I feel a warm, wet hand pull me. I let out a squeak as I'm pulled under the spray, and then his lips are on mine.

"How could something so simple be so fucking hot?" he groans against my lips.

"I don't know. But next time you better let me in." I feel his hard length against my belly, and I reach down and rub him. "Want to try a do-over?"

"Hands to yourself, little bird." He kisses me softly

and then spins me around so I have to let him go. "Shower up and then we're headed out."

"Where are we going?" I ask as he smacks my ass and steps out of the shower.

"Well, since you slept through dinner, food first. Then you get to come watch me spar with my team. Then we're going to my dad's."

He's got a towel around his waist now, and I make a point to look down at it and then back up to him.

He smiles and shakes his head as he leaves the bathroom. I make quick work of getting ready, seeing he already put all my stuff in here. When I hop out, I towel off and then quickly blow-dry my hair. Once I'm finished I walk into the bedroom to find him already dressed.

He's wearing a T-shirt with loose track pants and sneakers. He looks comfortable as he slips on a track jacket and zips it up.

"You know, the more you look at me like that, the more I think you're after me for my body." He winks at me and grabs his gym bag.

"You've discovered my secret," I say, dropping my towel dramatically and walking naked to the closet.

He's on me in point-three seconds, wrapping his arms around me and kissing my neck.

"You're the greatest temptation I've ever faced," he says, burying his face in my hair.

"Why didn't you wake me up last night?" I wondered that as soon as I woke up. Why hadn't he tried to make love to me? Even with the shower this morning, it's like he's trying to keep himself at a distance. "Are you afraid of getting serious?"

That's the real question, what's driving the fear that

sprouts in my stomach when I'm unsure of what he's after. Am I always going to be kept at arm's length?

He leans back and shakes his head. He tucks a strand of hair behind my ear and sighs. "No. I'm already serious with you, Jay. I've never been more serious. I just want to make sure..." He trails off and then shakes his head. "I want it to be special. As lame as that sounds. I don't want you half asleep or rushed for time. I want our first time to mean something."

"Are you blushing?" I ask, and I can't keep the giggle out of my voice.

He goes to pull away from me, but I cling to him. I'm sure he could break the hold if he wanted to, but he lets me have it.

"Jordan, that's the sweetest thing anyone has ever said to me. I'm just surprised. I had assumed you were pretty experienced with this sort of thing."

"That's pretty sexist to assume men can't be virgins." He leans down, giving me a kiss and then rubs his nose against mine. "Maybe you're not the only one who's been waiting for the right one."

With that, he gives me one last kiss and walks out of the closet. I stand there for a moment, dazed. Holy shit. Jordan is a virgin? And he's been waiting for the one? Am I the one? Now I have so many more questions rolling through my mind.

After a moment of standing completely still, Jordan pokes his head back in the closet. "Hurry it up, little bird. I've got breakfast cooking."

Going over to my side of the closet, I grab a pair of yoga pants and a tank top, with a zip-up hoodie and sneakers. I pile my hair up in a messy bun and then grab my bag off the dresser. I see my phone is lit up, and I scan the texts. I've got seven from my sister asking where my incense burner is, and then her telling me that she found something that would work. God help her, I hope she doesn't burn the whole building down.

I see that I have two more text messages from an anonymous number, and I click on them to open. At first, I think maybe they're not for me, but I read them again and the hairs on the back of my neck stand up.

Anon: Keep your fucking mouth shut.
Anon: Be careful little bitch

"If you don't get your pretty ass in here, I'm coming back there to get it," Jordan shouts from the kitchen.

There's no name, and I've never gotten a message like this before, so I delete them. They could have been meant for anyone. As soon as they're deleted I feel better and reply to my sister about fire codes in the building. She's a total flake.

I toss my phone in my bag and hurry to the kitchen. My stomach is growling, and I'm ready to see my man again. I push all thoughts about my phone aside and think about Jordan's admission. Somehow it makes me hotter and I want him even more.

Chapter Sixteen

Jordan

"Are we allowed to just bring chicks in here now?" McCoy says when I've got him in a choke hold.

"You know, that's probably why you're still single. You're afraid of pussy," Paige says from the side of the ring.

Ryan stands beside her protectively, but there's no need. She could take any one of us down, and we know it.

"I think she might be right," Jay says, and Paige high-fives her.

McCoy grunts, and I flip him over so he doesn't turn blue. He takes the opening, and we go back to wrestling.

We've been here for a couple of hours, and it's been fun having Jay watch me. She even got in the ring for a few minutes with Paige so she could learn some basic self-defense moves. I was impressed. She's a fast learner, and stronger than I realized. I didn't like the thought of all the guys watching her with Paige, but they were really helpful with instructing.

It wasn't until I got in the ring with McCoy that the shit-talking started. He thinks it will throw me off my game, but he didn't take into consideration that my woman can hold her own.

"You know, Paige, I've always wondered if it's easier to wrestle without balls. I guess I should have asked McCoy first."

I almost choke at Jay's trash talk, and then I hear everyone around the ring erupt into laughter. McCoy stands up straight and looks at Jay, pleading, with his hands out.

"Jay, what the fuck? What did I ever do to you?"

I take the opening and dive on him, pinning him down until I hear Sheppard hit the bell. I get up, still laughing, and help McCoy off the mat.

"Your girl plays dirty," he tells me, shaking his head.

"Poor guy. Did you get your feelings hurt?" I joke, poking him in the chest.

"All right, that's enough for today," Ryan says, and everyone starts packing up.

I climb out of the ring and go over to where Jay is and grab my gym bag.

"You headed to your dad's?" Sheppard asks.

"Yep. Taking my lady with me," I say, grabbing Jay's hand.

McCoy walks over and nudges Sheppard out of the way. "Just wanted you to know, even though you're evil and you cheat." He looks at me and smiles. "You've given all guys in the friend zone hope. And you cost me some coin."

"Thanks, I guess," Jay says leaning into me. "But the truth is, he put himself there. Not me."

"Wait. So are you admitting you cheated?" McCoy says, trying to spin this back in his favor.

"Sorry, buddy. You lost," I say, feeling smug.

"Never bet against Jordan. You know that," Paige says as Ryan carries her over his shoulder out of the building.

I don't even want to know what him carrying her is about, and we all ignore it. It's practically normal behavior for the two of them.

"Fine. We're out. See you tomorrow," Sheppard says as he and McCoy leave.

Since I'm the last one out, I lock up and then hold Jay's hand as we walk to the train.

"Nervous?" I ask, feeling her pulse on her wrist.

"Nope. Just excited," she replies as she tucks her phone back in her bag.

Chapter Seventeen

Jay

We take the train to Brooklyn, and Jordan leads me to a cute neighborhood with family homes on tree-lined streets. He tells me about growing up here as we walk, and I can picture it. Kids are still running the sidewalks and riding bikes.

"This is me," he says, pointing to a little brick house with a front porch and purple flowers lining the beds.

"It's adorable!" I exclaim, and I mean it. It's charming and sweet, and it feels like a part of him. So, of course, I'm going to love it.

Love him.

The words play over in my head as he takes my hand and leads me inside.

"Pop, we're here!" he shouts in way of greeting.

We walk down a short hallway, and he stops to kiss his fingers, touching them to a picture hanging on the wall. It's of a beautiful dark-haired woman, who I know instantly is Jordan's mom. Beautiful high cheekbones, straight nose and a small dimple.

"You look just like her," I say, wrapping my arms around his waist.

"Wait until you see my dad." He kisses the top of my head, and we walk through the kitchen and out onto a back patio.

"Pop!" Jordan yells as we step out.

All at once the mood changes from happy to panicked. Jordan's father is slumped over in his seat with blood on his head. We both rush to him, and all hell breaks loose.

"Call 911," Jordan says, and I do it without hesitation.

My hands are shaky as I hold the phone, and Jordan starts CPR on his father. The operator is in my ear, but it's all a blur. I have to ask Jordan for the address and then shout it into the phone and tell them to hurry.

Panic is rushing through me, and my heart is breaking as I watch Jordan work on him. He's counting out the beats, and I'm praying like I've never prayed before that help gets here in time.

This isn't supposed to be happening. This can't be real.

Before I know what's going on, the ambulance is here and they're telling Jordan to get out of the way. I hold on to him with all my strength so that the medics can get to his dad and help save his life. Jordan has done all he can do, and it's in their hands now.

"We've got a pulse!" one of them shouts, and I thank God.

They bring in a stretcher and then carry him out in a blur. Everything is happening so fast. I hold on to Jordan's hand as we follow them. Jordan climbs into the back of the ambulance and holds his hand out to me.

"Only one family member," the medic says, looking at me as they load up.

"Go. I'll lock up the house and be right behind you," I say.

I see the torn look in his eyes, and I want to go with him, but I can't.

"Right behind you," I say again, and he nods.

There's fear like I've never seen in his eyes, and I pray again that everything will be okay. I watch for a second as they pull away and listen to the sirens blare.

I run back into the house and make sure everything is turned off. There was a pot on the stove, so I'm glad I came back in. I straighten up the back porch in case Jordan comes back here later. I don't want him to have to take care of it.

It's then I realize that the chair was still sitting up when we came in. I had assumed Jordan's father had hit his head, but how could he have done that if he was still in his chair? It all happened so fast that now I'm not able to recall the detail properly. Maybe I'm mis-remembering…

After I've double-checked everything, I lock up the house and flag down a cab. I tell the driver the name of the hospital the medic said they were going to and text Jordan that I'm on the way.

Me: In the cab. Be there soon.

Jordan: I'm in the waiting room. They're in the back working on him.

Me: Do you need me to get anything for you on the way?

Jordan: No. I just need you. Hurry.

Me: I'm almost there.

I toss an extra twenty at the cab driver to speed it up, but he's still not going as fast as I need him to. Although he is breaking the speed limit and most traffic laws.

We pull up in the parking lot, and I jump out while the cab is still moving. I run inside and see Jordan pacing. He stops when he sees me and runs to me, wrapping me up in his arms.

"Is he okay? What's happening?"

"The doctor came out and said he has a severe concussion. They're going to put him into an induced coma until some of the swelling goes down."

"Oh God, Jordan, I'm so sorry. Are you okay?"

"I just want to see him. They said I can go back, but I was waiting for you."

"Go ahead. Don't wait for me. I'll be right here when you come out."

He shakes his head. "I need you."

His voice and his eyes are filled with a desperate plea.

"I'm right here. Anything you need. I'm not going anywhere." I squeeze his hands in mine, and he nods.

We walk down a quiet hallway, and the nurses at the end speak to us before we go in. They tell us to be quiet and that we can only stay for a few minutes. He's in ICU, but he's stable, and they'll monitor him overnight and see how the swelling progresses. We can touch his hand and talk to him, but don't touch anything else. We agree, and they show us to a private area, with the curtains pulled around to block out the surrounding bustle.

Jordan's hand squeezes mine as we walk closer.

His father looks small and frail in the bed, hooked up

to so many machines. Jordan must be having the same thoughts, because I see his face turn white.

I decide to help calm him and step up to his dad, taking his hand in mine. "Hey, Mr. Chen. It's not so great meeting like this. But I'm glad you're still with us and that I finally get a chance to say hello. Jordan made me pick out your scratch-off this week, so if it's not a winner, that's my fault. And he says you'll never let me forget it."

I look up to Jordan and see his eyes are red, but his tears are unshed.

"I made pecan pie because he said it was your favorite. I don't know how good it is. Don't worry. I'll save you a slice. You know how Jordan can be when it comes to food." I wink at him, and he smiles at me. "Anyway, we'll let you get some rest. We'll be back as soon as the nurses say it's okay, and then we'll check that ticket. I think I'm pretty lucky, since I managed to get this guy to ask me out."

I squeeze his hand one last time and step aside for Jordan to hold it now. He does, and I stand right behind him with my hand on his back.

"Pop," he says, and then stops. He takes a deep breath and lets it out. "Don't you dare do this to me. You get some sleep and then come back to me."

He takes my hand and places it on top of their joined ones. The three of us are in one hold.

"I love you," he whispers, and in that moment it feels like he's saying it to both of us.

Chapter Eighteen

Jay

A few days have passed, and I hate the little cloud that's hovered around Jordan. The doctor has given his father a good prognosis, but Jordan is still worried. They said the swelling is going down, but not as fast as they'd like. But for a man his age, it's to be expected. They hope to be able to wake him up from the induced coma this weekend and see the full extent of the damage.

I think that's Jordan's biggest fear, that his dad will wake up and he won't be the same. We've spent every chance we can at the hospital, staying for only a few moments at a time. I came back to work yesterday after Jordan insisted. I told him that I could take off as much time as I needed in order to be with him, but I think he wanted one of us to be productive. Sitting around worrying all the time wasn't doing either of us any good. Only now I'm sitting at work and worrying.

My afternoon consists of taking notes in a meeting with Miles and Mr. Spencer. I didn't tell Miles about what happened the last time he was here, and I don't plan to, unless another situation occurs.

Miles has sent me an email to let me know what

they'll be covering in their meeting, and I see it's got the Lannister file included. Clicking on the folder, I scan back through the documents to see why this one thing keeps popping up. Some of these documents have details on overseas deals that having nothing to do with us. I can't imagine why either of them would be talking about this, especially when the company that's processed this request also deals in foreign ammunition production. Osbourne Corp. doesn't contract with anything like this.

I click on the email and start to reply when my cell phone rings. Thinking it might be Jordan, I pick it up on the first ring without looking to see who it is.

"Oh my God, Jay, what kind of disgusting mail-order service are you a part of?!" Summer screams into the phone.

I rub my forehead and try to push away the migraine I know she's about to trigger.

"It's just my monthly snack box order. Put it to the side and don't eat it if you don't want to. I can come by and pick it up later. You know, opening someone else's mail is a federal offense." Jesus. Who knew she was going to be this much trouble? Oh, wait. I did.

"Are you shitting me, Jay? There's a dead fucking bird in this box."

"What?" My voice is barely above a whisper.

"I wasn't going to open your mail, because I'm not a complete asshole. But this one was starting to smell, so…" She lets that sentence hang in the air.

"I'm coming over," I say and hang up the phone.

I poke my head into Miles's office and say I need to head out to take care of some errands. I don't know why, but I don't want him to worry.

"You know you don't have to tell me. And you can take all the time you need," he says.

I nod and duck out, grabbing my bag and hitting the button for the elevator. Just as the doors open, Mr. Spencer steps off in such a way that I can't step on.

"Miss Rosie." He says my name wrong on purpose, and then licks his lips. "You know I was hoping I could make it right after our last run-in."

He leans in close to me, and I have no choice but to stand there. I can't get around him, and he's too big for me to physically push out of the way.

"How about I take you out to lunch? Or maybe dinner? We could go to my place. The view from the penthouse is spectacular." He brings his hand up to my shoulder, and I move to the side to avoid it.

"I need to go. I have a family emergency."

"Oh, is everyone okay?" He feigns concern. "Can I offer you a ride?"

"No, thank you," I say just as Miles comes out of his office.

"Is everything all right?" he asks, and when Mr. Spencer looks up, I duck around him and hit the button. I don't hear the rest of the conversation as the doors close, and I slide the card Jordan gave me to take me directly to the first floor.

Jordan. Shit.

I was supposed to have lunch with him today. He isn't back to work yet, but I thought it would do us some good to have lunch in the park. Get some sunshine and help him relax.

I pull out my phone and send him a quick text telling him my sister needed me to go by the apartment and I may be a little bit late.

Jordan: Want me to come with you?

Me: No, it's fine. You know how she is. I'll take care of it.

Jordan: Okay. I'll see you after. Better have my kiss ready.

I can't help but smile. He always knows how to make me feel better.

Me: Always.

I send twenty kiss emojis and think that maybe it's overkill, but I don't care. He can have as many as he wants.

We haven't done anything sexual since Sunday morning before we left his place. At night, we just hold one another. Sometimes he holds me and sometimes I hold him. I know he needs comfort these days, and I try to respect that. No matter how much my body begs for more.

By the time I make it to my apartment, my sister is in hysterics. She's such a ditz she thinks I ordered this for some kind of séance.

"Summer, in what world would anyone want a dead bird? Let alone find a place that delivers it!" I shout as she goes on and on about how I'm the reason there's so much negative energy in this space.

"You really need to clean your chi," she says, crossing her arms and looking at me like I'm a disgrace.

"Just…just call the building security if you have any more problems like this, okay? This isn't a normal delivery for my house. How did you even get it?"

"It was sitting outside your door," she says over her shoulder as she walks away from me. "Lock up on your way out."

I take the box with the dead bird and bag it. There was no note or return address, and the fact that it was outside the door makes me really nervous. How could someone just leave this outside my door? Is this some sort of sick joke?

I walk down to the front desk and speak to the doorman that's there. He doesn't have any information and says he can request the camera footage if I fill out some forms. I don't have time, but I take them with me, saying I'll drop them by later before his shift is over.

He takes the bag and says he'll dispose of it and contact the building management to see what they can do.

It's not much to go on, but at least it's something. I should tell Jordan about it, but with everything that's going on with his dad, I don't want to add to his stress. I know how protective he is of me already, and I can't imagine this would make it any better.

By the time I've got all of it taken care of, the sky has opened up and it's pouring rain. I'm in a cab halfway to the park when I get a text.

Jordan: Looks like our picnic is once again ruined.

Me: At least this time I didn't kick you in the balls.

Jordan: There's that silver lining I was looking for.

Me: Want to meet at the cafeteria at work?

Jordan: Don't think I can make it across town in time. I'm going to head to the hospital. I'll see you after work.

Me: Okay, tell Pop I said hello.

Jordan: XOXO

Disappointment hits me as I tell the driver to take me back to Osbourne Corp. Could this day get any worse?

Chapter Nineteen

Jay

I look at the clock on my computer for the millionth time, willing it to move faster. I swear it's taunting me. Normally I'm always on the move at work and the day flies by, but today my mind can't seem to focus.

Picking up my phone, I check to see if Jordan has texted me with any updates. I'm disappointed when I see nothing new. I don't know if no news is good news. I hate not being there with him, holding his hand while he has to go through all of it.

"Jay." I jump at the sound of Miles calling my name. I must've zoned out. "Why don't you head out?" he says, studying me for a moment. I glance back at the clock and see it's only a little after three. I still have a list of things I need to finish.

"Sir, I…" I want to leave. To go to the hospital and check on Jordan. I've felt off all day, and I want to be close to him right now, but I also know I've missed a few days already and there are things I need to take care of here. I still have a pile of emails to go through and a few reports to go over, as well.

"Jay, go. I know you're worried. You have a million

vacation days saved up." He's right. I do. I never use them. "This isn't a request. Do what you need to do, and go. Your mind isn't even here right now, so there is no point in staying."

"I promise I'll get all caught up—"

He raises his hand to stop me. "It's fine. You're my best employee. I know everything will be taken care of, and we have nothing pressing that can't hold off for a day or so."

"Thank you."

Miles nods and goes back to his office. I don't wait another moment before I grab my purse and shut my computer down. I pick up my phone, checking it once again as I head to the elevator and slide in the key card. The one I told myself I'd probably never use but now I can't seem to help myself.

When I get in the elevator, my phone dings with a text from Jordan. I hurry to open and read it.

Jordan: Take a cab.

I glance up at the camera and smile before shaking my head. I have a feeling Jordan can even pull up building security from his phone. I don't think there is anything he can't do with technology.

Me: You watching me?

Jordan: Always.

That should probably be creepy, but all it does is make me feel warm inside. I love that he worries about me enough to check in. I've never really had that before. When I lived at home, I was always the one doing all the worrying for everyone else. They all seemed to think I had it all under control, so no one ever bothered to see if I was okay. Having Jordan do this now is comforting in a way I wouldn't have expected.

When I exit the building, I grab a cab and head straight for the hospital. Traffic isn't too bad this time of day, and before I know it, I'm hopping out and making my way into the recovery wing, where Jordan's dad is located.

When I walk into the room, Jordan looks up, and I watch a smile pull at his lips. Some of the tension leaves his body as he stands, moving towards me. He looks like he hasn't slept much. I know at night in bed he tosses and turns until I stroke my hands through his hair. It's the only thing that settles him down, but I'd do it all night if it meant he finally had some peace. He's been a mess the past few days, and I know the stress is wearing on him.

"Hey," I say softly. He wraps his arms around me, pulling me closer into him. I bury my face in his chest, breathing him in. Some of the worry of the day fades away at his simple touch. I never knew having him in my life would offer me so much comfort.

"I missed you," he says against the top of my head, and I feel him kiss me there.

"I missed you, too," I admit. "How are things?"

I try to pull back so I can look at him, but he only holds me tighter, not wanting to let me go.

"They said he should wake up anytime now."

More relief washes over me. They're letting him wake up. That's good. Better than good. "So we wait?"

"We wait," he agrees as he picks me up and sits us

both down in the chair beside the bed. He cradles me in his arms, and I snuggle against him, feeling his hope seep into me.

"Jordan?"

"Rest," he says, stopping me from asking questions.

"You're the one who needs sleep," I insist, finally getting to really look into his eyes.

"I just need to hold you. Then I'll be good to go."

"Hmm," I mumble, burying my face in his neck. I feel even more tension drain from his body as his warmth surrounds me.

I must drift off, because the next thing I hear is a man's gruff voice. "You always going to hog her like that?" Jordan laughs quietly at the man's question.

I turn my head to see Jordan's dad is awake, and he's staring at me. In one movement, I'm up on my feet. "You're awake!" My eyes water as I step toward the bed.

Jordan hits the call button by the bed rail.

"Now why did you do that?" his dad huffs, clearly not pleased that the doctors and nurses will come in at any moment.

"Let them check you over, Pop. You scared the shit out of me." Jordan's words are filled with so much relief.

His dad reaches up, touching the spot where he got hit. "How long have I been out?"

Jordan sighs deeply. "It's been a few days."

His dad shakes his head. "I don't remember a damn thing." I can tell he's trying to concentrate, but it isn't coming to him.

At that moment two nurses come rushing in with a doctor, and all three of them start looking him over.

"I feel fine. Just a small headache," he reassures everyone once again. He says he's ready to go home, but

Jordan isn't having it. The doctor says everything is looking great, but they want to keep him a few more days to monitor his progress.

"The doctor wants to make sure you're okay. Please, Pop. It's for your health."

I step forward, placing my hand on his arms. "Please stay. We've been so worried and—"

"All right." Jordan's dad gives in to me easily.

It makes me smile, and Jordan shakes his head.

"Well, aren't you going to introduce us?" his dad adds, making me blush. "I always felt like I knew you. Even when he would try to keep it a secret, I knew." He gives me a teasing smile, and I watch Jordan duck his head shyly.

"Pop, this is Jay. Jay, this is my father, Rick."

"But you can call me 'Dad' or 'Pop,'" Rick adds. He reaches out, taking my hand and kissing it. His eyes soften, making him look so much like Jordan. He lets out a deep breath, and I know he's fighting sleep. The doctors put something into his IV to help manage his pain.

"Why don't you kids get home. Let this old man rest so I can get out of here soon. I still want my Sunday dinner."

"Maybe I should stay…"

Rick ignores Jordan and looks over to me. "Make sure he gets home and gets some sleep. He looks like he needs it."

"Hey, not all of us got to nap for the past few days," Jordan teases his dad, making him smile. I see so much love in his eyes for his son. He's more worried about him then he is about himself.

"Give me a hug." His dad leans up, opening his arms

for Jordan, and they have a long embrace before pulling back and saying they love each other. It's adorable how close they are. I wish I had that with my family. But I always felt like the outsider looking in on them.

"You too," he says. I lean down, and he wraps me in a tight hug. "Take care of my boy. I'm sure this shook him," he whispers in my ear. I give a small nod, and he kisses me on the cheek. Then Jordan is pulling me to his side. "See? He's going to try to hog you," Rick says, patting my hand. "You kids get home."

"See you in the morning, Pop," Jordan says when we get to the door.

"Bring me my coffee," Rick retorts, winking at us. Jordan agrees, and we leave.

"He's sweet. I already love him," I say as Jordan pulls me into his side, wrapping one arm around me and kissing the top of my head.

"Yeah, Pop has always had sway with people. He makes everyone feel welcome."

"I wish I had that with my family. You guys love each other so much." I sigh thinking about mine. "I can barely get my mom on the phone. Pretty sure she's dodging me." Not that I can blame her. She knows why I'm calling. Her daughter is driving me insane.

"Well, you do have us. We're yours, too. Pretty sure Pop is going to try to steal you from me. I can already see the giant dinners the two of you will be making every Sunday."

Jordan lifts his hand to wave for a cab. His words mean more to me than he knows. I'll be a part of a family that will actually like having me around. The cab pulls up, and he opens the door for me.

For a moment, he stills and brushes my cheek with

the back of his fingers. "Why the face?" he asks, staring into my eyes.

"I'm just happy," I tell him. No, I'm more than happy. Happy isn't a good enough word for what I'm feeling right now.

"Come on, let's get home and I'll make you even happier." He helps me into the cab, and I feel peace settle in my chest. Home. I love hearing him say it.

"I should probably do some work. Can I use your office, and maybe a spare laptop?"

"You don't have to ask to use anything of mine. I'll show you how to log in when we get there. You can work, and I'll get us food."

"Sounds perfect." I snuggle into him as we ride in comfortable silence. I feel better than I have in days. Even the rain has finally stopped.

When we get to his place, we walk inside and he gives me a serious look. "If you don't like it, we can change it."

"Hmm?" I ask, not understanding.

"I want you to like the place."

"I love this place."

It must be the answer he's after, because he leans down and kisses me. I try to deepen it, but he pulls away. "If you start that, I'll never be able to feed you, and you won't get to see your surprise."

"Fine." I give him a small pout, and against his own words, he kisses it off my face. Though this time, when I try to deepen it, he lifts me and throws me over his shoulder. It makes me laugh as all my hair falls into my face so I can't see anything.

Before I know it, I'm back on my feet and see I'm in Jordan's office. I glance around and see a new desk. It's white with silver trim and looks beautiful. On top of it is a computer, and beside that are dozens of notebooks.

"Jordan," I whisper. "How? Why? This is amazing."

He wraps his arms around me from behind. "We can change anything you want. I still need to put up some shelves for all your notebooks." He motions to a wall.

I turn in his arms and look up at him. "When did you have time?"

"I had some help, but it didn't take much. It was more having to order things."

I reach up and wrap my arms around his neck, making him bend down to kiss me. This time he deepens the kiss, and when my butt hits the desk, the notebooks fall to the floor. My legs fall open as he steps in between them.

I go for his shirt, trying to get it off him. I love when he doesn't have on a shirt so I can run my hands on his bare skin. He feels me tugging and helps me pull it from his body. Then he's rushing to get me out of my clothes. I lean back, helping him get my pants off, then my shirt goes next. Quicker than I thought possible, I'm completely naked on the desk in front of him.

"Fuck," he mumbles as his eyes roam over me. He drops to his knees in front of me, grabbing a hold of my thighs and pulling me to the edge of the desk.

"I've missed this. Missed you." His voice is deep and low against my sex, and he begins to devour me like he's starved.

I grab his hair, needing something to hold on to. I'm desperate to touch him.

"Jordan," I moan. I try to push up with my hips, wanting to be closer to him. I need to be wrapped around him as tightly as possible.

"So fucking sweet. No one knows just how needy and wild you get when you're turned on. And they never will. This." I look down at him, this giant man on his knees in front of me, pushing my thighs apart. "This is all mine. Forever."

"Yours," I admit, loving his words but needing his mouth back on me. "It's yours, Jordan. Please take it."

At my words, he covers my sex with his mouth. I rise off the desk, my orgasm fast approaching. From the second he took his shirt off, my body began to tighten for it. As he loves my clit, the muscles in my legs tense as he grips my thighs tighter. There's no escape for me, nowhere I could possibly want to go. The only thing I can do is cry out as he gives me the release I so desperately need.

I scream his name over and over again as he pulls the pleasure from me. Waves of it flow through my body, and I don't know if I have the longest orgasm of my life or if it's made up of several that roll together. It's passion unlike anything I've ever felt, and I'm certain the things he did with his mouth should be illegal in all fifty states.

My eyes fall closed, and I don't know how long I lie there, sprawled out on the desk. When I open my eyes, I see Jordan standing over me with a satisfied look on his face. You'd think he'd just had the orgasm, from the smile he's wearing.

He leans down and gives me a soft kiss. I can taste the pleasure he just gave me on his lips, and somehow that makes the kiss more intimate. I run my fingers through his hair, wishing we were in bed and I was cuddled in his arms.

"Now that was rude of me," he says, and I open my eyes.

"You can do rude things to me all the time, if that's what you consider rude."

He smirks down at me and shakes his head. "I ate, but you didn't." He pulls me into a sitting position, then picks his shirt up off the floor and slides it over my head.

"Put your finger here." He points to a little pad I didn't see on the desk.

"That is not where I want to put my finger right now," I sass, wanting us to go to the bedroom.

He chuckles, then lifts my hand and kisses my palm. He takes my finger and puts it on the pad. I watch as the computer comes to life. "Now you don't have to worry about fifty million passwords."

"I like that," I admit. It's pretty cool seeing it all open for me. I bring my hands back to him and rest them on his chest. "I like this, too." I start to trail my hands down his body, but he grabs my wrists.

"I'm going to feed you first."

"Forget the freaking food." I try to push for more, but my stomach isn't on my side. It growls, and Jordan raises an eyebrow. He's smug, and we both know he's won this round.

"I'll get the food. Play with your new toy."

I huff.

He leans down, getting but a breath away from my lips.

"I want you fed before I get you in that bed again, because I don't know when I'll let you out of it."

He gives me a kiss that's just deep enough to make me want more before he's striding from the room. I watch him go, wishing I had taken his pants off so he'd be walking around in just underwear. Damn it.

I jump off the desk and pick up the notebooks, then I sit down in the chair and start clicking on the computer. It looks like Jordan already set me up. All my tabs are there, and even my favorite websites are pinned to the desktop. I shake my head at how sneaky that man is.

I pull up my emails and start going through them, trying to clear as much stuff as possible. I really need to sit down with Miles and go over things that aren't adding up. Or maybe I could have Jordan look them over.

Time passes as I weed out the ones I need more notes on and the ones I can handle now. My email dings, and I freeze when I recognize the sender. I remember it from before, and a creepy feeling sets in. I hover over the email before finally clicking on it.

From: anonymous3640@gmail.com
Subject: none
Don't become the little birdy in the box.

I sit there, staring at the email, unsure what to do. Jordan walks into the room, and I pull my emails down, smiling at him. I really don't want to worry him with this right now. This is the first time in days he's really been smiling. The tension in his body has eased and he seems content. I don't want that coming back on him right now.

"Hey," I say, standing up. He looks at me a little funny.

"You ready to eat?" he asks.

I glance back at my computer, debating what to do. Jordan wraps his arms around me and nuzzles my neck.

"Let me feed you. Let me take care of you tonight like you did for me today."

I run my hands into his hair like I always do and nod. I will give him what he wants, because it's what I want, too.

"Sounds perfect," I tell him. I'm not ruining this day with threatening emails. I'll tell him about it tomorrow and let him take over. I won't keep anything from him. But as long as I'm in his arms, there's nothing that can touch me.

Tonight I'm falling into Jordan and forgetting everything else.

Chapter Twenty

Jordan

"Did you take the last wonton?" I ask, looking for it in the Chinese takeout box.

Looking up, I see Jay with her mouth full and her eyes wide.

"No," she mumbles guiltily and looks away quickly.

I narrow my eyes playfully. "Jay, did you eat the last one and not even ask me if I wanted it?"

She looks up at the ceiling as she chews and then swallows. She shrugs and takes a sip of her beer. "I don't know what you're talking about."

"I can't believe it. My little bird is a liar!" On the last word I lunge for her, and she squeals as she tries to get out of her seat.

I've caught her too quickly, and there's no escape. I pull her in my lap and dip her low so she's inches from the floor.

"Let me up! I'm going to fall!" she gasps between fits of laughter.

"Not until you admit that you stole the last wonton on the sneak!" I blow a raspberry on her neck, and she laughs so hard she has tears in her eyes. "Admit it. Admit it or else."

"I did it!" she gasps, and I can't help but laugh with her.

"I love you, but wontons are sacred."

She sobers at my words, and I smile at her, trying to catch my breath. It takes me a second to catch up to her.

"You love me?" she whispers, but I don't know why she suddenly looks so nervous.

I sit her up and place my hand on her chest, right over her heart. I didn't realize what I was saying when I said it, but it's exactly what I meant. "You know I do, Jay. I've never felt this way about anyone before. I love you."

I say it again so that she knows it wasn't a mistake. It wasn't a slip that I didn't mean. She's the love I've been waiting for.

"I love you, too," she says, and though her eyes are watery, she gives a small laugh and wraps her arms around me.

"Good. Now that that's settled, let's discuss your punishment for the food theft."

She squeals and wiggles out of my lap, taking off for our bedroom. I could have stopped her, but why deny her the thrill of the hunt?

Instead of stalking after her right away, I clean up our plates and turn out all the lights, then make my way to that end of the house.

"I hope your hiding spot is good. When I find you, there's gonna be hell to pay."

I slowly walk to the bedroom, checking doors and closets as I go. When I get to the master, I close the door and lock it behind me. I stand there for just a moment when I hear a muffled giggle come from behind the curtains.

Long drapes cover the floor-to-ceiling windows that line the room, so she could easily hide behind them. But the fact that her toes are showing at the bottom is what's truly adorable.

"I'm going to give you to the count of three. If you come out with your hands up, this will go much easier," I say, trying my best to keep the laugh out of my voice.

There's no response, only more muffled giggles. God, she's trying so hard not to laugh. She gets a gold star for effort.

"One." I begin to count, and I see the fabric twitch.

"Two." I say it slowly, giving her plenty of time.

"Three!"

Just as I shout the last number, she bursts from the curtain and runs straight at me, taking me by surprise. She leaps into my arms, and I don't catch her in time. We both go tumbling back on the bed, but I roll us over to soften her landing, and somehow I end up with her pinned under me.

"Ladies and gentlemen of the jury, I give you the Chinese-food thief. She's stolen not only food, but the plaintiff's heart. Clearly she's a menace to society," I say as I push the shirt she's wearing up her body and expose her breasts. "Just look at her. Temptation beyond belief. I think the sentence should be severe."

"I'll take the punishment I deserve," she says, biting her lip and pulling her shirt the rest of the way off. Her face turns solemn as she reaches down and pushes my pants off my hips. "Perhaps through rehabilitation and training, I could learn my lesson."

"Doubtful," I say as I lean down and bite her bottom lip before I run my tongue across it. "But I'm more than willing to try."

I take both her wrists in one of my hands and pin them above her head. I use my free hand to push down my underwear and then move between her thighs.

"I've waited a long time to have you under me, Jay. Too goddamn long."

The length of my cock rubs between her wet folds, and I have to press my forehead to hers and take a breath.

"I've never done this before. And from what you said, you haven't either, so we'll skip the safety chat and go right to me getting you pregnant."

Her cheeks flush, but as I slowly drag the ridge of my cock down her clit, she opens her mouth and moans at the friction.

"I'd love to slide into you bare," I say, lazily coating my cock with her honey. "And I'd love more than anything to make a baby on our first try."

Her eyes pop open and stare straight at me, but she doesn't say a word.

"But I understand that might be too much for you all at once." I press the tip of my cock to her opening, giving her a taste of what I want. Then I take it away and rub my length on her again. "So right now, you can tell me if you're on the pill. And if you're not, we can do other things. Or you can let me in that wet pussy for a little bit and then I can pull out."

I kiss a trail down her neck and feel her body shiver as she gasps. I'm moving on top of her, my thrusts making it look like I'm fucking her. One slip of my cock and I'd be balls-deep.

"Say the word and we'll go as far as we can. And

then we'll stop." I bite her earlobe as I hold her arms down and continue to thrust against her.

"I—" Her breath catches. "I was on the pill. But it got messed up when I left my apartment. I haven't been taking them since I came here."

"Yeah? So that means…?" I trail off, letting her think about it.

"You could get me pregnant." Any concern she has about it is belied by the moan that escapes her lips.

Slowly I move my cock to her opening, press in just a little, then take it away. The torment is killing both of us slowly, but it's too good to stop.

"I could," I say, kissing her collarbone and feeling the sweat break out on her skin. "I could slide into your tight little pussy and make a baby on the first shot. A baby with chestnut curls just like yours. And big chocolate eyes that match the ones I love so much."

"Oh God, you can't do this to me," she moans. "My ovaries are going to explode."

"I love you, Jay. You'll always be mine." I let go of her wrists to grab her hips. "There won't be a condom tonight or any night. But I'll stop when you ask me to. I'll pull out, if that's what you want. Just let me inside for a little bit."

I hold her still as I press inside her, but this time I don't take my cock away. Instead, I sink in a few inches and let her feel my cock inside her.

"I want to know what it's like to make love. And I don't want anything between that. You're it for me, Jay. I won't ever be with any woman but you."

"Oh God, Jordan. Don't stop." She grabs my ass and tries to pull me inside her.

Leaning down, I take her lips as I sink the rest of the way inside her. I try to go slow and gentle, but her legs wrap around me, and she forces all of me in in one thrust. She cries out into my mouth, but her pain only seems to last a split second as I hold myself inside her.

"Oh goddamn, I'm not going to last," I say, trying to pull out.

"No!" she protests and holds her body tight around mine. "Please don't stop. Please. It feels too good."

My body doesn't listen to anything other than her pleading as I move inside her.

"I'm going to come. Tell me what to do." The heat is building, and I don't know how much longer I can hold off.

Her legs squeeze tight as she rolls us over and grinds down on my cock. "Inside me," she whispers as she rocks her hips and rubs her clit.

The sight of her on top of me like a goddess from another world sends me over the edge. Her pussy squeezes me, and I push her hand out of the way and replace it with mine. She cries out at my touch and then opens her legs wider so that I can get her off with me.

It doesn't take long, and soon she's arching her back, bearing down as her passion takes over.

My warm seed fills her, and I watch as it spreads between us. The sight of her riding my hard length as my come coats her is the dirtiest thing I've ever seen.

"I will jack off to this image of you every chance I get for the rest of my life."

"You keep making love to me like this and you won't have to," Jay moans as she keeps moving.

Neither of us is sated by just one orgasm, and now that I've come in her once, what's a few dozen more times?

I flip us back over and get on my knees. I sit back

and pull Jay onto my lap so that I can hold her while I make love to her.

"You are the most beautiful thing I've ever seen," I say, wrapping my arms around her back and moving inside her.

"God, sex is amazing," she gasps, laying her head back and moaning.

"I'll take that as a compliment." I kiss her neck and then move my mouth to her breasts, sucking a nipple into my mouth and biting down gently.

"I want to do this forever."

"Until the end of time," I say.

We've sealed our fate tonight, and not just with chancing a pregnancy. I've admitted my love for her and gotten hers in return. But there's more than just love being put on the table. I'm telling her that this is it for me. She's my future, along with whatever comes out of our lovemaking. I want to put a ring on her finger and have her on my arm until the sun stops setting. I thought it might be too much for her to take in tonight, but from the light in her eyes, she's right there with me.

Her body tenses against me, and she's ready to come again.

"Being inside you is the most perfect thing I've ever felt. All those years of waiting were worth it. To have the woman I want to spend the rest of my life with wrapped around me is more than I could have dreamed of," I say as I move inside her. This is the reason I never went for second-best. "I'm grateful that my first time was with you and that it means something. Because I know it means something to you, too."

As I take her lips with mine and whisper how much I love her, we both find our release, wrapped in each other's arms.

Chapter Twenty-One

Jay

I snuggle deeper into the blankets, I don't want to get up. The last few days have been wonderful. I went ahead and took two days off work. We spent some of our time off with Jordan's dad and brought him home from the hospital. We helped him get his house back in order, and Jordan had a security system installed, complete with safety buttons all over the house for emergencies. He may have gone overboard with the safety features, but I didn't say a word. Because I may have gone a little overboard with food. I cooked enough to keep his refrigerator stocked and ready for all his visitors. We're all happy he's back home.

A few of his friends have come over every day, and we talked and had fun with them all evening. We'd do this each day until his dad would kick us out, telling Jordan he should be alone with his woman. It never failed to make me blush, and Pop would laugh at his victory.

Jordan didn't need to be told twice, because every day he'd bring me back home, and that's how we would end our days. We'd hardly left the bed when we were home, and now I know I need to get back to work.

I roll over, keeping my eyes closed and enjoying my last few moments in a warm bed wrapped in Jordan's smell. It's then I realize I'm not wrapped in him. I open my eyes and see a note on the pillow next to mine.

Went for a run and to grab breakfast. Be back in a few to take us to work.
I love you.
J

I pull the note to my mouth, kissing it. I'm totally keeping this. This is the first time he's said "I love you" in print. I shift a little, wishing he were still in bed. I love when he wakes me up by making love to me. It's always slow and sweet and takes my breath away.

Glancing at the clock, I know I need to get up. It takes some effort, but I pull myself from our bed and make my way to the shower for my morning routine. I even take the time to put on a little makeup and leave my hair down for once.

I slide on my glasses and walk out of the bathroom just as Jordan is walking into the bedroom. Gym shorts hang low on his hips, and his broad chest is covered in a thin layer of sweat. Even his hair is damp.

"Did you run like that?" I ask. He looks crazy-sexy right now, and a tug of jealousy shoots through me at the idea of other women seeing him like that. He shakes his head as he walks toward me.

"I went out and got you breakfast." He holds up a bag from my favorite bakery. He sets it down on the end of the bed before clearing the rest of the distance between us. "When I got back, I ran on the treadmill. In the house."

"Oh." It's the only word I can form, knowing I've been caught in my jealousy. My cheeks burn with embarrassment.

"You're so fucking cute." He leans down to kiss me, then yanks my towel off my body. "I'm going to shower. Eat your breakfast."

With that, he drops his gym shorts and goes into the bathroom. I don't know how long I stare after him, but then I giggle and grab the bag off the end of the bed and sit down to eat my muffin.

Not long after that, Jordan exits the bathroom as I finish eating. I should get up and get dressed, but I lean back on the headboard as I watch him look for something to wear.

"Little bird, I can't get ready with you doing that."

"What?" I say innocently, knowing what I'm doing. I'm completely naked. I bat my eyelashes at him. "I'm liking the view, so I'm enjoying it."

He mumbles something about being naked and only in my glasses.

Feeling a little bolder, I slide my hand between my legs, parting my thighs.

"Babe," he growls.

"I can't watch you? I mean, I didn't get my morning kisses and all, so…" I shrug and go back to what I was doing. I run my fingers across my clit and wish it was him doing it.

"Pretty sure I had you around three in the morning," he reminds me.

"Doesn't count if we go back to sleep," I tell him lazily, moaning a little.

"If I come over there, you know we'll be late." He

takes a step toward me. Then another. "You said we had to go in today."

"I can be fast."

"I don't like being fast with you."

"Jordan." I moan. I arch my back, offering my breasts to him. I'm getting closer to an orgasm, but I want him to finish me off.

"Fuck it," he growls. He moves across the room fast, and he's on me before I can gasp. His face goes straight for my sex, and I feel how hungry he is for me.

"Yes," I moan, letting my head fall back.

I try to raise my hips off the bed, but he holds me down. I sink one hand into his hair and grab on. It doesn't take much since I already had myself close. Arguing with him while he was naked and seeing his control snap was enough to send me to the edge.

"I'm coming!" I yell, as if he doesn't already know. My thighs clamp around his head as the pleasure washes through me. I let myself fall back onto the bed, feeling completely undone.

Jordan gives me a few more licks, making me jerk against him, before he rises over me. I think he's going to slide his cock into me now, but he doesn't. The bed jerks a little, and I look down to see him stroking himself. He pulls back even more, standing up beside the bed.

"Sit up," he commands, and I do. I reach out to touch him, but he shakes his head. I glare up at him, but he gives me a stern look.

"You got to touch yourself and mark me. Now I get to mark you." He licks his lips, and I know he's tasting me. I know he'll smell like me now. I stare up at him, transfixed.

"Tell me to mark you."

"Do it," I say quickly, my breathing picking up as he strokes himself. "Mark me, Jordan." His name comes out breathy, and I swear to God I might just come again from watching him jerk off in front of me.

"Jay," he groans as he starts to come. Hot spurts of semen hit my breast and trail down my stomach. God, that was hot, watching him like that. He got off on looking at me naked while I was still wrung out from the pleasure he gave me.

He reaches down and rubs his come into my skin. "Don't wash that off. You'll wear it all day as a reminder of what I'm going to do to you when we get home tonight."

I nod up at him. For some crazy reason, I love the idea that under my clothes today I'll have him on me. No one will know.

"That turns you on, doesn't it? That nobody suspects just how naughty you are for me."

He's so right. "I love it. I love you," I tell him. He leans down, taking my lips in a soft kiss.

"Love you, too, little bird. Now let's get ready." He pulls me up to help me stand from the bed before slapping my ass and pushing me toward the closet.

I want nothing more than to stay here with him.

"I don't want to go to work today," I grumble. This feeling is foreign to me. I've always looked forward to going into the office, probably because it was all I had. It's what my life was all about. Now I know that other things are out there. Like sex with the man I love.

"Why don't you just quit?" Jordan says. I look over to see him pulling on a pair of slacks.

"I can't just quit," I tell him as I roll my eyes and slip on a pair of dark blue panties with a matching bra.

"Yeah, you can. Not like we need the money. Plus, I haven't seen you write in any of your notebooks lately. Speaking of, I want to go get those from your old place," he says, buttoning up his shirt. Then he mumbles something about not liking my sister being so close to them or something.

I don't care for that idea either. What if she tries to read them? That thought makes me realize I haven't heard from her in days. Maybe she left town already. It's not unlike her to just pack up and leave and not tell anyone. The last time, she left while I was at work, and I didn't hear from her for months.

I shrug. "Maybe I haven't been writing in them because I'm living my own love story right now." I grab a pair of black slacks and slip them on, then pull on a dark blue top that I know will match the flats Jordan gave me. I turn around to see him sitting on the bed, his face soft.

"What?" I ask as I walk over to him.

"I like hearing you say that."

"Well it's true." I stand between his legs and lean down to give him a kiss. I trace his lip with my tongue as he caresses my hips.

"I can't wait for this day to be done," he sighs, and I step back, letting him get dressed. We both finish getting ready and head into the office. He gives me one final kiss, dropping me off at my desk.

I let out a deep breath and turn on my computer.

I cringe when I see the email from the other day still in my inbox. I need to talk to Jordan about it, and about the other one I got, not to mention that dead freaking bird, too. It's going to get him all worked up. I hate to burst the happy bubble we're in with something like this. My phone dings, and I see it's Jim from downstairs.

Jim: Incoming.

I go to the break room and hit the coffeepot in case he wants a coffee, but I'm pretty sure Miles has quit drinking it since he doesn't want Mallory drinking it because she's pregnant. I roll my eyes but smile while I do it. I walk back to my desk and sit down, making sure I have the things I need on my desk.

When the elevator opens and Miles walks off, I stand.

"Miles," I say, giving myself a pat on the back for not saying "sir."

"Everything better?" he asks. I can see the concern on his face.

"Yes, Jordan's dad is home. Thank you for asking."

"I'm ready whenever you are," he tells me with a smile.

I notice Mallory isn't with him, but I don't ask about her because I don't want to be nosy. But the difference in him since they've been together has been crazy. Miles was never mean or rude to me. We worked together like a well-oiled machine, but he would have never asked me about my personal life before. Never asked me to call him Miles. Mallory has melted a lot of his coldness away. I smile back. I'm getting it. I don't seem to get so worked up anymore either. Jordan has calmed me.

"Just need to make a few copies and I'll be right in." I lift up my folder and notepad. "You need me to grab you anything?"

"Nope, I'm good. See you in a few," he says and strolls into his office. I hear him whistle, and I have to hold back a chuckle as I make my way to the copy room, getting the last of the stuff I need before heading into his office.

I go over his schedule with him, canceling some appointments and moving others around. Then Miles jumps into wanting to back off some projects he's shown interest in in the past. I think this has to do with him slowing down. I nod, checking them off my list.

"Lannister," I finally say.

"I thought it was all wrapped up but the deal hasn't gone through?"

"I stopped it," I admit. "Mr. Stein gave us the final project portfolio, and we agreed. Well, while you were on your honeymoon he said something needed to be changed. The portfolio is over two hundred pages. He'd told me he'd mark the changes. I was reluctant to give it to him."

Miles leans back in his chair folding his hands together like he's thinking.

"I didn't care that he was going to mark the changes. I know he's been here a long time. Longer than me. I just can't blindly agree without knowing if something else was changed. My eyes go over everything before I hand you the final work."

"And that's why you're my assistant, Jay. I trust you, and something doesn't smell right. I thought the project was done. Mr. Stein even called to tell me things were wrapped up."

"What?" I grit my teeth. "I haven't signed off on it, and neither have you." I feel my anger grow and my face heats. That little fucker.

"I think he's changed something in there he doesn't want us to check. Getting it back from you while I was gone and then making me think it was done... I assume he was trying to push this deal through before we caught on."

"Yes," I agree. "I kept asking him for the project. He wouldn't respond. So finally, Jordan got it for me."

"He got it for you?" Miles asks with a smile.

I give a little shrug.

Miles chuckles. "Ever so persistent."

I don't respond because I know I am when I want something. I'll pick and pick and pick.

"I feel like he's telling you one thing and me another. Also, the files he gave me don't match the ones you had in the email you sent me. I was finally able to really go over it. It's not good. He needs to be fired and the whole deal needs throwing out." I shift in my seat. "In fact, there could be federal charges placed on him if he made those changes. I know they wouldn't be changes you would have agreed to, and normally I'd have caught this right away."

"It's almost like someone is trying to make sure both of us are busy during times we'd need to be on the same page. Me with my honeymoon. You with everything that's going on." He rubs his chin and thinks for a second. "And he's been out on family leave for how long now? This is all looking bad."

I hadn't thought about that. "The deal talked about foreign ammunition. There are so many copies of the portfolio floating around, I can't keep anything straight," I admit, feeling a little over my head.

"I'll make sure it's pulled. Then we can bring in the

team. I don't want the company left holding the bag on this."

"Maybe we need to look into some of Mr. Stein's other projects, as well." God, this is going to be a mess.

"I agree. Let's have Jordan do some magic for us. Maybe he can do some digging and see when the documents were time stamped. Who knows what else he'll find, but I'm sure he'll find us something." Miles reaches for his phone but puts it down when his office door flies open, hitting the wall. I jump up from my seat to see a very pissed-off Jordan standing in the doorway.

"Jordan?" Miles asks, but he ignores him.

"There something you want to tell me, Jay?" He steps into the office, and I pale a little.

"I was going to tell you, I promise, I just…" I trail off. What else is there to say? I wring my fingers together.

"What the fuck is going on?" Miles barks.

"She's been getting threatening emails," Jordan growls. "To her work email."

"And I got a box with a dead bird," I blurt out, wanting to lay it all on the table and get it over with.

Jordan lets out a string of curses that make me cringe.

"Jay." Miles says my name quietly, and I know I'm in trouble.

"I'm sorry! Things have been crazy, and, well…" Jordan stares at me, his eyes boring into mine. I've never seen him this mad before. He's always sweet and soft. Well, at least to me. Seems there might be another side to him.

"I'm sorry," I whisper.

I hear Miles pick up his phone and start talking.

"Justice, I need you to get my wife back here. When she gets in, my floor is on lockdown."

He's quiet for a second, and Jordan moves toward me. All that tension that had finally left his body is back. Maybe worse than ever. His fists are clenched at his side.

"Then I need you to meet Paige and Jordan in security. Seems my assistant has been getting threats and I might have an idea who's behind it. Or at least Jordan can start tracking the emails."

"I'm sorry," I whisper again, stepping closer to Jordan and closing the rest of the distance between us.

He cups my face, and some of the anger slips away. "I know I'm pissed. Real fucking pissed. And don't get me wrong, about twenty percent of it is your doing, but the real anger is due to someone threatening you. A fucking dead bird, Jay." His voice is hoarse and pained. He's the only one who calls me "little bird."

"I'm going to fix this," he tells me, and I nod, knowing he will.

"Okay, I want to go over some things I've learned with Jordan. All the programs are down in security. Let's go ahead and get started on what we can find," Miles says.

"Yeah, let's do this."

We leave Miles's office, but Miles stops at my desk. "You stay here and keep reading over these files. See what you can catch," Miles says.

"I want her with me," Jordan fires back.

"Justice and Mallory are on their way up. I'm locking down the floor. She'll be safer here than moving around the building."

I can see Jordan wants to fight him on it.

"I'll be fine." I try to reassure him.

"You keep your little ass in that chair, Jay," he growls, and I sit down exactly where he tells me. He shakes his head at me, and Miles steps back, clearly giving us some space.

Jordan leans down, caging me in. "I love you more than anything. Stay here where I can see you."

I nod. "I love you, too."

He lays a hard kiss on me before storming off, with Miles following him.

"Well, crap," I mumble to myself. I turn, picking up the folder and flipping it open. I don't make it two lines and my cell is going off. I see it's my sister and clear the call, but it rings again. I don't have time for this, but I know she'll just keep calling. Sighing, I answer, thinking maybe it will be a welcome distraction for a moment.

"What's up?" I say, still looking down at the folder and only half reading it.

"If you want your sister to live, you'll pick up that folder and walk out of the building."

"Who is this?" Panic hits me as the distorted voice echoes on the other end. It sounds like something out of a movie.

"Time's ticking, little bird. You better get off the floor before Justice and Mallory get there and the place goes into lockdown. Or you'll never see your sister again." I hear my sister scream my name in the background.

"All we want are the folders. Close it and pick them up." My hands shake as I do it. "Now use the special little card your boyfriend gave you and get to your apartment." I grab my purse and walk toward the elevator. "Don't use this phone again or I'll know."

Then the line goes dead.

I slide my card into the elevator, and the doors slide closed. My fingers twitch to hit the floor for security, but I don't know if whoever called me is watching. If I say something, he might hurt my sister. I just have to give him the folders. I can do that. When the doors slide open, I look up at the camera.

"I love you," I say before stepping off.

Chapter Twenty-Two

Jordan

"I don't understand why she didn't say anything to you before now," Miles says over my shoulder.

"I'm sure she didn't want me to worry," I respond, tapping my fingers. I'm waiting on the software I ran on Jay's computer to load and sorting through the mirror program I have that shows me all of her emails.

"You were able to get all this information just now?"

I look at Miles and then shake my head. "No. I copied her computer a long time ago." I shrug because I'm not the least bit sorry.

"Damn. I wish I had known this sooner. Remind me to talk to you about doing this for me later."

I smile, knowing a fool in love when I see one. Mostly because I see one every morning in the mirror. Tossing that thought to the side, I click on the Bluebird folder on my desktop and search the name Lannister.

"I've got all the correspondence saved on this file you were telling me about. I should be able to cross-check the data and see if anything matches. It's all too similar for it to be a coincidence," I say as I wait for the program to run.

"What's going on? Why are we on lockdown?" I look up as I see Mallory talking to Miles. Ryan, Paige and Skyler are with her. "We were shopping and then all of a sudden we had to come back. Is everything okay?"

"Why aren't you on the top floor, Mallory? I specifically asked you to stay there, where I know you're safe," Miles says, looking over at Ryan.

"The key cards didn't work. We thought we didn't make it back before you shut it down, so we came here," Paige says.

"Wait, what did you say?" I ask, cutting in. The hair on the back of my neck stands up. "We didn't issue it yet."

I click on the screen of my computer and bring up the feed for Jay's desk. She's not there.

"Fuck!" someone mutters behind me, and then I hear Paige shout for the building to go into code red.

The alarm sounds, and everyone is in motion. Everyone but me. My hand is shaky as I push back the footage and find the image of when she was last sitting there. I'm praying she just got up to go to the bathroom.

My stomach turns sour as I watch her pick up her phone and her face goes white. She walks out on shaky legs and gets into the elevator. I move the footage to when she gets off, and I can see her look up and mouth the words *I love you*.

"Oh God, no, baby. No." My heart feels like it's beating out of my chest. What the fuck is she doing?

The footage shows her exiting the building and getting in a cab. I can't see anything past the perimeter, and I stand up so quickly my chair falls to the floor behind me.

Someone gasps, and I'm shaking with rage. I grip

the edge of my desk, not knowing what to do. My first thought is to run out of this room and chase after her, but where do I go? I want to kick the desk over and break every piece of equipment in here, but that won't do me any good either.

"Chen," Paige barks, and I snap out of my downward spiral and look over to her. "You're the only one who can track her down. Find out where she went."

She's right. I can do this.

Pulling up the data on the nearest satellite, I hack into the cell tower and get her phone records. I remind myself to clone her goddamn phone just as soon as she's back in my arms.

It takes minutes for all of it to come up, and every second of that is pure agony. Finally, the last number that called her pops up. Her apartment.

"Her sister," I say, feeling another rock in the pit of my stomach. "I need to go to Jay's apartment." I stand up and start to push past the group of people behind me, but a short redhead is standing in my way.

"Jordan, let us go. You're the only one who knows how to do this shit," Paige says, waving at my computer. "If you go looking for her, what happens if she isn't there? Then what? You come back here and start again, losing precious time."

I want to protest, but I know she's right. I open my mouth, but she slaps something into my hand.

"You'll be with me the whole time. Captain?" she says, turning around to Ryan. "Get your gear. We're out in two."

They walk over to McCoy and Grant, and the four of them talk in low whispers. I feel like my hands are tied, but I know there's more I can be doing.

I get on my computer and pull up every trace I know. Everything is going to be okay.

If I say it enough, it has to be true. Right?

Chapter Twenty-Three

Jay

When I open my eyes, I feel the side of my head throbbing. The sound of my pulse is in my ears, and I'm disoriented. It's like that time I went on the Scrambler at the fair and couldn't walk straight afterwards. Only I can't even stand up now.

I look around and see light coming in from above. It's late in the day, and it looks like the sun is setting. Damn it, how long have I been unconscious? Hours have passed since this morning, when I was with Jordan and he was kissing me.

The thought of his name sends a bolt of lightning to my heart, and I sit up way too fast.

Leaning over on my hands, I feel like I'm going to vomit. I dry-heave and then cough, fighting the urge. "What happened?" I whisper to myself.

"Jay?" I hear a croaky voice and finally look around the room.

A sob bursts from me when I see my sister lying on the ground only a few feet from me. I crawl over, unsure if my legs will work yet or not.

"Summer? Oh God, are you okay? What happened? Where are we?"

She moans and covers her face with her hands. "They took us."

Suddenly images flash through my mind as the memories come back.

I went straight to my apartment and ran up the stairs as fast as I could. Just before I got to the door, I felt something hit me on the back of my head. Then I remember being dragged into the apartment, where there were two men, but I didn't recognize them.

Part of it is still foggy, but I remember being put in the back of a van, and at some point, I fought. I remembered some of the things Paige had taught me from our self-defense classes, but I was too disoriented to do them right. After that, I remember a pinprick in my ass, and then I passed out.

The thought makes me want to throw up again.

"Are you okay, Summer? Did they hurt you?" I reach out and hold her hands in mine, trying to will us to be okay.

"Yeah, I'm okay. One of them hit me a few times." She lifts her head, and I see a black eye already starting to form. "I'm so sorry, Jay. I didn't know what to do. They came to the apartment saying you had something they wanted. They tore the place apart, but I had no clue what they were looking for." Big tears roll down her cheeks, and she begins to shake. Panic is setting in.

"Shh. It's okay. You did the right thing," I say, pulling her into my arms and holding her while she cries. I feel my own tears run down my face as I try to comfort her.

One of us has to be strong, and I've been the one doing it my whole life. I can do it a little longer.

Looking around the room, I try to look for a way to get out. The space is about the size of my apartment, with no walls dividing it up. The only sources of light are the skylight in the roof and a bare bulb hanging down in the corner. There's a cot over on the other side of the room, and it looks filthy. I see a door, but it's hard to even call it that, because there's no handle on this side of it. There's a small window on it, but that's covered with a board, so we can't see out. For a moment I think about going over to it and trying to talk to whoever took us, but I'm not ready for that yet.

I can still feel my legs shaking, and I'm not sure I can walk on them.

"Who did this?" Summer asks, and I shake my head.

"I think I know, but I don't understand why. They got what they wanted."

"If you know who it is, it means you know their face. You could identify them." She shivers harder than before, and I can see where her train of thought has gone.

"Hey. Don't think like that. We'll get out of here," I say, and I hope that I'm not a liar. "I just need a few more minutes for whatever they gave me to wear off."

I hold Summer close to me, letting my body heat help with her shock. It's all I can do right now, but it's something. I keep scanning the room, looking for weaknesses.

There's a latch on the skylight, and I wonder how heavy it would be to push open. The ceiling isn't super tall, and I look at the bed, judging the distance from the skylight to the frame if I stood it on its side. I'm no MacGyver, but desperate times means looking at all your options.

What would Jordan do? Oh God, just the thought of

him is like a punch to the gut. How could I walk out of the building like that? Will he understand that I had no choice? That I had to save my sister?

I wasn't prepared for what happened, but how could I have been? I just wanted to give them what they asked for and make sure she was safe. But saving her may have cost me the love of my life.

Will he forgive me for what I had to do? Will I make it back into his arms?

More tears leak down my cheek, and I'm trying to be strong. I'm trying my best to hold it together. For Summer. For Jordan. For myself.

I pull all the strength I have left in me and focus on Jordan. He will find me. He would walk through hell and back to get me. He'll come for me, and when he does, I'll be ready. I won't curl up in the corner and cry. I'll fight to stay alive.

"Just hang on a little longer," I say to Summer. I kiss the top of her head and hold her close. "Everything is going to be okay."

Maybe if I say it enough, it will be true.

Chapter Twenty-Four

Jay

I snuggle deeper into Jordan, my head resting on his shoulder. My hand is on his bare chest, our fingers twined together. One of my legs is thrown over his hip, and I soak up all his warmth.

"I love waking up like this," he says.

I couldn't agree more. I've never slept better than I do with him. Each night my mind would race with things I needed to get done. Sometimes I'd even wake up in the middle of the night and do the thing I was so worried about. But not when he's in bed with me. He's all I can think about, and now when I wake up in the middle of the night, it's because he's making love to me.

"Me too." My voice is still full of sleep.

"Maybe we should paint this room lavender."

I open one eye at his words and look around a little. "You want to paint your room purple?" I laugh.

"Our room," he corrects, making me smile. "I want this to feel like your home, too. Your living room was lavender. I want you to love it here."

"I don't care where I live, as long as I live with you. And as long as you keep waking me up like you

did this morning." I wiggle, rubbing my naked body against him.

"I'd do anything to keep you here, so you've got yourself a deal." He strokes my ring finger gently, making my heartbeat pick up. Then he rolls us over, positioning himself on top of me.

"I want you again," he says against my mouth, already sliding into me.

I moan against his lips, wanting him too. I always want him. I will forever.

"Food!" I hear a shout, and it jolts me awake. My eyes fly open, and I look around, shocked. The sight that greets me makes me remember where I am. Not at home in the arms of the man I love, a place I may never be again. I blink a few times, trying to clear my eyes to see better in the darkness. I hear the door to our cell clang shut, and the lock clicks into place.

"I don't want to eat it," Summer mumbles, her head still in my lap. I have my back in the corner of the room, and I'm sitting cross-legged. I no longer feel groggy, but the concrete wall is doing a number on my back. At least my head isn't throbbing anymore.

"Scared it's not vegan?" I try to tease her. I don't want her to start crying again. As much as she can drive me crazy, I never want to see her cry.

"Ha ha," she says, rolling over to her other side, pulling her legs back into her chest and making herself into a ball. It's a little chilly in here, and she doesn't have much on but a tank and a pair of shorts. I rub my hand up and down her arm, trying to make sure she stays somewhat warm.

"I love you," she says, taking me by surprise. "You always took better care of me than Mom and Dad." I'm taken aback by her words. My eyes water, the emotions of the day weighing heavy on me. "I know I can drive you crazy, I just—"

"I love you, too," I tell her, cutting her off. Coming from a home where your parents are all about the free love, saying "I love you" to each other isn't that big. "To be honest, I thought I drove you crazy, too. Especially when we were little," I admit.

"Remember when Mom got those chickens?" Summer says with a small sad laugh.

"How could I forget? She kept them in the house." I want to be mad remembering it, but looking back now, I'm about to laugh, too.

"You ran around like crazy trying to clean up after them."

"God, that was a nightmare." I couldn't keep up with those chickens.

"A funny nightmare. You said you were going to cook them." Her tone is accusatory.

"Sorry about that." I shake my head. I wasn't really going to cook them, I was just annoyed. I'd keep putting them outside, and my mom would keep letting them in. "You lost it when I tried to cook their eggs. You ran around screaming and crying, saying, 'There are baby chickens in those!'"

We both smile for a moment. "Like the adult, you went outside and spent two days turning that old shed into a place for those chickens to stay."

"I wasn't going to let us all live in chicken shit," I say, shrugging.

"Yeah."

"You painted flowers and rainbows on the outside. You made it look pretty."

"I should have helped you build it. Not sit outside and doodle when you were doing the hard work. Like always."

"You were doing what you do, and I was doing what I do." My own words hit me.

My sister and I are day and night, and there's nothing wrong with that. We should accept each other, maybe even learn something from one another. Maybe I've been harder on her than I should have. We are both products of our raising. While I went one way, she went another, and I can see why someone would choose to go the way she did. It's easier to fit in. To feel loved.

"If we get out of here—"

"When," I correct her. I want her to stay positive. I don't want her having a breakdown.

"*When* we get out of here, I want us to be closer. To not fight so much."

"I want that, too," I admit.

"I'm tired of bouncing around, and I don't want to go back to Mom and Dad's. I want a home."

"Then you'll stay here. We'll come up with a plan for you."

"See? You're always looking out for me." I hear her sniff. I'm guessing this has really shaken her up. Made her rethink some things.

"Try to get some sleep. When we get a little more light, I'm going to try to get us out of here."

"I'll try," she says, and I start rubbing her arms again.

I keep looking up at the skylight. It's too dark for me to see the latch. I wish the moon would at least come out so I'd have some kind of idea how to open it.

We have to get out of here. If something happens to me, I know Jordan won't be able to take it. He's lost enough in his life. He doesn't need to lose more. A lump fills my throat. He's probably losing his mind right now. I have a feeling if he gets me back in his arms, he's never going to let me leave the house again. That thought makes me smile.

I never thought in all my life I would find someone like him. Someone who makes me feel like I'm coming home for the first time. Someone who takes care of me. We both have our odd habits, and we love those things about each other. He was made for me. I know it.

Time ticks by, and I don't know how long we've been here, but it feels like an eternity. I let my time with Jordan run through my mind. The memories make me want to smile and cry all at once.

I must doze off at some point, because when I glance up again I can see a hint of light starting to show. We haven't had anyone else come back to check on us, and the tray of gross food still sits by the door. I assumed it was probably drugged, and I'm not hungry enough to eat it yet.

"Summer," I whisper, giving her a little nudge.

"Hmm," she says, sitting up.

I point up to the skylight. "See that latch? We have to get up there."

Her eyes widen as she wakes up and nods. "Okay." She stands up. I see a little more fight in her eyes, and I think maybe our talk helped.

"Okay. We're going to move that bed over here, and I'm going to stand on it, then lift you."

"Maybe I should lift you. What if I can't get the latch?"

"You're smaller than me. It will be easier to pick you up. Plus, you do all that yoga stuff. You've got more muscle tone than me and can probably pull yourself up. No way can I do that."

"Okay." She walks over to the bed with me.

"We have to pick it up. We can't drag it. It'll be too loud on the concrete floor."

She nods and goes to the other side of me, and I gesture for us to both lift. It's heavy, but not impossible to move. We have to go slow, but soon we get it right under the latch.

"Now. When you get up there, slide it open, okay? And be as quiet as you can."

"All right."

I reach out and put my hand on her shoulder. "Summer, I want you to climb through and go. Do you understand me? I don't think you'll be able to pull me up, and we aren't wasting time trying. I don't know how much longer we'll have before someone comes back."

"I'm not leaving you." Her eyes search mine and begin to fill with tears.

"Yes, you are. You're going to run as fast as you can and you're going to get help."

"But—"

"You're not leaving me. You're saving us," I tell her. Suddenly she's grabbing me and pulling me into a tight hug. "You can do this. I know you can."

She takes a deep breath and pulls back to look at me. "Okay, let's do this."

I climb up on the bed, putting my feet on either side of the bed frame for support. She climbs up with me, and I hold my hands out like a cheerleader would to give a lift.

"I love you," I tell her.

"I love you, too."

She climbs up me, and I brace my legs, trying to be as sturdy as possible while on a cot. I can hear the bed groan under our weight. I close my eyes and give a small prayer, hoping like all hell this works.

She puts her foot in my hand and then steps up while I try to lift her. She puts her other foot on my shoulder and almost gets the other up to stand when the bed gives way. The frame snaps, and we both tumble down in a heap. I hit the dirty mattress that has fallen through the frame, and Summer lands on top of me, knocking the air out of my lungs.

I want to cry out, not just from the pain but from the fact that our last shred of hope has slipped away. It takes a moment before I can breathe normally again and my lungs aren't burning from the pain.

"Are you okay?" Summer asks, hurrying to get off me.

I tell her I'm okay and start to get up when the door to the room flies open. Both of us jump, going to the far wall as fast as possible, trying to put some space between us and the man in the doorway.

It only takes me a second to get my bearings, but once again the air is knocked right out my lungs when I see who is standing in the doorway.

"Mr. Spencer?" I say, as if I almost can't believe what I'm saying.

He reaches outside the door and flips a switch, and light floods the room. As he steps inside, my attention fixes on the open door. He must notice it, because he shuts it closed behind him immediately.

This guy has been into Osbourne Corporation more times than I can count. He used to be nice to me, but as time went on, he got sleazier and more aggressive. Did he do all this? How could he possibly be involved?

A sick smile spreads on his face as he glances around the room and looks down at our untouched food.

"Is our food not good enough for you, little bird?" At the use of the name Jordan calls me, my stomach tightens. "Nothing is ever good enough for you, is it?"

"Why are you doing this? I brought the files. That's what you wanted, wasn't it? Let us go." I stand a little straighter, trying to use the same voice I do when I'm at the office. I don't know if that's a good idea or not.

I'm not even sure what's going on at this point. I thought this was about the Lannister project. I was sure I'd end up seeing Stein, not Spencer. Unless they're in on this together. Now I'm worried who else might be in on this. How far through the company does this go?

"I think we both know there's something else I've been wanting to get my hands on for a while." At his words, I move to stand in front of my sister. I put my hands on my hips, not only trying to make myself feel bigger, but so he won't notice that my hands are shaking.

"I'll fight you," I tell him. And I will. I won't make it easy for him. My stomach turns, and I want to throw up. My skin is crawling. I still can't believe this is even happening. How could I feel like my life was finally perfect and now it's all falling apart? I only got a tiny taste of it.

He closes the distance between us. I look up at him, meeting his eyes. "I think I'll like it when you fight me." He gets right in front of me and lifts his hand, dragging a finger down my cheek. "It will be so much sweeter when I get you to break."

I smack his hand away, and he smirks.

"You'll have to fight both of us," my sister says, trying to step around me, but I block her with my arm.

"Two for the price of one. It's my lucky day."

"Fuck you." I reach up and smack him.

The smack echoes around the room, and my hand burns. When his face turns back to me, I see blood where my nails dug into his cheek. His face turns redder than I have ever seen. The deadly anger is clear in his expression. Yeah, I don't think he likes the fight, after all. I brace myself when he strikes me back. I almost fall backwards, but my sister catches me.

"You fucking bitch!" he bellows and lunges for me.

The door to the room flies open, and Summer and I use the distraction to move farther away from Spencer.

"That's enough." This new man's voice is deep and holds a tone of authority to it. Spencer stops immediately. I can tell he's fighting his orders.

"I can't have you messing her face up. We need her to be able to talk to that boyfriend of hers. Seems there are more problems."

"What kind of problems?" Spencer doesn't turn to look at the man. I glance over at the new guy. He's in a dark suit and fills up a lot of space in the door. I can tell that much. But his face is hard to see because he's not stepping into the room, and my eyes are still watering from the smack. My cheek throbs, and I want to hold it, but I want to have my hands ready in case Spencer comes at me again.

"Our guy is having problems getting some of the stuff removed from the Osbourne servers."

"Fuck!" Spencer grunts. His eyes harden on me. He walks over to me, grabbing me by the hair and pulling it. My sister tries to grab for him, but Spencer pushes her, sending her to the floor. I reach up, gripping his hand, trying to weaken his grasp.

"You're going to make a little call for us, aren't you." There's no question to Spencer's words.

"Yes," I say instantly, trying to seem agreeable. I know that if I say no they'll threaten Summer, and I can't handle that right now.

"That's a good girl." He leans down close to me, and he licks my face from my chin to my forehead. I have to bite back a gag when I feel his erection digging into me. "As sweet as I thought you would be." Then he lets me go, throwing me down to the floor next to Summer.

"We'll be back," he says turning to leave but stopping at the door. "Don't worry, though, Jay, we'll still get to have our fun soon enough." He reaches down and adjusts his crotch before turning and shutting the door. The lock clicks into place, and I finally let the tears come.

Chapter Twenty-Five

Jordan

My fist goes through the Sheetrock, and I welcome the burn on my knuckles. I pull back and do it again, the pain in my hand nothing compared to the pain in my chest.

"You going to let him keep doing that?" Ryan says behind me.

"It's either that or someone's face. Just let him get it out," Paige sighs, and I go back to beating up the wall.

It's been almost twenty-four hours. Miles wanted to call in the cops and report her missing, but Ryan and Paige talked him out of it. They explained that this is something we want to take care of in-house, and that means we can handle it how we want to when we find her. And find the bastard that took her.

I've been up all night, and I think most everyone else has been, too. Miles finally left with Mallory at some point in the night, and the rest of the team has been sleeping in shifts. I've done all I can do, and so far, nothing has popped up. I've caught a trace of someone trying to break into our system to wipe the servers, but both times they've slipped past me. That was the

first time I punched the wall. After that, I just needed
to do it every few minutes to give myself some kind
of release. I've almost destroyed one whole side of the
department, but nobody tries to stop me.

My scans finished an hour ago, and I couldn't cross-
reference any location where they might be holding Jay
with our files here. I was able to find all the dirty shit
Miles was looking for, so at least my time wasn't totally
wasted. There were all kinds of illegal deals slipped into
this contract that was set to make Stein a ton of money.
I don't know what kind of shit he got himself wrapped
up in, but now that the deal hasn't gone through, he
owes a lot of people.

My stomach churns, and I turn around, putting my
back to the decimated wall. I slide down it until my ass
hits the carpet, and then I put my head in my hands.

All I keep thinking about is Jay alone somewhere.
Scared. Hurt. Dead? A bubble of panic rises in my
throat, and I have to hold it down. I can't think like
that. It's not hopeless. Not yet.

I take a breath and start with what we know. The
Lannister deal was set up so that an international
company could funnel illegal ammunition through
Osbourne Corporation undetected. Stein took a huge
payment up front and blew through the money without
having the deal secured. Jay got suspicious, and when
she started poking around, Stein skipped out of work to
avoid getting caught. Then he tried to slide the deal to
Miles on the side so that it would get signed without a
fuss. If Jay hadn't caught it, no one would have known.
Stein wrote the deal himself, and he didn't have anyone
else checking his work. No one other than my little bird.

I rub my eyes, exhaustion hitting me. I want to close

my eyes, but I know if I do I'll be missing out on time I could be using to figure this out. What more can I do? There's got to be something.

When Jay caught the discrepancies, she kept hounding Stein. When he dodged her, I went after him and got it. When I showed up at his home, he was reluctant to give me all the paperwork, and I know it's because it wasn't wiped of all the illegal information. He must have handed it over thinking I was just a hired hand, and then Jay would turn it over to Miles. Miles even said he called to let him know it was all set and just to sign them. What Stein didn't count on was Jay. She's like a dog with a bone, and she won't let it go until she's good and ready. The part that scares me the most is that if Stein is looking for revenge, Jay is the one he would go after. If he's got her, then all I can do is pray we get to her before he reacts.

Summer had to be collateral damage. She was the bait to get Jay to come home, and she couldn't be left behind. If she's able to identify the person who took her, then she may not make it out alive. And the same goes for my Jay.

For a moment, a flash of her face drifts through my mind. Her smile as she's laid out on my bed, her hair a mess of waves around her. Her chocolate eyes looking straight to my soul. The ache in my chest burns like there's a knife inside, twisting in my heart. I don't know how much longer this can go on. She has to stay alive. She has to. There's no other choice.

I try to think of all the times I held her in my arms. I lean my head back and close my eyes, remembering the feel of her fingertips against my chest. I think about the curve of her hip as she lies on her side and tells me about all the places in the world she wants to see. I think about the sounds of her breathing as I wrap my body around hers and keep her safe. The memory of her legs wrapped around my waist as I sink deep into her body and make sweet love to her.

I'm jolted awake when my phone vibrates in my pocket. I look around, disoriented, and blink a few times. I must have fallen asleep. I reach down and grab my phone, almost dropping it as I slide the bar across the screen to answer it.

"Jay! Is it you, Jay?" My heart pounds in my throat, and I hear a throat clear.

"Jordan, it's Pop."

I sink against the wall as hope leaves me cold and alone. "Hey, Pop."

I called him late last night and told him Jay went missing. He took it almost as hard as I did, and we stayed on the phone for a while and he listened to me cry. As soon as I hear his voice now, I feel like doing that all over again.

"Listen, Jordan, I've been racking my brain all night."

"Me too, Pop. Thanks—"

"No. I'm trying to tell you I remember something." His voice is stern, and I sit up a little.

"What?" I can't understand what he means, but it could be lack of sleep.

"Last night I remembered something about my accident. It wasn't an accident. Someone was there."

My blood runs cold. "Pop, what are you saying?"

"There were two people. They came around the back of the house. Someone said the name Spencer. I didn't get a good look at either of them because it all happened so fast. I don't remember much else, but someone said the name Spencer, I'm sure of it."

"Do you think this has something to do with Jay?" I ask, and I see Paige looking over at me as I talk.

"I think it might. I don't know, Jordan, but I feel like it has to. Nothing was stolen from my house, they didn't break in. It was like they wanted to create confusion."

I'm nodding as he speaks. It has to be related. Why would someone harm my dad? It wouldn't be hard for the person who did this to find out Jay and I were together. She doesn't have much of a family to reach out to. So going after her parents wouldn't have gotten the kind of attention going after mine would. I rub my face, feeling like the fresh information has reenergized me.

"Okay, Pop. Thanks for telling me. If you think of anything else let me know. But this is enough for me to do some digging right now."

"I love you, son. Go find our girl."

"I love you, too, Pop. And I promise, I will."

I hang up the phone and grip it tightly in my hand. I've never lied to my dad before, and I'm not about to start now. I will bring Jay home.

Paige and Miles walk up to me.

I get up off the floor and look to the both of them. "The name Spencer mean anything to you?"

Chapter Twenty-Six

Jay

There's a noise outside the door, and I tense when I hear shouting. My body is stiff from being on the cold concrete, but there's no choice other than the filthy mattress. I'm aching and cold, but I'm not so far gone that I'm willing to crawl on it and pick up whatever diseases are lingering.

I feel Summer wake up at the sounds. We've been huddled up in the corner, trying to stay warm, but there's only so much we can do to prevent the chill from seeping in.

"What's going on?" she asks, looking at me with wide eyes.

"I don't know. Just stay calm." I don't want her to panic. I keep seeing it in her, so close to the edge.

She's like a skittish horse that's been thrown into a crowded street. Anything could set her off, and I want to make sure she stays as calm as possible. I can handle whatever comes our way, but I can't do that if I have to worry about her and how she'll react.

There's more shouting, and then I hear a loud bang

like a door slamming. Then our metal door is flung open, and the big guy in a suit from before looks at us.

"Get up. It's time to move."

I replay every *CSI* I've ever seen, and all of them are screaming at me that it's not a good sign if you have to go to a second location.

"Why?" I ask, not getting up.

The big guy comes into the light, and I see he's got blond hair and ice-blue eyes. They chill me right to the core, and I want to crawl farther back against the wall. My mouth has gotten me into trouble for most of my life, and right now I have to remind myself that it's not the time to sass.

He reaches inside his suit jacket, and when he pulls it out, there's a gun in his hand. A big black gun that scares the shit out of me.

"Is there going to be a problem?"

Summer starts to shake, and I stand up, blocking his view of her. "There's no problem. We'll come," I say, reaching behind me. Summer puts her hands in mine and gets up off the floor. "Please put the gun away. You're scaring her."

He looks past me, and something flashes in his eyes. I don't know what it is, but instead of putting the gun away, he holds it up and points it at Summer.

"You come with me," he says, and I step in front of her again.

"I said we'd come together." My voice is shaking now, my fear of being separated setting in.

Just then there's a noise behind him, and he glances back as Spencer walks in.

"We're all going together, Jay," Spencer says, coming over to me. He wraps his sweaty hand around my upper arm and squeezes it so tight I know it's going to bruise. He yanks me to his side and grabs my face. "You're going to sit in the back seat with me. She can ride up front with Michael."

Michael grabs Summer's arm in pretty much the same hold Spencer has me in. Only he holds the gun against her ribs and walks her ahead of me. I move my feet as fast as I can to keep up, but Spencer still has a hold of me. He grips my arm with one hand and moves his other hand from my face into my hair. The pain in the back of my skull is nothing compared to the panic I feel as we walk through the building and I lose sight of Summer.

The place they brought us to has narrow hallways with lots of turns. I think for a moment about breaking free of Spencer's hold, but I don't even know if could get away before he would catch me. The place is set up like a maze.

I decide to be calm and bide my time. There has to be a chance for escape. If he's taking us to another location, we must be going outside. There has to be people. One chance is all I need, and I'll make my move.

Just as I have the thought, I hear a scream from up ahead. The sound of Summer's fear races down my spine, and I cry out for her.

"Summer!" I shout, and Spencer elbows me in the ribs. The pain makes me gasp for air, but he doesn't stop pulling me by the hair.

After a few more feet, we come to an open area in the building. There's a Jeep parked in the middle of what looks like an airplane hangar.

Summer is standing next to the Jeep, holding her

face, while Michael stands in front of her, with his hand poised like he's about to strike her again.

When he hears us, he turns around and shrugs at Spencer. "This one doesn't have to stay pretty."

Fear for my sister overwhelms me. I try to go to her, but Spencer grips my hair so tight I feel some of the strands leave my scalp.

"Get in," he orders, shoving me into the back seat, then climbing in after me.

Instinctively I go to the far door to grab the handle. Only there isn't one. There's nothing on the inside to open the door. No locks, nothing.

"Come sit in my lap, Jay. The road may get a little bumpy, and I want you right here."

I look back to see Spencer rubbing his cock, and I cling to the door, as far from him as possible. He gets an angry look on his face and grabs me by the arm, dragging me over to him.

Just then, Summer is pushed into the front seat, and Michael walks around to the driver's side. I watch Summer buckle up and glance back to me in the mirror above her seat. When he gets in, he shuts his door and inputs a code into a keypad on the dashboard. The long metal door in front of us opens up, and sunlight streams in. It's at odds with what's happening to us right now. How can the sun shine so bright when all of this is so dark and dirty? This is a nightmare; how can it happen during the day?

When the Jeep begins to move, Spencer drags me onto his lap, and I can feel his stubby cock dig into my hip. I want to throw up on him so he pushes me away. But then I think he might get angrier and start hitting me again, and my face still throbs from before.

Instead I sit as still as possible and watch Summer to make sure she's okay. I see Michael reach over and put his hand on her thigh, holding it there and softly petting her. God, I don't know which is worse, the silent unknown of what he might do to her or the perverted asshole who at least tells me what he's going to do.

"Oh, that's it," Spencer says as we drive down a rocky road.

I feel bile rise in my throat, and though I don't want to throw up, I might not have a choice.

"I've been watching you for a long time, you know," Spencer says, leaning close to me.

I move as far away as I physically can with the grip he has on me. I don't answer him, fearing that the only thing that's going to come out of my mouth is whatever food I had to eat sometime yesterday.

"All you had to do was give me what I wanted. Just a little attention would have saved you from all this. Well, maybe not from everything."

I realize at this point I need to keep him talking. Maybe if he tells me what happened, I can figure out a way to get us out of this.

"So if I had flirted with you, I wouldn't be here?" I can't look at his face when I ask the question. All I want to do is smack him.

"No, sweet Jay. I wanted you to bend over that desk of yours and let me have my way. But you're a stuck-up little bitch, aren't you?" He reaches out and grabs my breast, squeezing it hard and then twisting.

I cry out, and then I hear Summer shouting from the front seat.

"Make him stop!"

She looks to Michael with pleading eyes, but he just shrugs.

"When I got asked to do a little work on the side to make some extra money, I never could have dreamed you'd be the icing on the cake."

I want to keep him talking, but the pain in my breast is throbbing almost as bad as my face, so I'm afraid that whatever question I ask is going to keep going this way.

The Jeep turns down another road and we're on a back highway lined with trees. I have no idea where we are. Headed to upstate New York maybe? They must have taken us out of the city when we were drugged, because none of this looks familiar to me.

I catch Summer's eyes in the mirror again, and I can see them narrow. She's trying to tell me something, but I don't know what. She glances down and then back up to me. She does it several times before I look down at her and notice her hand on her seat belt tighten. She's giving me some sort of signal about buckling up.

I nod imperceptibly, but she sees it and nods back at me before she stares out the window. I don't know what she's got planned, but I want to be ready.

"I think I'm going to be sick," I say, and put my head in my hands.

"We're not pulling over, so you can just throw up back here," Spencer says, shoving me off his lap. "Just don't get it on me."

God, if I had known that was all it took I would have said that from the beginning.

"We're almost there," Michael says from the front, and Summer looks back to me.

I reach over, grabbing the belt and putting it on. If Spencer notices anything, he doesn't say.

Michael turns down a dirt road, overgrown with trees and shrubs. I can hardly see the driveway from the road, even in broad daylight. On one side is a steep drop-off into a ravine. On the other is a path that leads down to a small cabin. There's a lake behind it, and if this were any other situation I would say how beautiful it was. But that cabin has the hair on the back of my neck standing up, and I know if we go in there, we're not coming out.

It's then that I look up and catch Summer's eyes again. She's thinking the same thing. I tighten my hand on the seat belt just as she nods to me.

It all happens in a split second, and though I see it coming, it still scares the shit out of me.

Summer reaches over with both hands and yanks hard on the steering wheel. Michael is taken by surprise as the Jeep spins out of control to the right and goes off the edge of the ravine. I brace myself as the Jeep flips and my ears start ringing. I don't know how many times we roll, but at one point the back door comes open and Spencer is ejected from the vehicle.

Summer screams, and the sound of metal crunching and glass breaking has me more terrified than ever before.

Suddenly the Jeep comes to a stop, and I gasp for air as both my hands are gripped tight around the roll bar. This type of vehicle was made to survive a fall like that, but not if you weren't harnessed in.

"Summer!" I shout, and she rolls her head back, moaning. I fumble with the buckle, ignoring all the pain I feel in my body, and reach for her. "Summer, talk to me."

"I'm okay," she says, and then coughs.

I look over at Michael, who is half hanging out of the Jeep. At some point he was almost thrown from the car, and he isn't moving.

"You okay?" Summer asks as she unbuckles.

Adrenaline courses through my veins, making it hard to determine exactly what is hurt on me. There's a pain in my left leg, but it doesn't feel broken. I look down and see my left wrist is at a funny angle and it's throbbing.

"I think my wrist is broken." I look around and up the ravine. "We need to get out of here."

Summer has to climb into the back with me because her door is crushed closed. When we wiggle out of the window on my side, we see that Michael is missing the top half of his body. I cringe at the sight, and Summer leans over and gags. I look around for the gun for half a second and then give up. There's no telling where it ended up, and I don't want to be next to the car in case it decides to blow up.

"Should we check the cabin to see if there's a phone?" Summer asks as we near the top.

"I don't know. Maybe? I'm scared to go in there," I admit, but the pain in my wrist is getting stronger.

"You've got a really nasty cut on your head. I don't know how much blood you've lost," Summer says as she rips off a sleeve of her shirt and holds it up to my scalp.

I hold the cloth to my head with my good hand and walk slowly. It takes a while, but Summer helps me most of the way. Just as we get to the top, movement out of the corner of my eye catches my attention. I feel Summer grab ahold of me to steady my feet as Martin Stein steps off the porch and walks right up to us.

Chapter Twenty-Seven

Jordan

"And you're sure that's him?" I ask Miles as I scroll through security footage.

"Yes," he says through gritted teeth. "How the fuck did we not catch this before?"

I pulled up the name Spencer on Jay's computer and got a ton of hits for the same person. Then I went through the camera feed on the dates he was scheduled on her calendar. During one of his meetings with Miles, he excuses himself from the boardroom. But instead of going to the restroom, he goes over to Jay's unattended desk and sticks something to it.

"That camera is the size of a goddamn pencil eraser. No way she would have noticed it," Ryan says from behind me, and he's right. Paige went up and pulled it off of there and brought it down for us to see.

My fist aches to punch the wall again, but I need my hands right now.

One of the next meetings Spencer shows up in, he does the same thing. Only this time he goes over to one of our cameras and attaches something to it as well. It all happens so fast there's no way we could have caught it in the feed. Not unless someone was staring directly at the screen all hours of the day.

I think about all the times I sat at my desk and watched Jay. If she was in a meeting with Miles, I usually never checked back in. She was a stickler for time, so it wasn't like she would get out of her meetings early. She was so regimented that I only checked on her when I knew her desk hours were listed on her schedule.

"Fuck. How did I miss this?" I say, guilt washing over me.

"We all did," McCoy says. "He used a tracker bracket on our system. It allowed him to access our digital feed and get into the entire panel with one clip. These things are military grade. He would either have to know someone who had that security clearance or gotten it on the black market."

"I'm going with knowing someone who had access," Paige says, and we turn to look at her. "Stein had contact with illegal weapons. I'm guessing Spencer was his in once he was no longer coming into work. He had to get his intel somehow. The only question I have is, why would Spencer go along with it? What did Stein have that Spencer wanted?"

"Jay," Miles says, and I grind my teeth.

The video feed plays out with Spencer cornering Jay and then Miles interrupting them.

"I knew something wasn't right, but she didn't say. Then she was out for a few days, and I forgot to bring it back up." Miles shakes his head. "Jordan, I'm so sorry."

"There's nothing we can do now but find the motherfucker," I say, and dig into his files.

I pull up everything I can on him and blast it across all the screens at my desk.

"These are his properties. We're looking for something close, possibly isolated, where he could have taken Jay and Summer."

"Are we sure it was a place he owned?" McCoy asks, and I nod.

"Stein is definitely involved, and he's been smart enough to slip us so far. There's no way he would use something in his name. And Spencer seems to be blinded by his need for—"

I stop myself, unable to finish the sentence. I can't put my love's name next to his. I'll burn his world to the ground for even daring to look at her.

"I think Spencer is dumb enough to use one of his houses as a location," I say, clicking on his real-estate holding.

"He invests in properties as a hobby. How are we going to find which one?" Paige asks.

"Like I said, we've got to do this based on a process of deduction. Stein wants his files, and he wants our server clear. That's the only way he can possibly make things right with the people he took the money from. I think it's his only chance for survival. So he's not taking Jay and Summer out of the country." I toggle a few things, and I'm left with only a few properties.

"Let's assume he stays in-state if he's willing to negotiate," Ryan says, and I click a few more, clearing off all properties except those in New York.

"He's going to be close, but rural," I say, and remove all the properties in the city.

I code all the addresses left with a map of New York, and there are two red dots remaining. I lean forward and stare at them, pulling up the images on Osbourne satellites.

The first is of a town house that's in a cul-de-sac. It's a family neighborhood, with sidewalks and a school right behind it. The second image shows an overgrowth of trees with a small cabin in the distance.

"There," I say, and get up from my chair.

Chapter Twenty-Eight

Jay

I want to fall to my knees and pass out at the sight of Martin Stein. I close my eyes and open them again, willing what I see not to be real, that the dream of help inside the cabin didn't just die. How do we keep going from one bad place to another? We can't catch a break.

"It's one problem after another with you, isn't it?" Stein says as he makes his way toward us. I don't see a gun or weapon on him at this moment, but I know he could easily catch us. I suspect he has a weapon within reach.

He doesn't look as put together as he usually does. His hair is perfectly styled, and his cocky arrogance is still as thick as ever, even though he doesn't look like he's slept in a few days. His polo shirt is wrinkled, and his jeans have seen better days. It makes me wonder if he's been hiding out in this cabin for some time, knowing everything was closing in on him.

"Bad guy?" Summer asks.

I can hear the defeat in her voice. I glance over at her. She looks like she's doing a little better than I am, but if I've learned anything in the past twenty-four hours, it's that our situation can change in a matter of seconds.

"Yeah, bad guy," I mumble.

Stein hates me more than Spencer, but at least I don't think he wants to rape me. His eyes roam over my sister, and I pray I didn't see them linger. What is it with assholes?

My whole body aches, but nothing feels worse than my wrist, not even my head. I use my shoulder to wipe some of the blood from my forehead. When I raise my arm, I see part of my blouse is ripped, exposing my light blue bra.

Stein pulls his eyes from my sister and looks past us, shaking his head. He's spotted the wreckage behind us down the road, and I wonder if Stein is going to go down there and check on them. I fear how mad he'll be when he sees Michael is missing half his body. I don't know how close the two of them were.

Suddenly an explosion rocks the ground, and I turn to look. With my glasses long gone, I can't make much out besides smoke and fire. A small smirk plays on my lips, knowing Spencer was down there. That's one less person I have to worry about. I feel no pity for either man. In fact, I think their deaths were over too fast. Maybe all of this has jaded me, because more than anything I would have loved what my Jordan would have done to them. I'm sad for him that he won't get that chance.

"Fucking hell!" Stein yells, and some of that cockiness fades. "Asses in the cabin right now before I kill you both." I glance back and see he's got a gun in his hand. Although the way he's holding it doesn't seem natural. I've watched Jordan clean his guns before and he handled them like they were an extension of his arm.

Neither I nor Summer fight it. We slowly do as he tells us, knowing there's no use. My body still feels the blows of when we didn't do as we were told earlier. I'm sure Summer is nearly as bad as I am. I'm not pressing my luck. I'm going to play along and not fight unless I see an opening. I'm not wasting any of the energy I have left.

We slowly make our way up the stairs, with Summer helping me when I feel dizzy. When we get to the top, Stein pushes us, wanting us to move faster. "Move your fucking asses. We don't have all day."

Summer opens the door, and once again Stein pushes both our backs, but my body doesn't care. I bump into Summer, and she catches me from falling. I hear Stein chuckle behind me.

"I think I'm going to pass out," I whisper. The room starts to spin, and black spots cloud my vision. I can't remember the last time I had a drink of water.

I try to look around the room as Summer holds on to me. It looks like we're in the living room. Glancing around, I see the ceiling, the walls, and the floor are all made of wood. The first spot of color I notice is a blue sofa. I want to sit down before my legs give out beneath me.

"Keep her awake," Stein barks, and I flinch, thinking a blow is going to come. When nothing happens, I sigh in relief. I think anything more traumatic right now and I'd pass out.

Summer moves me toward the sofa and sits me down. A moan of relief leaves my lips.

"I just want to sleep," I tell her. Just for a little bit.

That's all I need. To close my eyes for a moment. Maybe my mind will drift to another memory. I can soak it in and have a moment of sweetness.

"Jay, no," she barks at me. I can hear the panic in her voice.

Jerking my eyes back open, I see the room is fuzzy. "Stop yelling. It hurts my head." I reach up and wince when I make contact with my forehead. Pulling back, I look at the blood on my fingertips.

"Look at me."

I roll my head to the side and do my best to focus on her.

"I think you have a concussion. You can't go to sleep," Summer tells me softly. "You're losing a lot of blood." I can see the fear rising on her face.

"I once read head wounds bleed a lot," I tell her. "I'll be fine. I won't leave you." I don't know if that part is true or not. Right now, I'm not feeling so hopeful.

"You have a fucking call to make, so if I were you, I'd keep your ass awake. You don't want me waking you up to make it," I hear Stein say from somewhere in the room. I don't bother to look for him and keep my eyes on Summer. I can't find the will to care about his threat, and I'd rather not look at him as much as possible.

"Are you okay?" I reach up to touch her face. She winces in pain. The place where that bastard Michael hit her is already swelling. God, I wish I could have watched him go through that window. I feel my lips pull into a little smirk thinking about it. "You got the last laugh on him, didn't you?" I whisper the last part, not knowing if that will set Stein off.

She shakes her head, but I see a small triumphant smile tip her lips. "I'm fine, it's you I'm worried about."

She makes a move to stand, and I grab for her arm, not wanting her to leave my side.

"What the fuck do you think you're doing?" Stein asks, beating me to the question. Summer stills for a moment.

"I need to stop the bleeding from her head or nothing you did will wake her up!" she yells, and then turns to me and whispers an apology for being loud.

"There's a fucking towel over there."

Summer runs off to where he must have pointed.

"She's lucky I don't let her bleed to death after everything she fucked up. Stupid bitch." There's so much anger in his voice, and I'm terrified of what he might do in this moment.

He appears in front of me, glaring down at me. I want to look away from him, but I stare up into his cold eyes. They look wild, and I wonder if he's losing it, or if maybe he's on something. He leans down, getting into my face. He smells like he hasn't bathed in a few days. I'm sure I'm not any better, but at least I have a reason. "I'm not going to die because some stupid bitch couldn't keep her nose where it belonged."

I have to bite my tongue to keep from saying something smart back. The problem is that I had my nose exactly where it belonged.

I swear his eyes go darker right in front of me. I can feel the evil pulsing from him. "Maybe when I'm done here I'll pay your boyfriend a surprise visit. He'll never see me coming."

I feel the cold steel of his gun pressed to my temple. I close my eyes, thinking of Jordan and Summer, and pray for help.

"Stop it," my sister says. Her voice is shaking, and it breaks on a sob.

"Pop," he says loudly, making me wince. "He's dead."

A tear slides down my cheek. I hate how scared I am, and I hate that I gave him any sort of reaction. But I'm only so strong, and this is overwhelming.

"Look at that. The Osbourne ice queen has feelings. Who fucking knew." He stands there, not moving the gun, still holding it to my head. I can't bring myself to open my eyes. I know if I do, I'll want to lunge at him and claw his eyes out for what he said about Jordan.

"Move," Summer says, and I feel the cold metal leave my temple as Stein steps away. I finally open my eyes, and Summer is in front of me. Looking up, I watch Stein smile at me, then walk to the other side of the room. He sits down in a chair, leaning back and resting the gun on his lap. Summer sits next to me, putting the towel to my head.

My eyes start to close again, and I hear the worry in Summer's voice. "We need something to drink. She's going to pass out." She sighs, and her hands tremble. "You need her for something, and I know she needs to be awake for whatever it is."

Her voice is firm, and she uses a tone I've never heard her use before. While I seem to be weakening, she seems to be growing stronger.

I'm surprised when Stein stands and walks out of sight and a few moments later comes back with two bottles of water. He tosses them on the sofa next to Summer. She picks one up, opens it and hands it to me. I grab it with my free hand while she grabs the other for herself. We both start to drink but Summer tells me to slow down and not drink it too fast or it will make me sick. I want to chug it down but I know she's right. I had no idea water could taste this good. As I slowly sip it I already start to feel better.

"Now." Stein sits back down in the chair and leans forward. "You're going to make a call to your boyfriend as soon as my associate gets here."

"Why?" I feign ignorance. I want nothing more than to call Jordan. To hear his voice for even a moment would help me get through this, but I'm scared of what they'll make him do. I'm even more scared they might ask him to go somewhere and then he'll end up like me. I don't want him to get hurt. It would be too much to take, knowing I got him mixed up in this.

"I don't trust him to take care of what needs to be deleted. I want him to give us access into the servers and we'll do what needs to be done," he tells me.

I let out a breath, grateful that they aren't asking him to meet up somewhere.

"We haven't been together long. How do you know he'll even do it?" I ask. I still fear these people getting close to Jordan. I know he's looking for me, but I don't want them pulling him into this.

"Don't be fucking stupid, Jay." Stein stands, and I hold my breath. He doesn't move toward me but instead goes to a table where I see a bottle of liquor. He picks up the bottle and takes a long pull from it. After he's done, he doesn't put it down. He makes his way back to the chair with it and settles the gun in his lap again. "Trust me. I don't get it. All I've ever seen out of you is a total fucking bitch, but you had Spencer and Jordan chasing you around the office with their dicks in their hands."

I don't respond. What am I supposed to say to that?

"Then you give Jordan a lick of your pussy and he turns into a fucking pit bull banging down my goddamn door for you."

Now I don't know what he's talking about. Confusion must cross my face.

"You don't even know the crazy fucker you let between your legs, do you? Maybe that's what it is. You attract the crazy. Yeah, that makes sense."

Like he's one to talk. If Jordan is crazy, then I'm crazy, too, and I'm okay with that kind of love.

"If he never showed up at my door threatening me for that file because of you, none of this would have happened." Stein takes another swig from his bottle, this one bigger than the last. When he pulls the bottle away, a smirk crosses his lips. "But I got even. I was so happy to hear good old Dad made it," he says sarcastically.

A sob leaves my throat.

"See what you've done, Jay? You put that nose of yours too far where it didn't belong." He holds up the hand with the gun. "All of this." He waves it around in the air. "Is your fault. Everyone could be at home and none the wiser if you had just let it go."

He's right. I'm the reason hell is raining down on everyone I love. Everyone who has ever truly meant anything to me. My mom always told me I was going to get in over my head one day. I guess she was finally right.

I look over at my sister's face. It's darkening with bruises. She looks at me, trying to tell me something with her eyes. Stein mumbles to himself, and I look to see his eyes slowly starting to close. I glance back to Summer, who's now watching him, too.

We sit in silence for what feels like forever. I want nothing more than to lean my own head back and drift off, but I fight the pull, knowing that maybe we might have a moment to escape. Summer's gaze darts between Stein and me. She takes the towel from my head, and I think my wound has finally stopped bleeding. I can see the relief on Summer's face as she looks me over and nods approval.

Her eyes rush back to Stein, and then she leans in close. "He's sleeping," she mouths, and I look over to see Stein is passed out in the chair.

"Go," I tell her, looking over to the door. I feel like I'll only slow her down. She needs to run.

"Not going without you," she whispers, and I can see the determination on her face.

"Please." I try to plead with her.

"Get up," she whispers, standing up. I didn't know a whisper could sound so stern.

I lift my good hand, and she pulls me to my feet. I cup my injured wrist to my chest, and the pain isn't as bad as it once was, but the throb is still there.

I glance over at Stein. I want to grab the gun from his lap, but I'm too scared. He could wake up any second, and Summer and I don't have the power to fight him right now. Summer can read my thoughts and shakes her head.

"Let's run," she says, and I nod in agreement. I want to be as far away from here as I can get.

We walk to the entrance silently, and slowly open the door. The creak of the hinge echoes in the quiet cabin, and panic floods my body. I step out onto the deck only to be grabbed by my hair and yanked backwards. Without thinking, I scream Jordan's name. It's a cry for help because I want him more than anything right now.

I'm pulled back into the cabin and thrown onto the

sofa. Adrenaline pumps through me as I watch Summer throw herself at Stein. It takes him less than a second to throw her off, and then he hits her with the butt of his gun. She falls to the floor, and I scream. I don't seen any blood, but she doesn't move.

"Summer!" I cry out, but she just lies there.

Tears fall down my face, and I try to go to her, but Stein only pushes me back.

"You little bitch. Think you're so clever." He sneers at me.

He comes at me and tackles me to the ground, getting on top of me. I scream. The pain from my wrist shoots through my body as the weight of him lands on me. I try to fight, but there's no use. He's too big, and I've only got one good arm.

I cringe and brace myself for pain when I see him pull back his arm to punch me.

"Stop!"

Stein stops midair, and we both turn toward the voice. I look over to see a man I don't recognize standing in the doorway.

"She can't talk with a broken jaw, and we both know he won't do what we want unless he hears it from her."

Stein glares down at me, clearly wanting to give me what he intended. I look up at him and pray he listens. After a moment of hesitation, he drops his fist. I can tell in his eyes that he'll be coming for that blow. It might not be now, but he still wants it.

I look at the man standing in the door. Unlike everyone else we've come across, he's in jeans and a tight black T-shirt. He's small, maybe only as tall as I am, but it's clear Stein is scared of him.

Stein gives me one more hard look before getting off

me. I glance over to Summer, wanting to go to her. She rolls onto her side, but her eyes don't open. She looks as if she's asleep.

"Sit up," the mystery man says, walking in and shutting the door. I do as he says, moving up on the sofa and not saying a word.

"Here," he says to Stein, tossing him a phone. "Make the call and be done with this. You'll be lucky if I don't kill you afterwards." The man turns and walks back out the door.

Stein hands me the phone. "Call him and tell him to open the server."

My hand shakes as I take the phone from him. I don't want to make the call, but maybe if I do, Jordan can find me.

"Now," Stein barks, and I nearly drop the phone.

I slide my finger across the screen and I key in Jordan's number. I know it by heart. It barely has time to ring once before he answers.

"Jay?" His voice is panicked, and I can hear the fear through the phone. I have no idea how he knew it was me. Maybe he was just hoping.

"Jordan," I whisper back. Just hearing his voice makes me want to cry. I want to be near him. I want to be back in our bed and wrapped around his body. A sob climbs up my throat, and terror crawls over me.

"Baby. Talk to me." There is so much anguish in his voice, it makes my heart want to break.

But I have to be strong. I have to get through this so that Summer and I make it out of this cabin alive. I've got to hold it together for just a little longer.

"I'm supposed to tell you that you have to open the servers. They…" My voice trembles. Stein grabs me by the hair at the back of my head, and pain shoots through my scalp. I scream as the still-raw cut on my head throbs angrily.

"Jay!" Jordan yells into the phone, but his voice barely registers.

I blink a few times and take a breath, trying to get it together. "I'm here," I tell him through a sob. I try to stay strong, not wanting to hurt Jordan any more. But my voice gives me away. "You have to open the servers. They want to delete things," I finally get out. God, I hope that was what I was supposed to tell him.

"Okay, baby. I'll do it." His voice is tight. I can tell he's holding back. "I love you."

Tears stream down my face as I let go of all the ones I've been holding back. "I love you, too," I tell him. I don't know if I'll ever get to say those words to him again, and the ache in my chest tightens.

"I'm going to kill all of them," Jordan says through clenched teeth.

I glance over at Stein, who doesn't seem to care. He's texting on his own phone.

"Jordan," I sob.

"Listen to me, little bird. I'm coming for you," he says, then the phone is yanked out of my hand.

I look up and watch as Stein hits the end button. I cry out. I need the phone back. I want Jordan so desperately it's crashing on me like waves. He tosses the phone on the chair he was sitting on, and the front door opens. The man in the black T-shirt comes inside and looks at the two of us.

"Is it done?" he asks, and Stein nods.

"Good." The man walks across the room behind me, and I don't turn to watch. I want to seem as invisible as possible. "I've lined the house with explosives. I'm sure he traced the call. We only have a few minutes before we need to leave."

My body goes cold at his words. I had thought that Jordan could track the call and find me, but I didn't think that he'd set a trap for him.

I glance to Stein, who's smiling down at me. "How dumb do you think we are?" That stupid cocky smile is still on his face. "We knew he'd track us. We also knew you were the loose ends that needed to be taken care of."

I'm shaking. I just led the man I love to his death.

"Please don't do this," I beg. I don't care that I'm begging a man I want to see dead. I'll do anything to save Jordan.

Stein grabs my face. "Can I break her jaw now?" he asks the man.

I close my eyes, praying for this nightmare to be over.

"He opened the servers. We don't need her anymore," I hear him answer.

I replay Jordan's voice telling me he loves me, over and over.

Chapter Twenty-Nine

Jordan

"Jordan!" My name echoes through the forest, and I dig my feet into the dirt.

"Don't do it," McCoy says in my ear as he practically lies on top of me to keep me from running to her. "She's alive. Just hold on a little longer and we'll get her back. You go in there now and she's dead."

I know he's right, and I try to breathe through the panic. There are six of us out here on the ridgeline just a few yards from the cabin. McCoy, Sheppard, Grant, Ryan, Paige, and I geared up and made our way out here. Ryan put up a protest when Paige grabbed her guns, but one look from her and she was climbing into the truck.

We took a mountain trail that kept us clear of anyone who might be watching the roads. It took longer than I'd wanted, but we made it here undetected. After that, we hid the truck and came on foot to the edge of the clearing.

I take a breath and nod to McCoy that I've got myself under control. He and I are crouched down low, and we're the closest to the entrance. Ryan and Paige are a few yards to our right under some coverage with a clear shot of the road.

Sheppard and Grant are to our left and making their way slowly to the rear of the cabin. I press the device on my neck that lets us communicate to one another. The com clicks, and I struggle to keep my voice low.

"That motherfucker is mine," I say, and no one argues.

"We've got incoming," Paige says, and I turn my sights to where they're situated.

A black car with black windows pulls down the drive slowly. When it gets to the front of the house, a small man wearing jeans and a T-shirt climbs out. He doesn't have a weapon from what I can see, and I watch as he goes into the cabin.

"That makes two," Grant says on the com. "Nobody at the rear access point."

"Copy that," Ryan says.

All of the horrible scenarios that could be happening play through my head, and panic unlike anything I've ever felt takes over.

"She's breathing, Chen. Stay calm," Paige says over the com. "As long as she's breathing, everything is going to be okay."

Before I can let my mind go down any other path, my phone vibrates. I pull it out, knowing immediately it's her.

"Jay." I keep my voice low and hit the com so the others can hear what she says.

"Jordan."

Her voice is barely a whisper, and I can hear all the pain and terror in the one word. Every cell in my body longs to go in there, to kick in that fucking door and save the day. But we have to be ready. We have to make the right move at the right time so that Stein doesn't go off and kill her and Summer both before we can rescue them.

"Baby. Talk to me." I've got to help her keep her head. If she's talking, then she's not focusing on the what-ifs.

"I'm supposed to tell you that you have to open the servers. They—"

Her words are cut off by a scream, and I grip the phone so tight I'm surprised it doesn't crack. "Jay!" I yell into the phone, not caring how loud I am. I'm losing it. I'm so close to the edge of my control that it's starting to break.

"I'm on it," McCoy says, using his satellite laptop to open up the servers and drop the security to our entire system.

"I'm here," she sobs, and another piece of my heart breaks off. How much more of this can I take? "You have to open the servers. They want to delete things."

I take a breath and run a hand down my face. I'll take as much of this as I can if it means getting her back to me. She's my whole goddamn world, and I won't have it ripped from my hands.

"Okay, baby. I'll do it." I look over to McCoy, and he nods at me. "I love you."

"I love you, too."

Her words are like a balm to my soul, and I know that I will save her. I will get her back in my arms, and I will make everyone who dared to touch her pay for what they've done.

"I'm going to kill all of them." My voice is strong and calm.

"Jordan." The fear in her voice is rising, and I need to calm her down.

"Listen to me, little bird. I'm coming for you."

I hear a click, and the phone line goes dead. I look over at McCoy, and he shows me the screen.

"It's done," he says. "I ran the program to take the server down in case they check, but they'll be back up before they can get in there. And by that time, we'll be long gone."

"Yeah, we've got a problem," I hear Grant say over the com. "Evil short guy just wired the house with explosives."

"Fuck," Paige says, and we all agree.

Shit just got real.

"All right, new plan," Ryan says. "Jordan and McCoy, you guys ghost to the front porch and wait. Sheppard and Grant, on my signal, you guys go in the back and light the place up. Take out Stein and the evil short guy if you've got a clean shot. Then I want Jordan and McCoy going in hot. We clear?"

"Clear," we all agree, and I nod to McCoy.

"Paige and I will clear the explosive switches if we can, but don't bet on it. We're doing this fast, so in and out. Grab the girls and get them the fuck out. Nobody gets to be a hero. You hear me, Chen?"

"I hear you," I agree and tighten my grip on my gun.

"Everybody in position," Ryan says, and we make our move.

McCoy and I crouch down low and move silently across the shadows of the tree and onto the porch. I can feel the sweat trickle down my back as adrenaline thumps in my ears. Every sense I have is heightened, and I hold my Glock with both hands, ready to fire.

There's no sound made as we get in position by the front door and wait. I watch Ryan and Paige out of the corner of my eye as they move on the edge of the woods and to the side of the house. The two of them know the most about explosives, and I pray that they can take care of it before they go off.

Murmured voices come from inside the cabin, and I swear I hear a sob from Jay. But I don't let myself focus on that. Not when she's within my grasp.

"In three, two, one…" Ryan's voice commands over the com, and we wait, ready to go into action. "Move."

Reaching up, I grab the knob of the front door and swing it open, just as I hear the back door being kicked in. Shots ring out as I rush in and see Jay on the floor with Stein on top of her. I don't think of anything but Jay, and I rush at Stein, full-body tackling him to the ground. He's under me, and I sit up lightning-quick and punch him hard three times before he's unconscious.

Turning around, I see Jay against the couch, huddled up and in shock. She blinks a few times before she realizes it's me, and then we are both moving toward one another.

"Oh my God, Jordan," she sobs, and I pull her into my arms and look around for Summer.

She's already in Sheppard's arms and out the door, and I stand up with Jay to follow them.

Looking behind me, I see the short guy is lying on the floor with a bullet between his eyes, but I can't say for sure who did it. I don't remember shooting my gun, but I see it lying next to him. I reach down and grab it, tucking it into my holster while holding Jay close.

"We've got to get out of here," Paige says.

"I don't think he's dead," I say, looking back to Stein.

"He will be when this place goes up," Ryan says, getting everyone from the cabin.

"She needs to get to the hospital," Summer says, and I see the look of concern for her sister on her face.

Looking down at Jay, I really see her for the first time. I see the blood on the side of her face, and her eyes are almost completely closed. She's slipping in and out of consciousness, and I need to wake her up.

"Wake up, little bird. You've got to open your eyes a little longer," I coax, trying to keep her awake.

She opens her eyes, and they're glassed over. She looks at me for a second and then looks past me in the distance.

"Gun!" she shouts, and we all turn to see Stein stepping out of the cabin and waving it toward us.

Without thinking, I'm in motion. I pull out my gun, take aim, and fire off two bullets before anyone else has time to react. Stein drops dead in the doorway of the cabin right before the entire thing explodes.

"Jesus Christ!" Paige yells from behind me, and we all duck down.

We're far enough away that the debris doesn't hit us, but the heat from the blast is enough to scare the shit out of anyone. Too close for my liking.

I pull Jay back up in my arms and cradle her as I make my way to the truck.

"Let's get the fuck out of here," Ryan barks.

By the time we make it back to the truck, relief that I've got Jay in my arms again sets in. The panic I was feeling recedes, and some of the pain in my chest eases. She's safe. She's with me, and she's going to be okay.

Everything is going to be okay.

Chapter Thirty

Jay

He saved me. He's got me in his arms, and I'm going to be okay. Relief floods me, and just as I open my mouth to tell him how happy I am, he comes to an abrupt stop.

"Put her down or she's dead."

I turn my face away from Jordan's chest and to the truck up ahead. I'm completely shocked when I see Spencer standing there holding a gun and pointing it straight at me. He must have gotten it from Michael after the accident, because he didn't have one before.

"The six of us are armed and ready to kill you. Are you sure you're in a position to make those kinds of threats?" Jordan asks, but his grip on me tightens.

"Stand down," Ryan says to everyone, and nobody moves.

Spencer laughs, but it's bone-chilling and he looks crazed. The gun shakes in his hand, and if possible, it makes me even more nervous.

"Spencer, don't do this. Put the gun down," I say, trying to plead with him.

"If I put down the gun, I'm a dead man. But I guess I'm a dead man either way. You may have blown up those two, but the rest of them will come looking for their pound of flesh." He uses his other hand to steady the gun on me as he takes a step closer. "The least I can do is give them something in return. I'm sure a peace offering would smooth things over."

He licks his lips, and revulsion rises in my stomach.

"You're not putting a finger on her," Jordan says through clenched teeth. "There's only one way you're getting out of this, and it's in a body bag. How quickly that happens is up to you."

"Don't do this," McCoy says from behind us, and I don't know if he's talking to Jordan or to Spencer.

"If you kill me, I'll take your precious little bird out with me. Is that what you want?"

Jordan is shaking with rage, and it's all I can do to stay still and not panic.

"Don't you *dare* call her that!" he yells, and then he's moving.

My world is flipped upside down as Jordan spins his body and puts me behind him. I hear the gun go off, and screams ring in my ears, but I don't know if they're mine or someone else's.

My body hits the ground, and Jordan comes over on top of me, but he doesn't look right. His face has gone white, and his mouth is open with no words coming out. The light in his eyes is dimming, and I don't know what to do.

"Jordan? Jordan!" Hysteria takes over as I look down and see red blossom across his chest. It's spreading fast, and I place my hand over it to try to make it stop.

"Get him in the truck, now!" someone shouts, and his weight is lifted off me.

I climb in behind him, hands helping me to sit in the

seat as someone starts compressions and counting off for CPR. Someone else is on the phone, screaming for medics as the truck is in motion.

Everything is happening so fast, and suddenly my head is swimming. I feel like I'm going to throw up, but at the same time the truck is getting darker. It's like the sun is setting, and I blink it away to make it stop, but it doesn't work.

"Jordan," I mumble as the lights of the truck fade to black and I can no longer feel the beat of his heart in mine.

Chapter Thirty-One

Jordan

I gasp as I sit up in the bed, but restraining hands hold me back down.

"Where is she?" I shout as bright lights are shined into my eyes.

"Calm down, Mr. Chen. She's right beside you," the doctor says, but I can't see from being blinded by the lights.

"They moved Jay in here a few hours ago," a soft voice says, and I realize it's my dad's.

"Is she okay?" I ask as tears fall down my cheeks. "Tell me she's okay."

"She's fine. She's asleep right now. She had a bad bump on the head, and they're waking her every few hours. She's got a broken wrist, but it's a clean break, and they've already bandaged her up."

I breathe a sigh of relief, and I feel his hand in mine.

"Would you like to know about your injuries now, Mr. Chen?" the doctor says, and I hear my dad laugh. I nod, and she continues. "You had a through-and-through on your left shoulder. You're very lucky. A few more inches lower and it would have punctured a lung. We had to go in to remove some of the fragments, but you should make a full recovery. With some physical therapy, you'll be back to normal in a few weeks."

"Thank you," I say and close my eyes. "Did you treat my Jay, too?"

"Yes." There's a smile in her voice. "I treated Miss Rose's injuries as well."

"Then you saved me twice."

"From what the nurses tell me, you would have burned the hospital to the ground if I didn't."

I open my eyes and look at her in confusion.

"Even in your drugged state you demanded that she be treated by a woman and brought in here for safekeeping. I can't say that I liked the bossing around, but your dad is a sweetheart, so we accommodated your wishes."

"I should apologize?" I ask it as a question, because I don't really want to. But since she took care of my love, I could muster one up.

"Just get some rest. You're on some heavy pain meds for the next twenty-four hours. Enjoy the ride."

She speaks to my father and then looks over Jay's chart before leaving the room. A nurse comes in after her and goes to Jay's bed to speak to her in a low voice.

I watch as Jay stirs and then moans my name. It makes every protective instinct in me reach for her, and I look to my pop with pleading eyes.

"I'll take care of it, son," he says, and nods.

He walks over to the nurse and speaks to her. She looks at me and then back to Jay and nods. Walking around the bed, she clicks the wheels and then slides her bed over right next to mine. She lowers the arms that separate us, and I reach out, holding her hand in mine.

"Jay. Wake up, little bird," I whisper, and I feel her tense before her eyes open and she sees me.

She bursts into tears, and I pull her close to me as gently as I can.

"Shhh. Don't cry. I'm here. We're safe, baby. It's over."

"I thought I'd lost you," she sobs, and I try to calm her down.

"I'm right here. You're in my arms, and I'm never letting you go again."

"What happened?" she asks and leans back a little to look at me.

"Spencer is dead," Paige says from the doorway, and she walks in with Ryan on her heels. "The doctor said you were awake, so I wanted to come in and check on you."

Summer walks in behind them, and she looks much better than the two of us. Summer goes to her sister's side and leans down, kissing her on the cheek.

"Are you okay?" Jay asks her, and she nods.

"Yeah. Just a bit traumatized, but physically I'm good. They checked me over and released me within a few hours." She glances at me. "Thank you for saving my big sister, and for saving my life, too."

I nod, knowing there was no other choice. I had to save Jay or my life would have ended with hers.

"Do we have to call the cops or something?" Jay asks, breaking the sad moment, and Ryan smiles at her.

"We're all good."

I nod, knowing some of Ryan's background. He's got connections that go deeper than even I know, so I'm sure whatever took place at the cabin has all been wiped clean.

"The team wanted to come in and hang out, but we knew you guys might need some time. We'll be back in a couple of hours. I'll bring food." Paige winks at Jay and then squeezes my arm.

"I think food sounds good. I'll go with you," Pop says and stands next to Paige. I see Ryan pull her back away from him a little and narrow his eyes on my old man. I can't stop the smile that pulls at my mouth.

"You can sit in the back with me," Summer says, and puts her arm in the crook of his.

"She better be careful. He's a charmer," Jay says, and we say our goodbyes and she snuggles closer to me.

She's careful not to touch my bandages and to keep her wrist elevated as she wraps her body around me.

"I was so scared," I admit. "I was terrified of losing you."

"Me too."

"Don't ever do that to me again." I look down at her and wait for her eyes to meet mine. "Don't you ever run from me again."

"Never," she says, and I see the promise in her eyes. "I was wrong not to go to you, but they had my sister, and I just panicked."

I place a finger over her lips. "I know. I won't ever allow another situation like this to happen again. You'll be in my arms and under my protection for the rest of your life."

"Promise?" she asks as she pulls my hand away and leans toward me.

"Promise," I agree, and place my lips on hers.

The kiss is soft and warm and filled with promises of forever. I want to deepen it, to roll her onto her back and make love to her. To show Jay just how much I ached for her and how much she means to me. To make us alive and real as we connect. But we can't. Not here, and not yet.

But very, very soon.

Chapter Thirty-Two

Jay

It's been a week since Jordan saved me.

"Come here," he says, grabbing for me.

I dodge him, and he gives me the cutest grumpy face that almost has me giving in. It doesn't help that I want him just as much as he wants me, but I'm trying to hold back. The doctor said three physical therapy sessions and he would be cleared for sex. Today will be the third, and I'm trying to be good. But he's making it really, really difficult.

"One more session," I remind him, but he just isn't having it.

"How about I do my last session on you?" He reaches for me again, grabbing me this time when I don't fight him. I'm scared I might hit his shoulder wrong while I'm pulling away and cost us more time.

"Jordan." I try to put fight into my rebuff, but it doesn't work when his mouth comes to my neck and he starts kissing me. "Jordan," I try again, but he slips his hand into my shorts as he lifts me onto the kitchen counter. I want to tell him to stop. That he shouldn't be picking me up, but all that comes out of my mouth is a moan.

"Just need a little something to hold me over," he whispers in my ear as he runs his finger along my sex. My hips jerk, trying to get closer to him. "Always so greedy for me."

I am. Since we left the hospital I can't bring myself to be far from him. If he isn't holding me at night, I can't sleep. I dread when we might go back to work. I want to stay locked to him, where I feel safe and protected.

"Jordan." I say his name again, and this time I need to come.

"I got you, little bird," he growls before taking my mouth in a soft but intense kiss. I open my mouth for him, sucking his tongue and tasting him. I try to take over the kiss, but he doesn't let me. I slide my fingers into his hair as he strokes me back and forth, playing with my clit. My orgasm is so close. "Give it to me," he growls against my mouth as two fingers enter me and his thumb strums my clit. It's been so long since I've had him that I come easily. My body is wound so tight that even the slightest touch is setting me off. I've been on the edge of climax for days, and I desperately need this connection to him.

I pulse against him as he milks my orgasm from me. I cry out his name, unable to hold back any emotions.

"Fuck, I love watching you come for me."

"Hmm," I moan, feeling more relaxed than ever. He pulls his hand out from my shorts, and I watch as he licks his fingers clean.

"That taste is going to push me through this workout," he says before he kisses me deep and hard. I can taste myself on him, and his aggressive desire is turning me on again.

I push on him a little, and he steps back. "Jay…" he says, and I slide off the counter in front of him, dropping to my knees. I watch his chest rise and fall, his breathing growing heavy.

"Jay, my control isn't great." His voice is deep and rough and only turns me on more. He braces his hands on the counter, and I can tell it's taking everything in him to not reach out and grab me.

I look up at him through my lashes. His hair is a little longer than normal and hangs in his eyes. I reach for his gym shorts, slowly pulling them down, and I kiss a trail as I slide them off. His breathing grows heavy.

"Maybe I need a taste to hold me over, too," I say softly.

"Fucking hell," he mutters as his cock throbs in front of me. I grab a hold of him, and he jerks in my hand. "Baby, maybe…" His words trail off as I lean forward and lick the small drop of come on the end of his cock. His body stiffens at the contact. I didn't know someone could feel so powerful while being on their knees.

He's salty sweet, and I want more of him. It always turns me on when he wants the taste of me on his tongue. I want the same. I wrap my lips around him, taking him in my mouth. His arms above me look tense. I see every muscle and vein as he tries to keep himself under control.

I lean back, letting his cock slip free of my mouth. "Let go. Use me," I tell him. The idea of him taking over and claiming his pleasure sparks something deep inside me. I want him to stop fighting what he wants.

"Open," he snarls as his hands leave the counter and

slide into my hair. He grips it with a hard hold, and I can feel the shift in power. "Take me in." I do as he says, wrapping my mouth around him. I try to move my head, but he doesn't let me. He keeps his tight hold on me as he jerks his hips back and forth, fucking my face.

It's so erotic watching him use me, taking what he wants and being rough. "Fuck," he growls and moves faster. I dig my fingers into his thighs, holding on to him. "I'm going to come. And you're going to take it." It's not a request. He's demanding that I pleasure him, and I'm eager for it.

I feel myself start to throb. I let go of his thighs and slide my hand down my shorts, needing relief.

"Fuck, always so greedy for it."

I moan around his cock because he's right. Something about him always calling me greedy does it for me. I'm his and only get like this for him. It's almost like a little secret we have together.

"Swallow," he commands through gritted teeth as he starts to come in my mouth.

I do as he says. My finger over my clit continues to move as I come. I taste his release in my mouth, and it makes mine all the more intense. He jerks against me, pushing all the way to the back of my throat. I moan as my own orgasm takes over.

He slowly pulls back. His eyes are hooded and filled with passion. He's looking at me with so much love as his cock slips free. I see a trace of come still on the tip, and I greedily lean forward, taking him back into my mouth. I want to make sure I get every drop of him.

He grunts, his hips jerking, then I'm being pulled to my feet.

"Jordan." I try to scold him. He shouldn't be lifting

me, but he ignores me and takes my mouth in a deep kiss. "I don't know what I did to deserve you," he says when he finally presses his forehead to mine. He lifts my hand to his mouth, sucking my fingers clean.

"That's mine," he says as he does it.

"You're such a caveman lately," I tease.

He's been a little more controlling lately, but I like it. I know he's still on edge about everything that happened. Yesterday I had to maneuver myself to get out of his hold while we were sleeping. It took me ten minutes to break free. I barely made it to the bathroom and he was freaking out looking for me because he woke up and I wasn't in bed.

"Your caveman."

I roll my eyes then hear the doorbell ring, and I duck under his arm. He tries to grab me, but I slip free heading for the door. I already know who it is.

"John," I say in greeting when he walks in.

"Jay." He nods and smiles at me. "Is he a bear today?"

I glance over at Jordan, who's now in the entryway. "You didn't check the peephole," he scolds, and I ignore him.

"I thought I'd gotten him toned down, but I guess not." I shoot a glance back to Jordan, and he's still giving me a stern look. I have to bite my lip from smiling, knowing that will only make it worse. "I'll leave you to it," I tell them, turning to leave.

"Little bird," Jordan growls. I turn to look at him. "Come here."

I should tell him not to boss me around, but my body doesn't listen. I think Jordan knows if he says anything in a growl to me, my body will obey. When I get to him, he slides his hands in my hair, pulls me close, and kisses me.

When he breaks the kiss, he rests his forehead on mine. "Check the peephole." I can feel the strain in his body.

"Okay," I tell him, and he visibly relaxes. I want to tell him no one can get up here unless they are approved, but I know small things will make him feel better. So I give it to him. Plus, he's right; I should have checked the peephole.

He reluctantly lets me go when John clears his throat. I give him one more quick kiss, and he grabs me back for another, and I know what he's thinking. His eyes bore into mine. When this physical therapy session is over, he's coming for me. I turn to leave, excited and praying the next hour doesn't feel like twenty. I need Jordan just as much as he needs me. I need his weight on my body. We need to mend our bond and join our bodies in the most primal and intimate way possible.

"Are you looking at her ass?" Jordan clips out from behind me, and I roll my eyes.

"If I'm going to look at anyone's ass around here, it would be yours," John says in response to Jordan. I snort at that.

When I get back to the bedroom, I make the bed and go about tidying up. I glance at the clock and see only ten minutes have passed. I groan and flop down on the bed then grab my phone from the nightstand and call Summer.

"Hey," she answers, sounding chipper. As bad as everything was, this whole ordeal seems to have changed our relationship for the better.

"Hey," I reply. "How is everything?" It's so different

to be able to call my sister for no reason, but that's what we've been doing. We've talked on the phone every day since I left the hospital.

"Great! I got an interview next week," she tells me.

"That's great. Where is it at?"

"Some yoga studio a few blocks from your old place. The pay isn't great, but I know I'll enjoy it."

"That's awesome. I'm happy for you."

"Thanks. How's your arm?"

I smile. She's been kind of doting on me since it happened, and I can't say that I don't like it. There's something about our roles reversing that feels different but nice.

"Still the same. At least they've given me a smaller cast now, not that big clunky one."

"All the better to move with," she says and I can picture her eyebrows wiggling.

"Dork," I say, and laugh at her.

I'm glad she's feeling more settled. She, out of everyone, has seemed to have dealt with what happened the best. She and Pop are best friends now. She goes over there all the time to help out with anything he needs. I don't think Pop needs the help, I think my sister really enjoys his company. I get it. Pop is so different from our parents. He actually makes you feel like he's your dad and he cares and loves you with his whole heart.

When I called and told our parents what happened, my mom gave me the *"I told you not to move to New York"* line. Nothing more. I thought she would at least try to come out, maybe even check on us a few times. But neither of us heard anything.

She lets out a little sigh, but it sounds happy. "You

guys need anything? I can bring over food or something."

"Nope. We're all good," I confirm. Food is the last
thing on my mind. All I can think about is the clock. I
glance over again and see the hands have barely moved.

"All right." I hear the laughter in her voice. She
knows what today is, and now I have a feeling she's
teasing me. She knows I didn't want anyone to come
over today.

"Whatever," I mumble, making her laugh harder.

"Hey, at least you know you're going to be getting
some. It's a dry land over here, and I don't see the rain
coming anytime soon."

That makes me laugh. I love that we have this now.
Those forty-eight hours were the worst hell I've ever
been in, but at the end of it I got my sister. We've formed
a bond now, and we actually feel like a family.

I hear the doorbell. "Hey, someone's here," I tell her,
rolling off the bed.

"Call me later."

"'Kay. Love you."

"Love you, too," she says before hanging up the
phone.

I make my way down the hall to see Jordan heading
for the door, too. I beat him to it this time, stopping to
look through the peephole.

"This is really barbaric. Shouldn't my hacker boyfriend have a camera out there and all I'd have to do is
check a monitor?" I tease, pulling open the door. He
picks me up by the waist and places me behind him,
grunting a little.

"Dang it, Jordan, don't hurt yourself or you really

won't be getting any!" I give him a smack on the back. He grunts again like I really hurt him, but I know better.

"Pop," Jordan says, and I blush when I realize what I said in front of him. Pop laughs, and I bury my face in Jordan's back.

"Whatever," I moan as a laughing Jordan pulls me forward. I try to reach out to hug Pop, but he doesn't let me go. "Was he always this much of a caveman?" I fake a sigh.

"I never let my wife out of my hands either," Pop says, leaning down and kissing my cheek. The word "wife" makes my heart flutter in my chest.

"Don't you have something you should be doing?" I look up at Jordan. He has a sheepish look on his face.

"I sent him home," he finally admits. I reach out and grab Pop to look at his watch.

"You had another twenty minutes!" Jordan just shrugs. "Come in," I tell Pop, pushing Jordan out of the way. "Do you want something to eat?" I ask him.

"He's not hungry," Jordan answers for him. I turn around and give him a hard look that seems to do nothing.

Pop just laughs.

The doorbell goes off again. "Fucking hell," Jordan mutters. I have to bite the inside of my cheek to keep from laughing. Pop sits down at the breakfast bar.

"What's wrong with him?" My face pinkens at the question, not wanting to tell Pop Jordan is horny and wants me in bed.

"He…ah…" I'm saved when Jordan comes back into the room with Ryan and Paige.

"Company," Jordan grunts. I don't know if I want to laugh or cry. Laugh because he's acting like an adorable grumpy bear that can barely talk, or cry because I, too, want to be alone with him.

Paige takes me by surprise, walking in and wrapping me in a hug. "I'm so sorry," she says. When I pull back, she has tears in her eyes.

"I'm fine, I promise," I try to reassure her.

"It's my job to make sure everyone is safe. I—"

"Stop," I tell her. "It's my fault, too. I should have said something sooner." That guilt still weighs on me, so much so I'm not sure I should go back to Osbourne Corp. to work. I messed up. I should have told someone about the emails.

"Stop, both of you," Pop snaps. We all turn to look at him. "No one can control crazy. This isn't anyone's fault. Trust me. I've been there. The ifs, ands, and buts will get no one anywhere but stuck in a place you don't want to be."

Pop's words sink in, and I know he's right. We need to let it all go. Living in it only gives the ones who hurt us more power.

I look over at Jordan, whose eyes are on me like they always are. I don't think it will be that easy for him. His possessiveness seems to be growing each day. He reaches for me and pulls me to him. I go to his side, melting into him. I know he understands what his dad is saying, but I'm not sure how much is really sinking in. I think he still needs more time.

"We wanted to let you know to take as much time as you need," Ryan says, breaking the silence. "Miles said he doesn't want to see you back for a while," he adds, looking at me. I nod. Everyone at work has been so sweet to us. I'm not used to having so many friends and people around. It's a lot to take in. To get used to.

"Okay, fuck it," Jordan finally says, his impatience getting the best of him. "Everyone has got to go."

Everyone turns to look at him. My face warms, but it's clear he's at the end of his rope. "I've been waiting all week for this." I feel like my eyes are about to pop out. I can't believe he just said that in front of his dad and his boss.

"Jordan!" I yell.

"Nope, little bird, I'm done sharing. Everyone out. I want to be alone with my woman," he says. I feel like I'm going to die of embarrassment, but when I look around at everyone, they are all smiling. Well, not Jordan, because people don't seem to be moving at a speed that makes him very happy.

I go to smack his chest, but he grabs me by the wrist, bringing my palm to his mouth. Our eyes lock as he kisses me there, letting his lips linger. I get lost in his eyes for a moment, forgetting everything else around us. I don't even realize that everyone has left until I hear the click of the front door.

He cups my face and kisses me. I drown in him, thinking how for a few hours once upon a time I thought I'd never get this again. "I love you so much," I tell him when he pulls back. "You're why I held on. Why I fought when the darkness wanted to take me. When, for a few moments, I wanted to give up," I tell him. Tears cascade down my face.

"I would have followed you into the darkness. I'll never be without you," he says, lifting me up. I should yell at him and tell him he shouldn't want that, that if something ever happened to me he should want to live, but I know my words will fall on deaf ears.

"You're going to hurt yourself," I tell him in a half-hearted protest. He should put me down, but I know he's not going to. Not until my back is on the mattress, at least. So I wrap myself around him, holding him tight as he carries me through the house after relocking the front door.

"Your dad knows we're having sex," I mumble into his neck.

"He's probably saying a prayer right now that I'm knocking you up."

"Jordan." I try to sound shocked, but he's probably right. Pop has brought up being a grandpa more than once, always in a jokey manner, but I know it's something he really wants, and soon. I wouldn't mind either. With everything that's happened, I know life is short, and being a mom is something I want. I'd never given it a ton of thought before, until Jordan came into my life and made me his. Now it's something that flutters through my mind often, but he hasn't asked me to marry him.

My back hits the soft mattress. I expect Jordan to start ripping off my clothes, but he looks down at me. "I wanted you for so long. Since the moment I saw you. Then to have you and to think I almost lost you…" He leans down, his lips brushing mine. "For so long I've been drifting in life. Doing my day-to-day, and then there you were, making life feel important. Making me feel like I had a reason."

My eyes fill with tears. I reach up, running my hands through his hair. "I never thought I belonged until you made me feel that way. You're the first person in my life to make me feel normal, Jordan. Like I fit somewhere."

"You're not normal," he corrects. "You're perfect."

Chapter Thirty-Three

Jordan

She is. She's the most perfect woman I've ever laid eyes on, and any man who passed up a chance to be with her was a fool. But it's by design that they missed their opportunity, because now she's mine and they'll never have another chance for her attention. It's all for me.

"I can't hold back much longer, Jay," I say, kissing her softly.

"I know." She rubs my chest before she gathers my shirt and pulls it off me.

I push hers up, needing her skin against mine. It's been so long since we've had contact like this, and I'm starved.

At night when we would come to bed, she insisted on wearing one of my shirts and a pair of shorts. She knew if she was naked, there was no way I'd keep off of her, and it's been torture ever since.

The feel of her bare stomach against mine is so fucking erotic I almost come in my shorts. I can't control myself as I pull down the cups of her bra, revealing her breasts so that I can press them to my chest.

"Fuck, I've missed your nipples on me," I moan, and I hear her laugh.

I rub my upper half against hers, needing the contact. I should take the time to remove her clothes, but I've got a one-track mind right now. She wiggles under me, and then more skin is exposed. I look down and see she's gotten her shorts and her shirt off, but her bra is still pulled down below her tits.

"Get your cock out." Her face is serious now, and I see that her need has risen as high as mine.

"Yes, ma'am," I grunt as I reach down and unzip my shorts.

I don't have them halfway off my ass before I'm seeking her wet heat and thrusting home.

"Oh God," we both moan at the same time.

"It's better than I remembered," I say, and she pulses around me. I know it's only been a week, but it's felt like an eternity. "I can't last."

My words are choked as I hold myself still, trying desperately to think of baseball and horror movies. Nothing is working, though. The image of Jay under me, legs spread, filled with my cock, is too much. I make the mistake of glancing down at where we're joined, and I groan in agony.

"Fuck, that's so hot. Seeing you take all of me."

"Move, Jordan, please," she begs and presses her chest up as she squeezes her eyes tight.

She's aching for me to make love to her. Her body needs it, and I'll be damned if I don't give her what she needs.

"Grab my shoulders, little bird."

She does as I say, and I slide one arm under her lower

back, lifting her hips. The other hand goes to her hip and grips her hard as I start to thrust.

"I'm going to come, but I'm not going to stop," I say through gritted teeth.

Her eyes lock with mine, and she clenches around me. She gets so turned on when I release inside her, and seeing her turned on is a drug for me.

I use her body to give her what she wants, and I feel my orgasm rush out of me. Warmth spreads between us, but I don't stop thrusting. She looks down at where we're connected and licks her lips, and I swear I pulse more come into her at the sight.

Holding her hips just right, I make sure that her clit is being rubbed every time I enter her. The feeling of her warm channel coated in my seed is enough to bring me back to the edge in seconds. She's gripping me tight and begging for just a little more as I see she's approaching the edge.

I keep my thrusts hard and steady as her nails dig into me. "Jordan!" she cries out as her body locks up, but I don't stop my rhythm.

I ride her hard as the pleasure washes over her. I can see the peaks, and when she gasps for air, I make sure another is there waiting on her. Her orgasm goes on and on, and I come with her, too. But my release does nothing to soften my cock, and I use the thick, hard length to give her endless paradise.

When her arms fall to the bed and her eyes are almost closed, I kiss her softly and slip free, moving to her side.

"More," she mumbles sleepily and smiles as I kiss her neck.

I bury my face in her hair, smelling her sweetness

and running my hands over her lush curves. "Rest, little bird. I've got more waiting when you wake up."

She mumbles something about doing it while she sleeps, and it makes me laugh. She's so cute when she's drunk on love.

"Just a quick nap. Then I'm waking you up," I say, and she nods in agreement.

She's snoring before she gets the second nod, and I kiss her forehead.

I've got a plan for later on today, and it would help if she's completely exhausted. I'll give her ten minutes to sleep, then I'm getting more of what I've been missing. As soon as she's unable to walk, I've got a few things I need to take care of.

Chapter Thirty-Four

Jordan

My thighs ache as I walk toward the house. I smile, thinking about why they're hurting so much. I spent hours making love to my woman in every position we could get into without hurting her wrist or my shoulder permanently.

The thought of our injuries makes me want to turn around and run back home, to crawl into bed and make sure she's safe. But I can't. I've got to do this, and then I can go to her.

"It's me, Pop," I call out as I use my key to get in the house.

He's sitting in the living room with a book in his lap. It's nighttime, but I knew he'd still be up.

"What are you doing here?" he asks as he watches me kiss my fingers and then place them on the picture of my mom. "Are you here for some pointers? I know you were supposed to have a big day with Jay." He wiggles his eyebrows, and I groan.

"Gross, and no."

I look down at my watch, thinking how long I've left her alone. I know I checked the locks a few times and made sure the security guard in the building knew no one was allowed up. I could probably call and check to see if she's okay, but this is supposed to be a surprise. Anxiety picks up, and I wonder how fast I could get back to her. What if something went wrong again?

"Jordan!" My dad's tone snaps me out of my train of thought. "Sit down. I know why you're here." I try to interrupt him, but he raises his hand to make me stop. "You know how much I loved Mom."

I nod, waiting for him to get to the point.

"She was my world until you came along. Then it grew. She was the absolute light of our lives. I didn't know what love was until she gave it to me. I didn't know what it meant to have someone consume your whole being and to worship every inch of someone's soul."

"I know, Pop. She loved you, too."

"Then listen to me when I say this, Jordan." He sets his book on the table beside him and leans forward. "If you love Jay the way I love your mother, don't take her light away."

I'm confused and open my mouth to speak, but he stops me again.

"Jay has a light inside her, just like Mom did. A light so bright you can't help but be drawn to it. It will consume every part of you it touches and make you feel warmth like you can't imagine. But if you stand over her and smother it, it will go out."

He gives me a hard look, and I feel a pain in my chest.

"You've both been through something traumatic, but life doesn't stop. You can't predict the future, and you can't change the past." I see tears form in his eyes. "I would trade everything I have for one more day with your mother, but living in fear that the same might happen to you doesn't honor her memory."

"I know. She would want you to be happy," I admit.

"She would want me to live," he says. "I worried about you every time you got in a car after the accident. Every time I saw the scar on your face, it was a reminder of what we both lost. But I couldn't keep you from getting in cars. I couldn't stop you from going out into the world. It wouldn't have been fair to your spirit. And it's not fair to Jay's."

He's right. I drop my head in my hands and take a deep breath.

"It's been a week, but I see how you've isolated her. Don't let it continue, Jordan. Let her light be the thing that guides you, not what terrifies you."

"I love her so much." There's pain in my voice when I look at my father. Pain that comes from the fear that I can't protect her, the way he couldn't protect his wife, the way I couldn't protect my mother.

"Then love her how she deserves to be loved." He opens the drawer beside him and pulls out a small box. "The woman who wore this before her shone brighter than the sun. Let the next woman who wears it do the same."

I take the ring box in my hand carefully. I nod and look up to see Pop giving me a soft smile.

"It was only a matter of time after you met Jay that you'd come to get the ring. I've been waiting, and after all you've been through, I think you're finally ready."

"I don't want my fear to push her away," I admit. It's been the thing that keeps me up at night since the kidnapping. "I have to have her, and I have to keep her safe."

"You're a smart boy. You take after me." He winks at me, and it makes me smile. "You'll figure it out. You love her, and I know you'll do the right thing."

I hold the ring box tighter and nod. "Thank you."

"Your mother would have adored her. She always wanted a daughter."

I smile, remembering Mom saying she wished there had been another female in the house to be on her side. "She would have," I agree.

"Honor your mother and her memory by treating Jay with the same respect and kindness. If you can do that, there's no greater love."

I stand up and go over to Pop, kissing him on the cheek. "Go to bed, old man," I tease and walk toward the front door.

"Go make me some grandbabies," he says from behind me as I close the door.

I shake my head as I walk to the end of the block and wave down a taxi. I feel better leaving than I did when I got here. I know I'm on my way back to Jay, but my dad is right. I can't control everything, and I have to stop trying. The reason I fell for her was because of her strong personality and independence. That, and she's insanely hot. But if I try to change her life and keep her locked up in my building, it changes what I love about her.

I know that she's my forever, and we need to be able to grow together as we grow older. But I don't want to change things about her in order to make that happen. I will be by her side no matter what the future holds. Pop is right, just like always. I can't smother her light.

Leaning back in the cab, I open the ring box. The large diamond was an extravagant gift from my father, but I remember him telling me that my mother deserved to have a piece of jewelry almost as beautiful as her. Seeing the stone sparkle in the night on the plain gold band makes me anxious to get it on Jay's finger.

But like my dad said, I can't let fear rule me. I've got a plan, and I'm sticking to it.

Chapter Thirty-Five

Jordan

"No. No, no, no, no. Not happening," Jay says, and crosses her arms.

I smile at her and wait with my hands outstretched.

"Damn it, Jordan, I don't want to go through this again." She looks at the horse carriage and then at me.

"I've double-checked the horse to make sure he's okay, and I promise this time will be better."

Jay looks at me and then bites her lip. "Do you really want to have a do-over?"

I nod and reach out, pulling her in my arms. "You deserve to have the date you always dreamed of. The first got ruined, so I'm going to make it better."

"If it means that much to you..." she mumbles against my chest.

"It really does. I want to make all your dreams come true."

She looks up at me and smiles, placing a hand on my cheek. I lean into the touch, and she nods.

"All right, handsome. Let's go for a spin."

The past two weeks have been heaven and hell for

us. Heaven because we've spent every day together, and hell because I've had to loosen my control.

We've both decided to go back to work in two weeks, so we've spent our days lying around the house or going to the park. It's been amazing, talking and laughing and making love. I can't get enough of her, and the more I have, the more I want.

Her sister called one day last week and asked to go see a chick flick. I offered to go with them, but I could tell that Jay wanted some one-on-one time with Summer. I could have followed them. I could have waited outside the movie theater until she was finished. I could have gone with them and seen another movie. But instead I chose to trust Jay and listen to my father.

By the time she came back home to me, she was practically running through the door and in my arms. I made love to her on the floor right in the entrance because we couldn't wait to get to the bedroom. I don't think my anxiety about being away from her will ever leave me, but at least I'm able to control it long enough for her to see a movie. I'm a man who's obsessed, so I can't expect too much.

Her wrist only had a small break and is healing quickly. She was released to go back to work next week, so we're sticking to the plan. I know Jay has her own fears about what happened to her, and working for Osbourne Corp. again. But Miles called her last week and they talked for a long time about how much he wanted her to come back to work.

She agreed to try it out again and see how it goes. With Miles cutting back some of his work, she's not needed as much as she was before, so this is a good time to start. She can work part-time and still be able to keep busy while figuring out if this is what she still wants to do long-term.

She started writing again, and to walk by the office and see her typing away warms my heart. She looks so intense but happy, and that's all I want for her. For the both of us. Maybe one day she'll do something with her stories, but until then, I know she's happy just writing.

I've thought about proposing to her a million times in the past two weeks, but I wanted it to be perfect. The carriage we had on our first date was hired for commission out of state. So I had to wait until it came back into the city before I could reserve it again. Now it's here, and this time nothing is going to go wrong.

I help Jay into the carriage, and her hands are clammy. She looks worried as I sit down beside her and we pull away from the curb.

"Are you okay?" I ask.

"Yeah, I'm just really nervous."

"It will be fine," I say, running my hand over my pocket to be sure the ring is still safely inside.

"I love you," I say, and kiss her lips softly.

She smiles at me, and some of her nerves drop away. "I love you, too, Jordan. So much."

The carriage rides along the park, and it's a beautiful Sunday afternoon in New York. The birds are singing, the sun is shining, and I've got my soon-to-be wife at my side.

The ride is a little bumpy as we go over some of the rougher pathways. There's some sort of race happening today, so there are a lot of people passing by us. It's not as private of a ride as I'd like, but it's New York, so there's never much privacy.

As we near the lake, I turn and look at Jay. She's

worrying her lip, and I can see a little color has left her cheeks.

"What's wrong?" I ask, concerned she's not having a good time.

"Jordan—"

"And here we are," says the driver of the carriage as we stop by the lake. He grabs the picnic basket and stands there, waiting on us.

Jay stands up, and I help her down, taking the basket and walking to the spot we sat at last time.

"See, already better than the last ride. Now just don't kick me in the balls and we'll ace this."

I'm able to get a smile out of her on that, but something is bugging her. There's something she's not telling me.

I spread the blanket out, thinking that maybe if we sit down for a little bit she'll be okay and can tell me what's bothering her. Maybe it's the fact that I haven't proposed yet. She made a few small comments this week about getting married, but I didn't want to spoil the surprise, so I just played them off and talked about something else. Maybe she thinks I've changed my mind, which is absolutely insane.

We sit down, and I open up the picnic basket. "I've brought a few things I think you might like," I say, trying to entice her with food.

She gives me a sideways glance and then nods. It's unlike her not to get excited about sharing a meal with me. Usually she can't wait to eat. It's one of the things I love most about her. But her mind is somewhere far from here.

I open the food containers and set them down. The

smell of her favorite dried meats and cheeses floats between us as I take her hands in mine.

I'm just going to get it out in the open. I've been stressing about it for two weeks now, and I know she must be thinking the same thing. She didn't want to do this carriage ride today, and I've forced it, so I'm going to propose to her and tell her what an idiot I am for going through this charade. I don't want confusion to be the reason she's worried. I want to set her mind at ease.

"Jay, since the day you walked into my life—"

At that moment, Jay inhales the smell of the food, and instantly her face turns green. Before I can finish my sentence, she leans over and throws up on the blanket.

'I'm pregnant," she says and then looks up at me and bursts into tears.

"Marry me," I blurt out, totally overwhelmed by what just happened.

There's a pause, and we both begin to laugh. God, this would only happen to us.

"Are you saying that because I'm pregnant?" she asks, laughing through the tears in her eyes.

"Damn it, woman, you know me better than that." I pull the ring out of my pocket and slide it on her finger. I grab a bottle of water and lean down, picking her up. I carry her over to the bench nearby and sit down with her in my lap. I cradle her in my arms, feeling the warmth of her body against mine.

"Jay, my sweet little bird. Why didn't you tell me?" I kiss the top of her head as my heart grows. "We're going to have a baby?"

"I was trying to find the right time. I just found out this morning. You had this whole thing planned, and

I was feeling sick. I didn't want to tell you yet, but I didn't know how to say I wasn't feeling good without you going crazy."

"I've been planning this as a proposal. I had to wait on the damn carriage to come back to the city."

"Stupid carriage," Jay mumbles. "I thought you changed your mind." She looks up at me, and I can see the worry that was there fade. "You were just playing me."

"How could you possibly think I could ever change my mind? You're the love of my life."

"Hormones?" she says, and shrugs like it's the answer to everything. Maybe it is.

"So, is that a yes?" I ask, looking into her chocolate-brown eyes.

"Yes!" she squeals, and throws her arms around me. "Oh God, Jordan. It's all happening so fast."

"We're not on a timeline. We do things our way and at our own pace. I've known you for a long time. And I knew from the moment we met we'd get to this point." I tuck a strand of hair behind her ear. "You've been mine since the beginning. I laid claim to you long ago."

"You did." She nods in agreement.

"Do you want to go back home so I can get you some ginger ale and rub your feet?"

She smiles at me and nods, then looks over at the picnic. "I'm sorry this was ruined again."

I shake my head. "It just gives me another chance to try again. Third time's a charm, right?"

"Oh God." The worry is back, but it's playful this time.

"Home," I say, and tuck her into my arms as I carry her out of the park.

Chapter Thirty-Six

Jay

"Five more minutes," I moan, as I wrap myself around Jordan. I cling to him, not letting him get up from the bed. I don't want to let go of his warmth. Nothing feels better than being in bed with him.

"Little bird, I'll give you all the minutes if you really want to stay here."

I sigh, knowing he would, but I told Miles I'd be back today. Even if I choose to quit and keep writing while being a stay-at-home mom, I know I still need to transition. I have to find him someone to take my place. Miles has been good to me, and I won't leave him high and dry. I have months before the baby comes. I need to get everything lined up and taken care of.

"Shower," I murmur.

He stands up with my body still wrapped tightly around his. He goes into the bathroom and turns on the shower, stepping in. I still don't let go of him as the warm water washes over us.

"You feeling okay?" he asks me.

It's the same question he asks most mornings. My

morning sickness doesn't normally come until later afternoon, but he still worries.

"Yeah," I tell him, still not letting go of him. I want to stay latched on as long as possible.

"Come on, little bird. Get down and I'll take care of you."

I sigh again, reluctantly easing my feet to the tile floor. More than anything, I've been tired. Every now and then I feel sick, but most of the time I want sleep. I want to lie in bed cuddled next to Jordan and do nothing else.

He puts some soap in his hands and begins washing me. I love how much he enjoys taking care of me. I moan as his hands massage my hair, and I close my eyes. "Use your body wash on me," I tell him. I want to smell like him today. I know it will help with being away from him.

He chuckles but still does what I say.

"We have dinner with Pop today," he reminds me. We had to cancel our usual Sunday dinner yesterday. Well, Jordan canceled because he refused to wake me from my nap to go. I woke up and the sun was already setting. I was disappointed.

My eyes fly open. "I'm so excited." We haven't told anyone I'm pregnant yet because we wanted Pop to be the first to know. I was going to tell him yesterday, but I guess that didn't happen.

"God, I love how happy you get with my dad." He cups my face sweetly. "I swear you're the light of our family now."

I blink back tears and smack his chest playfully. "Don't say stuff like that. I'll cry forever."

I seem to cry about anything right now. Him telling

me I'm the center of their family is really going to do me in. I've always stood on the outside of things in life, never really fitting in. Not with them, though. I fit in. It's like I've always been there.

He kisses my cheeks. "I'll make sure you don't cry." He drops to his knees in front of me. I lean back, knowing what he's going to do. Jordan always knows how to make me get lost in him and how to make everything else melt away to where it's only him and me.

I run my fingers into his wet hair. He grips my thighs and parts them. His mouth lands on my core, making me moan out as he licks and sucks me.

I jerk against him. My body tingles. I love that there's no tease with him. He's giving me what I need and making my body pulse with pleasure.

"Never thought I'd see this, you naked with my ring on your finger, my baby inside you."

He slides one hand up to rest on my stomach. I look down at him, my hands still tangled in his hair. I never thought I'd see this either, the man I've wanted for so long on his knees in front of me, worshipping my body, giving me everything and more than I could have asked for. I didn't know life could be this perfect.

His mouth lands back on me, his tongue going straight for my clit and making me come undone. Pleasure shoots through my body, forcing me to cry out his name over and over. He holds me tight, making sure I stay on my feet. All too soon he's pulling me from the shower and sitting me on the bathroom counter. I feel warm and fuzzy, and I never want to move again. Although I know I have to.

I go to get up, but he stops me. "Let me," he insists, and brushes my hair before blow-drying it. I didn't know a man could be so attentive and that I could be the center of his world.

"You going to dress me, too?" I tease, loving how he's doting on me.

"If you let me."

I smile up at him. How am I supposed to go back to being an assistant when I now have someone taking care of me all the time?

"You'd probably dress me in your clothes." Whenever I ask him to grab me a shirt, he always brings me one of his. "I bet you'd layer me in them."

"You love wearing my clothes." He gives me a little grumpy smile.

I laugh. I do love wearing them. I love smelling like him, feeling like he's always around me. "I do, but I'm not sure it's really work attire."

He shrugs like he doesn't care.

"Kiss me." I barely get the words out and he's got his lips on mine. I'm going to miss being able to demand kisses all day. Though I'm sure if I send a text he'll be at my desk giving me more than I asked for.

"Get ready, little bird. I'll get you breakfast," Jordan says, giving me one last kiss and pulling me off the bathroom counter. I watch his tight ass as he walks out of the room and wish I could drag him back to bed.

I turn and look at myself in the mirror. All the bruises on my face are gone, and my wrist doesn't hurt anymore. I'm back to my old self, but somehow I think I look different. People say pregnant women glow, but I thought it was a silly old wives' tale. But looking at myself now, I think they might be right. I feel like I'm glowing. I'm not sure if it's from the pregnancy or the love I feel.

I hurry up and get ready, putting on light makeup and a simple blue dress. I pause when I see new flats embroidered with little blue jays sitting in the closet. My last pair got ruined when Summer and I were taken. It had broken my heart to see them trashed. I hadn't said anything about it, but it seems Jordan noticed.

Smiling, I slide them on. I don't know how I got so lucky to have a man like him. He seems to notice everything.

When I get to the living room, Jordan is walking toward me, handing me a to-go cup and a bacon-and-egg sandwich.

"I think you might be the most perfect man in the world," I tell him, taking a bite of my breakfast.

"I better be the only man in your world." He smirks as he picks up my purse. I move to take it from him.

"Eat. I got it," he tells me.

"You're going to carry my purse around?" I ask. I know the security people he works with will likely give him crap if they see this.

"I don't give a shit. My woman needs to focus on eating her breakfast and keeping it down, not on her purse that I can carry for her."

I lift up on my tippy-toes and plant a kiss on his mouth, thinking all those years of feeling like men never noticed me were now worth it. I didn't have to go through the mess of dating. I got my perfect man from day one.

Jordan opens the door, and we head out. The traffic to work is light for once, and I'm at my desk before I know it. Jordan looms over me, and I can tell he doesn't want to leave.

"Last time I left you at your desk…"

"I know." I hate that he feels so worried about leaving me and that we had to go through that.

"I, ah…" He trails off, reaching into his pocket.

"What?" I ask, reaching for the box he's pulled out.

"It's a bracelet," he says as I open it. It's a thick, solid silver band with a giant bow on it, covered in diamonds, and a little bird sitting on it.

He takes the bracelet from the box and slips it onto my wrist.

"It has a tracker in it." The words stumble out, like he thinks I'm going to be upset about it. "Also audio," he adds.

"So you can always hear me?" I tease. He points to his ear, and I see a clear plastic device there. I burst out laughing.

His cheeks turn a little pink, and he shrugs.

"I love it," I tell him. I reach out and take his hand. "It's us."

We've always been a little odd. I've forever loved that he checks my work calendar and watches me on the camera. If this bracelet makes him feel more okay, then I'll wear it forever.

He leans down and kisses me. It's soft and sweet, and I know he still doesn't want to leave.

"Am I going to have to move your desk to this floor?" I pull back at the sound of Miles's voice.

"Sir," I greet him. Normally I know when he's coming, but this time I was distracted. Mallory's standing next to him with a giant smile on her face.

"Miles," he corrects.

"I, ah—"

"Don't worry about it, Jay. If anyone gets it, it's him," Mallory says before turning and kissing Miles. "Glad everything is okay," she tells me, pulling me into a hug before heading to her office.

"When you're done…" Miles nods toward his office door and then walks away, leaving us alone.

"I'm so getting fired," I mumble to Jordan, who looks happy at the idea.

I know I'm not really getting fired, but I'm not on my A-game anymore. Something in me has shifted. I used to be crazy about work, making sure everything is done and perfect, but that spark isn't there anymore.

"Look at me." Jordan tilts my face up to meet his eyes. "If anyone knows life is short, it's us. Quit. I know you want to. You don't have to be out of here today, but you can start that path. I have more money than we'll ever need."

"I'll talk to him." I glance over at Miles's office doors.

"I'm going to talk to Ryan and Paige, too. A lot of what I do can be done from home. I want to be a hands-on dad like mine was. I want to be a part of all the firsts we have." His hand slides to my stomach. In this moment I know what I have to do. My passion for work has shifted. I know I'm a driven person, but my drive is now somewhere else, not here.

"Kiss me." I use his own words. He leans down and does as I ask. "Go to work," I tell him.

He stares down at me, and I know he doesn't want to leave me. "I promise I won't leave this floor until you come get me for lunch." I lift up the bracelet. "Go listen to me quit my job."

He smiles and gives me another kiss. "I love you."

"I love you, too," I say instantly. He straightens and

pulls out his wallet, getting his elevator card out. I snatch it from him. "Lost mine."

He gives a little chuckle. "Guess I'll wait like a commoner." He winks at me as he makes his way to the elevator.

I smile, watching him leave. Letting out a deep sigh, I pick up my notepad and make my way to Miles's office. I give a small knock before opening the door.

"Come in." He motions for me to sit in the chair in front of his desk. I take my seat, unsure of where to start. Luckily Miles goes first.

"We've worked side by side for a while, and I know what's coming," he says, taking me by surprise. "I know we aren't what people might call friends, but you've been with me making sure anything and everything Osbourne Corp. might need is handled. You've been my right hand a lot of times. You might not see it, but to me you have been my friend. I don't get close to a lot of people. If anyone knows that, it's you. But you are my friend, and that's why I'm letting you go." He pauses for a second. "You're fired," he says, tossing an envelope in front of me.

"I…" I'm shocked. Was I given a compliment and fired at the same time?

"Pick it up," Miles says, gesturing to the envelope. I reach out and pick it up. "It's your severance package."

I open the envelope and see there's a check inside. I glance over the zeros, and all the air leaves my lungs. It's for five million dollars.

"Sir!" I scream.

"And she's still calling me sir," Miles says with a laugh.

"Well, technically I don't work for you anymore, so

I can do as I wish," I tell him, only making him laugh more. My heart is in my throat. This is way too much money.

"Don't fight it. Take the check," he says. "You know it's a drop in the bucket for me, and you earned it. You've helped the company become what it is." I look across the desk at him and feel my eyes moisten. Stupid pregnancy hormones.

"Thank you, Miles. You've always taken good care of me." I tuck the check away and put it in my lap. "I'd like to stay on to train someone new. Someone to replace me," I tell him.

He smiles and shakes his head slightly. "No one could ever replace you, Jay."

Chapter Thirty-Seven

Jay

"Little bird," Jordan says to me, placing a hand on my leg. I can't stop from bouncing it. I feel like I'm going to burst with excitement. Today has gone better than I thought it would. Between Miles being okay with me wanting to leave, to seeing Pop… I know he's going to be just as excited as we are about my being pregnant.

"I can't help it," I tell him, beaming over at him. Jordan has been excited about the baby, too, but I know this is going to be different for Pop. He's all about family, and this is us growing that family.

"You take your vitamins?" Jordan asks for the third time today.

"Yes. Pretty sure you already asked me." I pretend to be annoyed, but I do love how doting he is about me being pregnant. He leans over, burying his face in my neck and kissing me there. I tilt my head, letting him have his way with me. I get lost when Jordan has his mouth on me, thinking about nothing but how he makes me feel.

My neck is a weakness. He kisses it and I forget everything else. "We're here, little bird," he whispers in my ear. The cab comes to a stop in front of Pop's. He tosses the cabbie some money, then hops out, coming around to open my door and pulling me from the cab.

"You distracted me," I tell him. I love how he can do that. I get so worked up about something and he calms me down by letting me get lost in him. No one else in the world can do that to me but him. He's my calm.

"Hmm." He kisses me as the cab pulls away.

"Pop is going to be so excited," I tell him. I feel like I'm going to burst. Grabbing Jordan's hand, I start pulling him to the house, where Pop is already opening the front door to greet us.

"I'm pregnant!" I scream, unable to control myself and launching myself at him, but Jordan grabs me and holds me back, stopping me midair.

"No jumping," he tells me sternly. I roll my eyes. Pop smiles, and I see tears form in his eyes.

"Give her to me," he tells Jordan.

Jordan grunts before reluctantly letting me go. I go to Pop and wrap my arms around him. He picks me up, swinging me around and making me laugh.

"You don't know what this means to me," he whispers in my ear before putting me back down on my feet. "You're giving this family light."

Jordan grabs me, pulling me back to him. Pop laughs, a knowing smile on his face.

"Come inside," he says, ushering us inside. Jordan stops to kiss the picture of his mom. I look at him and do the same.

"Thank you." I tell the picture. This woman gave me the man who has made my life. Jordan turns me in his arms, his mouth landing on mine in a soft, sweet kiss.

"I love you so much," he whispers against my mouth.

"Stop hogging her," Pop says. I smile against Jordan's mouth. I've never felt more loved and wanted than I have with this family. My new family. I didn't even know families could be like this.

"I want to try out this new recipe," Pop says, taking my hand and pulling me toward the kitchen. Jordan follows us. When we get to the kitchen, Jordan picks me up and sits me on the counter. He thinks I can't do anything but eat now that I'm pregnant.

"You taste and watch," he tells me.

I lean back, watching my men go to work, thinking I've never been happier. I've never felt like I belonged more in my life.

"Hey!" I hear as Summer comes walking in. She gives Pop a kiss on the cheek before coming over to me and giving me a hug. I love how much she has molded into this family with me. I want her to be a part of it, too. We've never had something like this, something that feels so stable.

"You look like you're glowing," she tells me. As she stands in front of me, she looks happy, too.

"That's because you're going to be an aunt!" Her face lights up and she starts jumping up and down, making me laugh. She grabs my hands, locks her fingers with mine, and steps between my legs.

"Being kidnapped was the best thing to have happened to us. I know it was terrible, but I got a family out of it. It made me grow up," she says. "I don't want for you to feel bad for one second about me getting wrapped up in what happened. Oddly, I'm thankful for it." She drops her forehead to mine. "I love you, and I'm going to be the best aunt in the world."

My eyes grow wet. "I love you, too," I tell her. When

we pull back, I see Pop and Jordan watching us both with smiles on their faces.

I didn't know life could be so perfect.

Epilogue

Jordan
Two months later...

"Did you feel that?" Jay asks excitedly as Pop presses on her growing belly.

"Wow! She's going to be a strong little girl," he exclaims, and I see them share a look.

We haven't found out what we're having yet, but they both swear it's a girl. I don't care either way, as long as both Jay and our baby are healthy. Although I wouldn't mind a little girl running around our home. I can picture it with a little boy, too, and my heart can't decide. Good thing we can always have more.

Checking my phone to make sure everything is in place, I walk out on the balcony, where they're sitting. Pop looks up at me and winks. He's almost as excited as I am for the surprise.

"Here you go, little bird," I say, holding out the drink.

She looks up at me with confusion and then shakes her head. "You know I can't have a margarita."

"It's virgin," I say, holding it out to her.

She still doesn't get it, looking at Pop now and then

back to me. "Jordan, it's ten in the morning. Why are you bringing me a margarita?"

"Because it's your birthday, and I always keep my promises."

I watch her for a second, and then I see the memory click. A promise to bring her a margarita and take her away to an island on her birthday.

"Jordan." She says my name with warning and excitement. "What did you do?"

"We better go. Our drive is waiting downstairs."

She takes the margarita from me and stands up, looking at me and then at Pop. She's speechless. Then I see tears form, and I shake my head.

"Aww, Jay, don't do that. Don't cry."

"I'm just so happy," she sobs, putting a hand over her mouth.

I pull her to my chest and try to hold back my laugh. God, my woman is so hormonal. But I wouldn't have her any other way.

"You better go, honey. I'm going to take care of things here and I'll see you in a couple of weeks," Pop says, and leans over, putting a kiss on Jay's cheek and then on mine. "Love you both. Be safe, and take care of my granddaughter."

"Oh God, Jordan, I'm pregnant," Jay says, popping up and looking at me with panic.

"Yes, I'm aware." I'm the one who's confused now.

"Can I travel in this condition?" She's worrying her lip, and I swear she's never looked cuter.

"Yes. You're just over three months along. This may be the perfect time. And the last time for a while with the baby coming."

We were married at city hall with a few friends

and family present. Summer was Jay's maid of honor, but her parents weren't able to make it. Jay was disappointed but not surprised. When my father offered to give her away, I think that might have been the best part of her day. Well, other than marrying me.

The wedding was so quick that we didn't have time to plan for a honeymoon, and Jay said she wanted to wait until after the baby was born. But I know her, and I knew that she was just afraid. I asked all her doctors and called the place we're staying about seventeen thousand times to make sure we had everything we needed. They know me by first name now, but I don't care. I want her to have the best time possible, and putting her worries aside would do that.

When I saw her birthday was coming up, it worked out perfectly, and I've done all of this without her knowing.

She's spent the last two months training two people to come in and take over her job at Osbourne Corp. She loves to rub it in Miles's face that it took two people to make one of her. But they seem to have it figured out. At least once a week Miles calls and gives her hell, but I think mostly he just wants to check in. Through everything that happened, it bonded all of us. Even me with the security team. We've all created our own little family, and it's growing by the day.

I take Jay's hand and lead her off the balcony and inside.

"Jordan, I haven't even packed." She tries to pull from my grip, but I shake my head.

"You specifically said that you wouldn't need clothes. And I've got plans to keep you from getting tan lines." I watch her blush as she looks over to where Pop is, but he ignores us. "Just you and me in the island sun. Think you can handle that, little bird?"

She presses her body against mine and gets on her tiptoes. "If you say it's okay, then I know it's handled. Take me to paradise."

The travel time is hard for Jay. Hell, it's hard for the both of us. But I know once we get to the island it will all be worth it. It's a twenty-hour flight, and then a small water plane to the remote location. When we arrive, I don't know what day it is, but the sun is still shining.

We're greeted by several people who work on the island getaway, including a doctor from the mainland. I hired him to come meet us here, just to check Jay over after the journey. It may have been overly cautious, but better safe than sorry.

Contrary to what I told Jay, I did pack her a bag, but it's a small one. Someone grabs them for us, and I end up carrying Jay to the house, and any sort of protest she made was half-hearted. She's exhausted, and even the short distance from the shore to the house has her passing out in my arms.

The house is large with glass windows lining one side. I carry her straight to the master bedroom and lay her down on the bed, opening the doors that lead onto the sandy beach and smooth water a short distance away.

The doctor comes in, and they talk for a moment. He listens to her and reminds her to drink plenty of fluids. He leaves me with some nausea medicine just in case and shows me how to work the satellite phone for emergencies. Jay is asleep before he's even said goodbye to her, having reassured us both that everything is okay.

The staff takes me through the house, showing me the things I need, including the stocked kitchen. If we don't have something we need, we can call for it. Otherwise they'll see us in a few days to clean and restock. I've booked this place for three weeks, wanting a quiet place to love my woman in peace.

I walk down to the boats and watch everyone leave, making sure we're completely alone. Once they're gone, I go to the kitchen and grab a couple of bottles of water and return to the bedroom. I set them on the side Jay is lying on and look down at her.

She's so tired, but her hand is stretched out on the side of the bed I usually sleep on. She's looking for me, even though I'm right here.

My eyes fall to where her shirt has ridden up, and the small baby bump that's formed makes my heart fill with love.

Kneeling down beside the bed, I press my lips to her belly and then nuzzle it with my nose.

"I love you," I whisper to our baby and then feel Jay's fingers in my hair.

Leaning into her touch, I close my eyes and listen to the sounds of the ocean. Already I'm more at peace than I have been in a long time. I love the city, and I don't want to leave, but being able to get away and knowing there's no one here but Jay and me is intoxicating.

When I open my eyes, the sun is streaming in and Jay looks like an angel. Her face is content as she sighs, and I need to make love to her.

Reaching under her skirt, I find the edge of her panties and slowly pull them down her legs. She lies still, tired and turned on as I move her thighs apart and settle between her legs.

She hums with appreciation when my mouth covers her center. Her flavor is warm and sweet, just like she is. I lick her slowly, making love to her with my mouth. I'm gentle and coaxing, neither of us in a hurry.

"I've waited so long to have you like this," I say, tasting her lower lips and then teasing her bud. "You are so fucking beautiful." I stare between her thighs and let my eyes roam up her body before they lock with hers.

I keep contact as I lower my mouth to her sex, and this time, there is no tease. This time, I lick her exactly how she likes it, wanting to get her off.

I'm so attuned to her that when her climax approaches, I know it. With every twitch of her fingers, with every hitch in her breath. I know that her body is primed for release, and I give her exactly what it craves.

As long as I live, I will give her what she needs, and that includes her body's passion. I'll never take for granted the privilege of being between her legs and being allowed to touch something so pure and perfect.

When she gives herself over to the demands of my mouth, I drink down her sweetness. The taste of her orgasm in my mouth and the sight of her clawing at the sheets are enough for me to lose control.

Reaching down, I pull my cock out as I move up her body and slide inside her while she's still pulsing from her release. The feel of her honey-soaked pussy wrapped tight around me is pure heaven.

She pulls at my shirt, and I take it off while thrusting inside her. She always demands skin on skin, and it's another thing I'll never deny her.

"Give me your mouth," I order, and she tilts her chin up, opening for me.

I need to kiss her while I'm inside her. I have to have

my whole body bound to hers in every way that I can. Something about the taste of her on my tongue while I fill her body is primal and raw.

"I love you," she moans when I move down her neck and to her breasts.

They're so sensitive now that she's pregnant, and I can't wait to see them full of milk. To be able to taste what her body can give our babies is another way for me to bond to her. Another way that I will know her intimately, and in a way that's just between us.

Sucking her nipple into my mouth, I graze it with my teeth as she cries out in pleasure. I do the same to the other one, then kiss my way back up, whispering my own words of love.

Her body is wound tight again so quickly, and mine has been ready since the day I saw her. Reaching between us, I rub her clit as my cock dips in and out of her.

Sweat and sex spread from one another, and it's so fucking sexy. It's raw and real, yet it's safe and loving. Making love to Jay is the most intense and beautiful thing I've ever experienced.

"Come with me," she moans, and pulls me down for a kiss.

She gasps into my mouth as her climax hits her, and I have no choice but to follow. The edge is steep and my release is intense as I hold myself deep in her body and come with her. Just as she told me to.

It takes me longer than I imagined to catch my breath, feeling wave after wave of pleasure wrack my body. The combination of being exhausted and having an orgasm is enough to have me nearly blacking out.

Instead, I pull myself off of Jay and kick the rest of my clothes off.

"Come on, little bird. You can't sleep yet."

"Why the hell not?" she mumbles into the pillow as she rolls over and shows me her naked ass.

"Because it's daylight, and unless you want to be wide-awake tonight, we need to stay up just a little longer." I kiss her back, and she swats her hand at me.

"Maybe you should have thought of that before you gave me that good loving."

I laugh and shake my head. "I'll be back," I say in my best Terminator voice.

I go into the kitchen and get a tote bag out from one of the drawers. I fill it up with snacks from the pantry, then grab some more from the fridge.

My woman loves to snack, so when I think I have enough food for the both of us, plus enough to feed at least ten more, I step out onto the beach.

The water is only a few yards away from us, so this is perfect. I grab a blanket and lay it out under some trees, and then grab some pillows off the chairs nearby.

When I go back inside, Jay's skirt is still bunched around her hips and she's giving me suspicious eyes.

"You're naked. Where did you go?" she asks, sitting up.

I smile because I can't tell if she's curious or mad that someone could have seen me. "We're all alone. Come with me and see."

Walking over to the bed, I strip off the rest of her clothes so she's naked with me.

"This feels a little weird," she says, looking around when we step outside.

"It's our very own private naked island," I say, winking at her. "I made us a naked picnic."

"Is everything going to have the word 'naked' in it?" she asks, giggling at me.

I scoop her up in my arms and carry her over to the blanket, laying her down on the pillow. "Potentially. I've got a naked movie and dinner planned after this, if you want."

"I'm liking the sound of that. At least this way I can keep an eye on your balls so I don't go kicking them by mistake."

I can't hold back my own laugh. "You can keep anything you want on them." I pull her feet into my lap and then bring one to my mouth, kissing the top of it.

"What are we going to do for three weeks?"

"Not a damn thing," I say, sighing and leaning back, rubbing her feet. "That's the point."

She looks out onto the water, and the way the soft sea breeze blows her hair is like something out of a movie.

She rubs her belly as her naked breasts warm in the shaded sun. I could look at her for hours. And I intend to.

The light reflecting off my wedding band catches her eye, and she reaches out and takes my hand, placing it on her belly with hers.

"You've made me the happiest woman on the planet. You know that, right?"

"That's all I ever wanted to do, little bird."

"I want to name her after your mother," she says as she continues to stroke her belly.

I nod, thinking it would be a beautiful tribute to my mother if our baby does turn out to be a girl.

"I'd like that. And you know Pop would, too."

"Thank you. Not only for this, but for giving me a family."

"You've given me one, too, Jay. I know you think you were on the outside for a long time and didn't have much in the way of friends. But I didn't either. And it was just me and Pop until you showed up. Then you brought in Summer, and now our baby. Our family is growing, and it's all because of you."

"Don't make me cry," she says, fanning her eyes as the tears well up. "You know how I am."

I laugh and lean down, kissing the happy tears away. "I'm just saying, you think this was all because of me, but it was you and me together. Just like this baby is. A perfect blend of us, and our future."

"This is so romantic," she says, laughing and wiping away the last of her tears.

"It's naked romantic," I say, wiggling my eyebrows.

I spread her legs and move between them, coming over the top of her body.

"We're never going to make it to naked dinner if you give me any more orgasms."

"Guess I'll just have to keep you on edge until it's time," I say, leaning down and kissing her neck.

"You know better than that." Her voice is smug, but damn it, she knows she's right.

"Anything you want, little bird. Anything at all and it's yours."

"Make love to me," she whispers to me so softly I can barely hear it over the ocean.

I nod, and once again I send us into paradise.

Epilogue

Jay
Five Years Later...

"Come here." Jordan pulls me further into him, like there was much space to begin with between us. He's probably not going to let me far from him. I might have dressed up a little. Wearing a low-cut dress that hugs tight to my body but flares out at my hips. I even put on some makeup and left my hair down. I'm not going to lie. I didn't dress up because I was itching to. I did it to get Jordan worked up. I love when he gets extra possessive of me. It turns me on and tonight we don't have any kids when we get home so we can be as loud and wild as we want.

We have the night out. Pops pretty much kidnapped our two girls. They were more than excited to go. Sometimes it's even a fight to get them to leave his house after our Sunday dinners. They love it over there because he spoils them rotten. Pops can't go more than a few days without seeing them and the days he doesn't get to, he's FaceTiming them at night and reading them a book.

It could be two in the morning and they want pancakes and he's out of bed making them for them. As much as I roll my eyes about it I really love it. I even know Summer is going over there to cookout with them. I love this little family we have made and how my sister is a part of it. Our parents still don't really have much contact with us. They haven't ever even asked to come out and meet their grandchildren.

"How did you know I wanted Italian?" I ask him as he pulls me into the restaurant. His arm locked around me.

"When don't you want Italian?" he asks. It's the truth. I became addicted to it with my first pregnancy and the addiction never stopped. Sometimes I even ate it for breakfast.

"Two," Jordan tells the hostess. Then leans in, kissing me under the ear as she grabs the menus. We follow her to a table in the back. Jordan pulls my chair out for me.

The waitress comes over. I notice she keeps her eyes on Jordan, paying me no mind whatsoever. "Two dry white wines and a bruschetta to start," Jordan says before she can even really talk, not taking his eye off the menu.

"Okay," the waitress says a little tartly but she doesn't move from the table.

"Little bird, I think you'll like the stuffed chicken or maybe the angel hair tossed in oil," he tells me, still studying the menu. Anytime we go out the first thing he's looking for on the menu is what I'll like.

"Give us a minute," I say to the waitress, who's still standing there staring at Jordan. I feel my anger start to grow. I know my Jordan would never give another woman the time of day. Even one that looks as pretty as this one but still I don't like how she's eyeing him.

He looks up as if just now noticing the waitress was still standing there. "Can you put in what I already ordered please. My wife is hungry," he says, dismissing her before going back to the menu.

"Maybe I should just order you both. We can take the extra home with us." He looks up at me and reaches across the table, tucking a piece of my hair behind my ear. "Can't wait to have you in our bed with no worries of little ones climbing in. Miss you sleeping naked on top of me." I agree with him but I wouldn't change it for the world. Our girls are everything to us.

At the word "home" my stomach warms because that sounds nice—and not because of the women checking out my husband, but because lying in bed with to-go boxes and being alone for the night sounds wonderful. But I know Jordan wanted to take me out on a date night.

"I'm going to go to the bathroom. Order for me," I tell him. Jordan stands before I can, pulling my chair out for me. He grabs me, taking me into a hard, long kiss. I get lost in him for a moment. "Jordan." I half gasp his name when he finally releases my mouth and I remember that we are in the middle of a busy restaurant.

"Just making sure everyone knows you belong to me before I let you leave my side." I roll my eyes at him but I can't stop my smile. I walk to the bathroom and see the waitress that's been eyeing Jordon watching us. I give her a smug smile. Look all you want but that man is more than mine. I don't even have to worry about you.

I slip in the bathroom and check my lipstick before washing my hands. I look in my purse for my phone, making sure Pops hasn't called before slipping out of the bathroom. When I open the door I see a very pissed-off Jordan standing there. The same waitress from before staring at him with a panicked face.

"No, what you're going to do is step back from me." Jordan's eyes come to me. "Then you're going to say sorry to this woman I'm with who is clearly my wife or I'll be talking to your manager."

The woman looks over at me and stutters out a "sorry" before rushing away.

"I'm so sorry, little bird. I had no idea she'd follow me back here then hit on me." He grabs me, pulling me into his body. His hands cup my face before his mouth lands on mine in a deep but soft kiss.

"Why were you even back here?" I ask. The men's restroom is on the other side. A sheepish look hits his face.

"Just checking on you," he finally says. I can't help but laugh. I was gone maybe three minutes. "You wanna go home? Order takeout and eat in bed?"

"There's nothing more in the world I want to do than that," I tell him before taking his mouth in a kiss this time.

* * * * *

First Meeting

Jordan

"Hey, do you mind taking this up to the top floor for me? I'm on my way to lunch, and you know how Paige is with food," Ryan says, holding out a folder.

I look over his shoulder and see Paige hitting the button for the elevator, then impatiently hitting it three more times in a row.

"Yeah. She's hangry as hell," I say, taking it from him and shaking my head.

She's got that man all kinds of twisted. I've never seen him so far gone before. But he looks happy as hell, so I guess I can't be mad. Deep down, though, I'm really just salty.

I've never had anything even close to the look Ryan has on his face. It eats me up even more when I watch him walk over to Paige and put a possessive hand on her hip. I have to look away, because it makes me so envious and angry. I'm a goddamn virgin, for crying out loud. Not that anyone would know that. I don't talk about my personal life much at work. I don't really talk about much of anything. I keep to myself, and I like it that way.

At least that's what I keep telling myself.

Shaking my head, I stand up, deciding to take the folder upstairs now and grab lunch after. No sense in putting it off. I hop on the elevator and scan my card so I can go straight up without stopping.

On the way, I think about what I'm going to eat and then about seeing Pop this weekend. I need to make sure he's got his posts in for the garden. He'll be ready to put his tomato plants out any day now.

When the elevator doors open, I take a step, then stop dead in my tracks.

I've been up here only once before, and the desk was empty then. I just had to drop the paperwork the CEO was asking for and leave. But this time, there's a woman sitting in front of me, and every cell in my body has just been electrocuted.

Her dark brown hair is in a knot at the back of her neck. She's tucked away a few loose strands to keep them out of her eyes. Her black-framed glasses are on the edge of her nose, and she pushes them up as she reads over something on her desk. Her hand scribbles a note with a pen she's holding, and I think about how delicate those fingers are. How small they would look pressed against my bare chest.

She hasn't looked up to notice me, yet everything in my world has suddenly been swept away by a tsunami. How did she not see it happen? One second I was normal, regular Jordan just like every day before. And then I was hers. There's an invisible line that's just tethered me to her, and I'm forever a changed man. My insides have genetically mutated into a man made to become hers. On the outside, though, nothing has changed.

The doors to the elevator try to close and end up

squishing me. I let out a grunt, pushing on them to make them open, and step off the elevator fully. When I look back to her, I see she's staring at me.

Chocolate-brown eyes meet mine, and my mouth falls open. Jesus Christ, how can one woman be so beautiful? Is this legal? Are there petitions going around to ban this sort of attractiveness? She can't be real.

"Can I help you?" she asks, smiling at me like an angel.

Her lips are kind and indulgent, and God help me I want to ravage her like some sort of romance hero. I want to reach over and push everything off the desk, then crawl over the top of it and claim what belongs to me.

She clears her throat, and I blink, realizing I've just fallen down a rabbit hole of total desire.

"A file," I say, and her perfect brows draw together in confusion. I lick my lips and try again. "I've got a file."

"I can see that," she says, looking down at my hand and then back to me.

There's a list forming in my head of illegal things that I would do in order to have those eyes look at me for the rest of my life.

"It's for Mr. Osbourne," I say, taking another step forward.

She stands up from her desk, and God she's so short. I bet if I were on top of her she'd disappear under me. The thought sends a warm tingle down my spine, and then my mind wanders to how easy she would be to pick up, how slight she is compared to me. I could protect her and keep her safe without much effort.

I blink and see she's got her hand out, waiting on the folder, but she must have been in that position for quite some time because she drops it and walks around the desk to take it from me. I feel the file slip from my fingers, and panic begins to take over. I'm not ready to leave.

"Hmm. This is the Lannister folder," she says, flipping it open and thumbing through the pages.

I clench my fists so tight my knuckles turn white as I itch to tuck a strand of hair behind her ear.

"I swear this deal is going to be a pain in my butt. I can already see it. It's got to go back to Stein and he's always avoiding my emails. I know most of the time I'm just hungry, and you know what they say about not eating. It makes you more irritated. Hangry, that's it!" She looks down at her watch and then back to me. "I'm about to starve to death. Do you want to go downstairs to the cafeteria and eat with me? I don't know you, but you work here, and there's never anyone on this floor to go with, so I thought I might as well ask the only other person I've seen. Are you hungry, or did you already eat?"

Her voice washes over me, and I stand there like an idiot. She asked me a question, but she's going a million miles an hour and I don't know where to begin. I think I must nod, because she smiles at me, and I want her to keep doing it.

"Great. I'll grab my wallet. Oh, and let me make sure the coffeepot is off. There's nothing worse than the smell of burnt coffee. I forgot once and left just a tiny amount in the bottom, and the warmer was still on. It scorched the bottom of the pot, and it took me a week to get the smell out. And it's not like you can just open a window on the top floor."

She flits around the office, and all I can compare

it to is a bird. She's talking nonstop, but I love it. The sound of her voice, the way she's buzzing around the room. It's like she's a tiny tornado of love that's been sent to turn my world upside down.

She comes over beside me when she's done and looks at me expectantly. "Ready?"

I guess I nod again, because she hits the elevator button and we step on.

"Oh, I'm Jay, by the way."

"Jordan," I say, and she smiles even bigger at me.

Could I repeat my name to her over and over? Would that be weird? I just want to see her smile like that forever, and I don't care how it happens.

Her voice fills the elevator as she talks about what will be down there to eat today. How it's gotten so much better since Mr. Osbourne had the whole thing redone. I listen, not wanting to miss a word, but having a hard time concentrating when the woman of my dreams is inches away from me. I'm trapped in a metal box with the person I've been waiting my whole life for, and I can't do anything about it. This is truly what torture is.

"Oh good, the line isn't long," she says once we exit and grab trays.

She piles her plate high with food, and I'm actually impressed. I love a woman who can eat, and for someone her size, she isn't afraid of food. I put extra on mine, thinking about what she's going to eat after she's finished with hers. What if she gets hungry later? Who will provide for her?

Then the thought that she might have someone in her life makes me livid. I look down at her finger and don't see a ring. She could be married, but if a man were with her and not smart enough to mark her as taken, then he doesn't deserve her. I never thought about breaking up a marriage before, but there seems to be a time and a place for everything all of a sudden.

"Husband?" I ask as we stand in front of the soups.

"That's a weird choice," she says, looking down in all the pots.

"Do you have a husband," I ask, and she lets out a laugh.

"Oh!" she says, and waves her hand. "The Italian wedding soup. I see what you did there. No, I'm not married. You?"

I shake my head, and she smiles. "Well, I guess it's good we're friends now. We don't have to eat alone."

She takes her tray to the cashier, and the word *friends* echoes in my ears. Hold up. Did she just send me directly to friend zone? I didn't get to pass go or collect a phone number at least? How is she not holding herself back from ripping my clothes off? Am I the only one who feels what's happening right now?

I look around the room and see everyone going about their day. I want to slam my tray down and ask why the hell no one notices that I've just fallen in love with the most beautiful woman in the world. How come this isn't headline news?

"Jordan?" Jay says my name, and suddenly I'm putty in her hands.

I walk over and set my tray down beside hers, pulling out my wallet. "I've got this," I tell her, and hold out my money for the both of us.

"That's so nice of you. Thank you," she says as we walk to a table in the corner. "I didn't ask you so you'd treat me."

"Friends," I say, rolling the word around on my

tongue. I sound like fucking Tarzan learning English with her.

"Sounds good to me," she says as she reaches her hand over and pats the top of mine.

I sit frozen as she takes her hand back, and I want to reach out and yank it over to me. I want to take it and press it to my face and tell her all my deepest, darkest secrets.

"Oh wow, this soup is awesome. Good choice."

I watch her eat and then talk to me. She's completely comfortable, and I could sit here for hours. The sound of her voice is like music, the most beautiful symphony I've ever heard. Her eyes see straight into my soul, and I can't look away.

"Aren't you hungry?" she asks, looking between my full tray and hers, almost halfway finished.

As if she's given me a command, I do as she says and start to eat. When she starts telling me all the places in the city she loves to eat, I make mental notes about each and every one of them. Why didn't I bring a pen and paper? I don't want to forget anything.

I make it my life's mission right then to make sure that I know as much about her as I can. To absorb every little detail so that when I make her mine, I'll also make her happy.

My tray is almost empty, and I've got an extra cookie for her on it. I pick it up and put it on her tray, and the beaming smile she gives me is almost enough to do me in.

"You know the way to a lady's heart," she says, taking a bite of it.

Food is the way I'll make her fall in love with me. My pop always told me that was the secret of his happy marriage to my mom. He kept her fed and remembered all her favorites. Could it really be that simple? I'm starting to think the old man was right.

She glances down at her watch, and her eyes get big. "Damn, I'm late. This was so nice, Jordan. I'm glad to have finally made a friend at work. Do you want to do lunch again tomorrow? I don't think I have anything planned, but sometimes my calendar shifts around. I could always email you since I know where you work." She laughs at her own joke, and I just nod dumbly. "Okay, perfect. I'll shoot you an email tomorrow. This is always quick and easy for me, so is the cafeteria okay?"

I nod again, and this time she gives me a shy smile. "I know I talk a lot. Maybe next time I'll let you get a word or two in."

She clears up her empty tray and waves over her shoulder as she heads for the elevator.

I don't know how long I sit there, but it must be a while because when I look up, Paige is standing over me.

"Seriously, Jordan? I had to check the camera to find you."

"Sorry, I was having lunch," I say, and stand up to see the room empty.

"Yeah. And now it's time to go," she says, looking at me like I'm an idiot.

Sure enough, the sun has set, and I've been sitting here all day thinking about my brown-eyed beauty and how I've just met the woman I'm going to marry.

"Hey, you okay?" Paige asks as we leave.

"Yeah," I say, smiling. "I've never been better."

Her eyes narrow, and then they get big. "Oh shit," she exclaims, shaking her head. "I know that look."

"What look?" I ask.

She laughs mirthlessly. "Sorry, buddy. I hate to be the one to tell you, but you just got claimed."

I feel the smile pull at my lips, loving the sound of it. Jay definitely claimed me.

For more books from Alexa Riley,
visit alexariley.com.

Acknowledgments

We say thank you a lot to Carina Press, but they're the reason you've got this book in your hands. They took a chance on the two of us, and brought the For Her series to the light of day. We are forever grateful that you believed in our stories, and in us. A special thanks to our editor Angela James for letting us be us and not complaining about all the times we went overboard. Oysters and drinks soon, doll face!

Thank you to our entourage that kept us sane in the group chat, sent us food when we needed it most, and never let us forget that we are loved. You'll never have any idea what you mean to us, and our books. We wouldn't be here if it wasn't for our bird, panda, and sensei leading the way.

To our readers. Everything For Her was a giant leap of faith and we are so happy that you took it with us. Thank you for all of the kind emails, messages, and hugs you've given us as this series has grown and become more than we could have dreamed possible. You are the reason we put the words on the page…because most of the time you won't stop yelling at us until it's finished! We are forever humbled by your praise.

To our husbands…grab the tequila. It's time to celebrate!

About the Author

Alexa Riley is a pseudonym for the sassy dynamic duo of Melissa King and Lea Robinson. Both are married moms of two who love football, doughnuts and obsessed heroes in novels. They bonded over their love of steamy reads in the summer of 2013 and haven't been able to stop talking since. As a team, they are *New York Times* and *USA TODAY* bestselling authors.

Alexa Riley specializes in insta-love, over-the-top sweet and cheesy love stories that don't take all year to read. If you want something safe, short and always with a happily-ever-after, then these are your girls.

Connect with Alexa Riley!

AlexaRiley.com
Facebook.com/AlexaRileyAR
Twitter.com/_AlexaRiley
Instagram.com/AuthorAlexaRiley

*Love your heroes a lot on the protective side
and totally in love with their women?
Meet the* MEN OF HAVEN
*Jace will go to any lengths to protect
and care for Vivian in*
ROUGH & TUMBLE *by Rhenna Morgan*

*"Rough & Tumble by Rhenna Morgan will warm
your heart and melt your panties."*
—*#1* New York Times *bestselling author
Audrey Carlan (Calendar Girl series)*

Chapter One

Nothing like a New Year's Eve drunk-sister-search-and-rescue to top off a chaos-laden twelve-hour workday. Vivienne dialed Shinedown's newest release from full blast to almost nothing and whipped her Honda hybrid into a pay-by-the-hour lot in the heart of Dallas's Deep Ellum. Five freaking weekends in a row Callie had pulled this crap, with way too many random SOS calls before her current streak.

At least this place was in a decent part of town. Across the street, men and women milled outside a new bar styled like an old-fashioned pub called The Den, with patrons dressed in everything from T-shirts and faded jeans, to leather riding gear and motorcycle boots. Not one of them looked like they were calling the party quits anytime soon.

Viv tucked her purse beneath the seat, stashed her key fob in her pocket, and strode into the humid January night. Her knockoff Jimmy Choos clicked against the aged blacktop, and cool fog misted her cheeks.

Off to one side, an appreciative whistle sounded between low, masculine voices.

She kept her head down, hustled through the dark double doors and into a cramped, black-walled foyer. A crazy-big bouncer with mocha skin and dreads leaned against the doorjamb between her and the main bar, his attention centered on a stunning brunette in a soft pink wifebeater, jeans, and stilettos.

The doors behind her clanged shut.

Pushing to full height, the bouncer warily scanned Viv head to toe. Hard to blame the guy. Outside of health inspectors and liquor licensing agents, they probably didn't get many suits in here, and she'd bet none of them showed up in silk shirts.

"ID," he said.

"I'm not here to stay. I just need to find someone."

He smirked and crossed his arms. "Can't break the rules, momma. No ID, no party."

"I don't want a party, I want to pick up my sister and then I'm out. She said she'd be up front. About my height, light brown, curly hair and three sheets to the wind?"

"You must mean Callie," the brunette said. "She was up here about an hour ago mumbling something about *sissy*, so I'm guessing you're her." She leaned into Scary Bouncer Dude's formidable chest, grinned up at him, and stroked his biceps with an almost absentminded reverence. "May as well let her in. If you don't, Trev will spend closing time hearing his waitresses bitch about cleaning up puke."

Too bad Viv didn't have someone to bitch to about getting puke detail. Callie sure as heck never listened.

Bouncer dude stared Viv down and slid his mammoth hand far enough south he palmed the brunette's ass. He jerked his head toward the room beyond the opening. "Make it quick. You might be old enough, but the cops have been in three times tonight chomping to bust our balls on any write-up they can find."

Finally, something in her night that didn't require extra time and trouble. Though if she'd been smart, she'd have grabbed her ID before she came in.

"Smart move, chief." The woman tagged him with a fast but none-too-innocent kiss, winked, and motioned for Viv to follow. "Come on. I'll show you where she is."

An even better break. The last search and rescue had taken over thirty minutes in a techno dance bar. She'd finally found Callie passed out under a set of stairs not far from the main speakers, but the ringing in Viv's ears had lasted for days. At least this time she'd have a tour guide and an extra pair of hands.

The place was as eclectic on the inside as it was out. Rock and movie collectibles hung on exposed brick walls and made the place look like it'd been around for years even though it reeked of new. Every table was packed. Waitresses navigated overflowing trays between the bustling crowd, and Five Finger Death Punch vibrated loud enough to make conversation a challenge.

The brunette smiled and semi-yelled over one shoulder, never breaking her hip-slinging stride. "Nice turnout for an opening week, yeah?"

Well, that explained the new smell. "I don't do crowds." At least not this kind. Signing her dad's Do Not Resuscitate after a barroom brawl had pretty much cured her of smoky, dark and wild. "It looks like a great place though."

The woman paused where the bar opened to a whole different area and scanned Viv's outfit. "From the looks of things, you could use a crowd to loosen up." She shrugged and motioned toward the rear of the room.

"Corner booth. Last I saw your girl she was propped up between two airheads almost as hammered as she was. And don't mind Ivan. The cops are only hounding the owner, not the customers. My name's Lily if you need anything." And then she was gone, sauntering off to a pack of women whooping it up at the opposite end of the club.

So much for an extra set of hands. At least this part of the bar was less crowded, scattered sitting areas with every kind of mismatched chair and sofa you could think of making it a whole lot easier to case the place.

She wove her way across the stained black concrete floors toward the randomly decorated booths along the back. Overhead, high-end mini sparkle lights cast the room in a muted, sexy glow. Great for ambience, but horrid for picking drunk sisters out of a crowd. Still, Viv loved the look. She'd try the same thing in her own place if it wouldn't ruin the tasteful uptown vibe in her new town house. Funky might be fun, but it wouldn't help with resale.

Laughter and a choking cloud of smoke mushroomed out from the corner booth.

The instant Viv reached the table, the chatter died. Three guys, two girls and the stench of Acapulco Red— but no sister. "You guys see Callie?"

A lanky man with messy curly blond hair eyed her beneath thirty-pound eyelids and grinned, not even bothering to hide the still smoldering joint. "'Sup."

The redhead cozied next to him smacked him on the shoulder and glowered. "She's after Callie, Mac. Not stopping in for a late-night chat." She reached across the table and handed Viv an unpaid bar tab. "She headed to the bathroom about ten minutes ago, but be sure you take this with you. She stuck me with the bill last night."

Seventy-eight bucks. A light night for New Year's Eve, which was a damn good thing considering Viv's bank balance. She tucked the tab in her pocket. "Which way to the bathroom?"

The girl pointed toward a dark corridor. "Down that hall and on your left."

Viv strode in that direction, not bothering with any follow-up niceties. Odds were good they wouldn't remember her in the morning, let alone five minutes from now.

Inside the hallway, the steady drone of music and laughter plunged to background noise. Two scowling women pranced past her headed back into the bar. One glanced over her shoulder and shook her head at Viv. "May as well head to the one up front. Someone's in that one and isn't coming out anytime soon from the sound of things."

Well, shit. This was going to be fun. She wiggled the knob. "Callie?"

God, she hoped it was her sister in there. Knowing her luck, she was interrupting a New Year's booty call. Although, if that were the case, they were doing it wrong because it was way too quiet. She tried the knob again and knocked on the door. "Callie, it's Viv. Open up."

Still no answer.

Oh, to hell with it. She banged on the door and gave it the good old pissed-off-sister yell. "Callie, for the love of God, open the damned door! I want to go home."

A not so promising groan sounded from inside a second before the door marked Office at her right swung

wide. A tall Adonis in jeans and a club T-shirt embla-
zoned with The Den's edgy logo blocked the doorway,
his sky blue eyes alert in a way that shouldn't be possible past 1:00 a.m.

Two men filled the space behind him, one shirtless
with arms braced on the top of a desk, and another
leaning close, studying the shirtless guy's shoulder. No
wait, he wasn't studying it, he was stitching it, which
explained the seriously bloody shirt on the floor.

"Got more bathrooms up front. No need to break
down the damned door." Adonis Man ambled toward
her, zigzagging his attention between her and the bathroom. "There a problem?"

Dear God in heaven, now that the Adonis had moved
out of the way, the shirtless guy was on full, mouthwa-
tering display, and he was every book boyfriend and in-
decent fantasy rolled up into one. A wrestler's body, not
too big and not too lean, but one hundred percent solid.
A huge tattoo covered his back, a gnarled and aged tree
with a compass worked into the gothic design. And his
ass. Oh hell, that ass was worth every torturous hour in
front of her tonight. The only thing better than seeing
it in seriously faded Levi's would be seeing it naked.

"Hey," Adonis said. "You gonna ogle my brother
all night, or tell me why you're banging down one of
my doors?"

They were brothers? No way. Adonis was all…well,
Adonis. The other guy was tall, dark and dirty.

Fantasy Man peered over his injured shoulder.
Shrewd, almost angry eyes lasered on her, just as dark
as his near-black hair. A chunk of the inky locks had
escaped his ponytail and fell over his forehead. His
closely cropped beard gave him a sinister and deadly

edge that probably kept most people at a distance, but his lips could lull half the women in Texas through hell if it meant they'd get a taste.

Viv shook her head and coughed while her mind clambered its way up from Smutville. "Um…" Her heart thrummed to the point she thought her head would float off her shoulders, and her tongue was so dry it wouldn't work right. "I think my sister's passed out in there. I just want to get her home."

Adonis knocked on the door and gave the knob a much firmer twist than Viv had. "Zeke, toss me the keys off the desk."

Before either of the men could move, the lock on the door popped and the door creaked open a few inches. "Vivie?" Callie's mascara-streaked face flashed a second before the door slipped shut again.

Months of training kicked in and Viv lurched forward, easing open the door and slipping inside. "I've got it now. Give me a minute to get her cleaned up and gather her stuff."

Adonis blocked the door with his foot. The black, fancy cowboy boots probably cost more than a month's mortgage payment, which seemed a shame considering it didn't look like she'd be able to pay her next one. "You sure you don't need help?"

"Nope." She snatched a few towels out of the dispenser and wetted them, keeping one eye on Callie where she semi-dozed against the wall. "We've done this before. I just need a few minutes and a clear path."

"All right. My name's Trevor if you need me. You know where we are if you change your mind." He eased his foot away, grinned and shook his head.

"Oh!" Viv caught the door before it could close all

the way and pulled the bar tab out of her pocket. "My sister ran up a tab. Could you hold this at the bar for me and let me pay it after I get her out to the car? I need to grab my purse first."

He backtracked, eyeballed Callie behind her, and crumpled the receipt. "I'd say you've already covered tonight." He turned for the office. "We'll call it even."

Fantasy Man was still locked in place and glaring over one shoulder, the power behind his gaze as potent as the crackle and hum after a nearby lightning strike.

She ducked back into the bathroom and locked the door, her heart jackrabbiting right back up where it had been the first time he'd looked at her. She seriously needed to get a grip on her taste in men. Suits and education were a much safer choice. Manners and meaningful conversation. Not bloody T-shirts, smoky bars and panty-melting grins.

Snatching Callie's purse off the counter, she let out a serrated breath, shook out the wadded wet towel, and started wiping the black streaks off her sister's cheek. A man like him wouldn't be interested in her anyway. At least, not the new and improved her. And the odds of them running into each other again in a city like Dallas were slim to none, so she may as well wrangle up her naughty thoughts and keep them in perspective.

On the bright side, she didn't have to worry about the tab. Plus, she had a fresh new imaginary star for her next late-night rendezvous with BOB.

Damn if this hadn't been the most problematic New Year's Eve in history. It wasn't Jace's first knife wound, but getting it while pulling apart two high-powered, hot-headed drug dealers promised future complications he didn't need. Add to that two more customers arrested at his own club, Crossroads, in less than three days, and nonstop visits from the cops at The Den, and his New Year wasn't exactly top-notch.

Thank God his brother Zeke wasn't working trauma tonight or he'd have had to have Trev stitch him up. That motherfucker would've hacked the shit out of his tat.

"You 'bout done?" Jace said.

Zeke layered one last strip of tape in place and tossed the roll to the desk. "I am now."

"Took you long enough." Jace straightened up, tucked the toothpick he'd had pinched between his fingers into his mouth and rolled his shoulder. It was tight and throbbing like a son of a bitch, but not bad enough to keep him from day-to-day shit—assuming he didn't have any more drug dealer run-ins.

"I don't know. Our straitlaced partygoer didn't seem to mind me taking my time." Zeke packed his supplies into one of the locked cabinets, the same triage kit they kept at every residence or business they owned. It might have been overkill, but it sure as hell beat emergency rooms and sketchy conversations with police. "Thought for a minute there the sweet little thing was going to combust."

"Sweet little thing my ass." Trevor dropped into his desk chair, propped his booted feet on the corner of his desk, and fisted the remote control for the security vids mounted on the wall. "I'd bet my new G6 that woman's got a titanium backbone and a mind that would whip both your asses into knots."

Jace snatched a fresh white club T-shirt from Trev's grand-opening inventory and yanked it over his head, the wound in his shoulder screaming the whole time.

"Based on what? Her courtroom getup or her uptight hairdo?"

"Like I judge by what people wear. You know me better than that." Trev punched a few buttons, paused long enough to eyeball the new bartender he'd just hired ringing in an order on the register, then dropped the remote on the desk. "You ask me, you're the one judging. Which is kind of the pot calling the kettle black."

The setback hit its mark, the Haven tags he wore weighting his neck a little heavier, a reminder of their brotherhood and the code they lived by.

It's not where a man comes from, or what he wears, that matters. It's what he does with his life that counts.

Twenty-seven years he and Axel had lived by that mantra, dragging themselves out of the trailer park and into a brotherhood nothing but death would breach.

"He's right," Zeke said. "You're letting Paul's campaign crawl up your ass and it's knockin' you off course."

Damn, but he hated it when his own mantras got tossed back at him. More so when he deserved it. He let out an exhausted huff and dropped down on the leather couch facing the string of monitors. "Play it again."

Trevor shook his head but navigated the menu on the center screen anyway.

"Not sure why you're doing this to yourself, man." Zeke pulled three Modelos out of the stainless mini-fridge under the wet bar and popped the tops faster than any bartender. God knew he'd gotten enough experience working as one through med school. "Paul's a politician with a grudge, nothing else. Watching this again is just self-inflicted pain. Focus on the real problem."

Jace took the beer Zeke offered as the ten o'clock

news story flashed on the screen. The third-string reporter's too-bright smile and pageant hairdo screamed of a woman with zero experience but eager for a shot at a seat behind the anchor desk.

"Dallas's popular club, Crossroads, is in the news again this New Year's Eve as two additional patrons were arrested on charges of drug possession with intent to distribute. Undercover police are withholding names at this time, but allege both are part of a ring led by Hugo Moreno, a dealer notorious in many Northeast Texas counties for peddling some of the most dangerous products on the street."

"She's not wrong on that score." Zeke plopped on the other end of the couch and motioned to the screen with his bottle. "The number of ODs coming in at Baylor and Methodist the last six months have been through the roof. The guys from DPD swear most are tied to some designer shit coming out of Moreno's labs."

Trevor leaned in and planted his elbows on the desk, eyes to Jace. "You think Otter's going to hold out long enough to waylay Moreno?"

If Jace knew the answer to that one, he'd be a lot less jumpy and minus one slash to his shoulder. Pushing one pharmaceutical genius out of his club by strong-arming him with another was a risky move at best, but it sure as shit beat ousting Moreno on his own. "Otter's a good man with a calm head on his shoulders and a strong team. If he says he'll only let weed in the place and keep Hugo at bay, I'm gonna give him all the backing he needs. DPD's sure as hell not going to help. Not the ones in Paul's pockets, anyway."

"Paul doesn't have any pockets," Trev said. "Only his daddy does."

Right on cue, the camera cut to an interview with Paul Renner as reporters intercepted him leaving another political fundraiser.

"Councilman Renner, you've been very vocal in your run for U.S. Representative in supporting the Dallas Police Department's efforts to crack down on drug crime, and have called out establishments such as Crossroads in midtown Dallas. Have you heard about the additional drug arrests there tonight, and do you have any comments?"

Renner frowned at the ground, a picture-perfect image of disappointment and concern. Like that dickhead hadn't been trying to screw people since his first foray from the cradle.

"I continue to grow more concerned with establishments like those run by Jace Kennedy and his counterparts," Renner said. *"It seems they continually skirt justice and keep their seedy establishments open for business. It's innocent citizens who end up paying the price, courted by heinous individuals peddling dangerous substances and amoral behavior. My primary goal, if elected to the House of Representatives, will be to promote legislation that makes it difficult for men like Mr. Kennedy and Mr. Moreno to escape justice."*

The toothpick between Jace's teeth snapped in half. He tossed it to the coffee table in front of him and pulled another one of many stashed in the pocket of his jacket.

"It's official, now." Trevor raised his beer in salute and tipped his head. "You're an amoral son of a bitch leading innocent citizens to ruin."

Motion registered in one of the smaller security screens, the bathroom door outside Trevor's office swinging open enough to let Little Miss and her seriously drunken sister ping-pong down the hallway. The two were about the same height, but you couldn't have dressed two women more differently. Next to Little Miss, her sister was best suited for a biker bar, all tits, ass and wobbling heels. Not that she was bad to look at. She just lacked the natural, earthy grace of the sober one.

Damn it, he needed to pace. Or get laid. Just looking at the ass on Little Miss in tailored pants made him want to rut like a madman. Never mind the puzzle she presented. Trev wasn't wrong—she had a shitload of backbone blazing through those doe-shaped eyes. The combination didn't jive with her image. Nothing like a paradox to get his head spinning.

"Guess we found one way to get his head off Renner." Zeke knocked back another gulp of his beer.

"What?" He back-and-forthed a glare between his brothers.

Trevor chuckled low and shifted the videos so Little Miss's trek to the front of the bar sat center stage. "Zeke said the only thing you've done amoral was that freak show you put on with Kat and Darcy at last month's barbecue."

"Fuck you, Trev."

"Fuck her, you mean," Trev said. "No shame there, brother. You didn't even see her up close. If you did, you sure as shit wouldn't be sitting here rerunning sound bites of asshole Renner."

"Hell, no," Jace said. "A woman that uptight is the last thing I need. Or did you miss her casing not just Zeke patching up my shoulder, but the bloody shirt on the floor, too? You'll be lucky if the cops don't show from an anonymous tip called in."

Little Miss and her sister stumbled into the front
section of the bar, the sister's arm curled around Little
Miss's neck in a way he'd bet would still hurt tomorrow morning.

Nope. Sweet hips, fiery eyes and a good dose of mystery or not, she was the last thing he needed right now.

Two men blocked Little Miss's path.

The women stopped, and the drunk sister swayed
enough it was a wonder she didn't topple onto the table
beside her.

One of the men palmed the back of Little Miss's
neck, and she jerked away.

Jace surged to his feet, grabbing his leather jacket
off the table. "I'm headed to Haven. You hear more
from Axel at Crossroads or get any more grief from
the cops, let me know."

Both men let out hardy guffaws and waved him off.

"Twenty bucks says our buttoned-up guest gets some
help on the way out the door," Trev said.

Zeke chimed in behind him. "Yeah, let us know if
Sweet Cheeks tastes as good as she looks."

Bastards. The sad thing was, Trev was about to score
a twenty from Zeke, because Jace might not be willing to curl up with Little Miss, but he wasn't watching
men paw her either.

Chapter Two

Viv tightened her arm around Callie's waist and shook off the not-so-shy behemoth of a man gripping the back of her neck. His height alone was enough to make him intimidating, but paired with his shaved head and leathers, the scary vibe packed an extra punch. "I appreciate the offer, but we'll be fine."

"Ah, come on, darlin'." He stepped closer and shot a quick, conspiratorial grin at his cohort in crime, a much smaller guy who more than made up in the shaggy hair department what Cue Ball was missing. "Just trying to help out. Can't have a pretty thing like you out on the streets alone this time of night."

Stupid, stubborn men. One thing about guys who lived and breathed a hard life, they seemed to think the word *no* was a coy version of *maybe*. She feigned an innocent smile as best she could with Callie wrenching her neck. "Well, before I take you up on that, I should warn you, Callie's probably about five minutes from puking on anything or anyone within a twenty-foot radius. Seeing as how I'm right next to her, that would include me. You still up for helping?"

The mood killer worked even better than she expected, dousing the naughty gleam in both men's eyes faster than the people at the table behind them downed their shots. The big guy stepped back and waved her through without another word.

Viv half laughed and half scoffed, leaning into her first few steps to get some extra forward momentum.

Callie staggered closer and nuzzled next to Viv, her words coming out in a drunken, sleepy slur. "Thanks for coming to get me, Vivie." The scent of tequila and other things Viv didn't want to contemplate blasted across her nose and riled what little was left of the snack she'd pilfered at the New Year's Eve party. "You're a good sister. I can always count on you."

An uncomfortable pang rattled in her chest, memories of coming home to an empty apartment when Mom and Dad should've been there clanging together all at once. Family was supposed to be there for one another. To love each other and have their backs, not leave them to grapple with life all alone. "Yeah, Callie. I'm here. Always."

The bouncer who'd let her in took one look at her sister and stepped out of hurling range. "See you found your girl."

"I did, thanks." She shouldered the main door open and braced when Callie stumble-stepped down to the sidewalk. A little farther and she'd be home free, or at least in a place where she could battle the rest of the night barefoot in a comfy pair of sweats.

Behind her, the bar door chunked open, and a few of the people crowded in front of the bar called out goodnights and wishes for a happy new year to whoever had come out.

Viv stepped out onto Elm Street, Callie pinned to her hip.

Midstride, Callie lurched and waved to someone across the street. "Stephanie!" The unexpected happy dance knocked them both off center. Callie fisted Viv's hair in a last-ditch grasp to stay upright, but wrenched Viv's neck before she went sideways.

Viv stumbled, heels teetering on the blacktop and arms flailing for purchase.

Callie smacked her head on the curb.

Viv braced for her own impact, but strong arms caught her, her back connecting with a warm, solid chest instead of the painful concrete she'd expected.

A deep, rumbling voice rang out behind her. "Get Zeke and Trevor out here. See if Danny's still around, too."

She clenched the leather-clad arms around her waist and fought to catch a steady breath.

The bouncer hurried into the street and kneeled beside Callie, gently lifting her so her head rested on his lap.

This fucking night. This horrid, embarrassing, fucking night. Behind her, murmurs and giggles from bystanders grew by the second. Her mind pushed for her to get up, deal with Callie, and get home where it was safe, but her body wouldn't move, mortification and the flood of adrenaline rooting her in place.

The man behind her tightened his hold as though he sensed her self-consciousness. "We got this, sugar." The tiny movement made the leather of his jacket groan. His scent permeated her haze, a sea-meets-sun combination that made her think of Mediterranean islands and lazy days on the beach, not at all what she'd expect from a man coming out of the dive behind her. He sifted his fingers through her freed hair, moving it to one side of her neck, and a stray bobby pin clattered to the asphalt. "Your neck all right? Your sister gave it a hell of a snap."

That voice. Every word radiated through her, grated and deep like the rumbling bass of a stereo cranked up too loud.

He stroked her nape, the touch confident and not the least bit platonic.

Her senses leaped to attention, eager for more of the delicious contact. It was all she could do to hold back the moan lodged in the back of her throat. She swallowed and blew out a slow breath instead. "Yeah, I'm fine."

He lifted her upright, and the muscles in his arms and chest flexed around her, tangling what was left of her reasonable thoughts into a hopeless knot.

A man jogged up, hunkered down beside her sister, and opened up a leather duffel. Not just any man, the guy who'd stitched up the hottie in the office.

She surged forward to intervene, but firm hands gripped her shoulders and pulled her back. "Give Zeke a minute to check her out."

Viv twisted, ready to shout at whoever dared to hold her back—and froze. Her breath whooshed out of her like she'd hit the pavement after all.

Fantasy Man grinned down at her, a toothpick anchored at the corner of his mouth. His tan spoke of far more hours in the sun than the surgeon general recommended, and his almost black eyes burned with a wicked gleam that promised loads of trouble. And not necessarily the good kind, judging by the vicious scar marking the corner of one eye.

"Zeke's a trauma doc," he said. "Perks up like a bloodhound if anyone so much as stubs a toe."

Callie moaned, and Viv spun back around to find the doc prodding the back of her sister's neck.

"I know it hurts," Zeke said. "Can you tell me your name?"

"I don't feel so good," Callie said.

Zeke carefully moved Callie's head back and forth and side to side. "I imagine you don't. Still want to know your name though."

"Callie."

"That's a pretty name." Zeke dug into his duffel and pulled out a penlight. "You know what day it is, Callie?"

Callie's eyes stayed shut, but she smiled like a kid at Christmas and threw her arms out to the side, damn near whacking Trevor as he sat on the curb beside her. "Happy New Year!"

Trevor chuckled and shifted Callie away from the bouncer so she rested against his own chest. "I got her, Ivan. See if you can't find the crowd something else to gawk at."

"You know where you're at, Callie?" Zeke checked her sister's pupils for responsiveness.

As soon as Zeke pulled the light away, Callie blinked and focused on Viv. "I'm with Vivie."

Fantasy Man's voice resonated beside Viv's ear, the tone low enough it zinged from her neck to the base of her spine. "Vivie, huh?"

A shudder racked her and she crossed her arms to combat the goose bumps popping up under her suit jacket.

His arm slipped around her waist from behind and pulled her against his chest, his heat blasting straight through to her skin. "You okay?"

Hell, no, she wasn't okay. Her sister was hurt and

bystanders lined both sides of the street waiting to see what happened next, but all Viv could think about was how his voice would sound up close and in the dark. Preferably between heavy breaths with lots and lots of skin involved. She'd chalk it up to exhaustion, but her nonexistent sex life was probably the real culprit.

"I'm fine. Just tired." She forced herself to step away and faced him, holding out her hand. "And it's Vivienne. Vivienne Moore. Or Viv. Callie's the only one that calls me Vivie."

He studied her outstretched palm, scanning her with languid assessment, then clasped her hand in his and pierced her with a look that jolted straight between her legs. "Jace Kennedy."

Figured that Fantasy Man would have a fantasy name to match. It sounded familiar, too, though with all the pheromones jetting through her body she couldn't quite place where. Maybe wishful thinking or one too many romance novels. She tugged her hand free and stuffed her fists into her pockets. "Thanks for not letting me bust my ass in front of everyone."

He matched her posture and shuttled his toothpick from one side of his mouth to the other with his tongue. "Pretty sure I got the best end of the deal."

Zeke's voice cut in from behind her. "I think she's fine. Just a nasty goose egg and too much booze."

Viv turned in time to see the two men guide Callie to her feet. She weaved a little and looked like she'd fall asleep any second, but the pain seemed to have knocked off a little of her drunken haze. Her floral bohemian top was wrinkled and askew on her curvy frame, and her golden-brown hair was mussed like she'd just had monkey sex. Otherwise, she fit the rest of the crowd a whole lot better than Viv.

Pegging Zeke with a pointed look, Jace cupped the back of Viv's neck. "Check Little Miss out, too. Didn't like the angle her neck took when her girl went down." He focused on Viv and held out his hand, palm up. "Keys."

"What?"

"Keys," he said. "Give 'em to me and we'll bring your car around."

"You don't need to do that." She pointed at the lot across the street. "I'm just over there, and Callie looks—"

"It's almost two in the morning, your sister's hammered, and you both took a fall. Fork over the keys, we'll get your car, pull it around and load your girl up."

Four unyielding stares locked onto her—Zeke, Trevor and Jace, plus a new guy with black hair and a ponytail nearly down to his ass. The way the new guy trimmed his goatee gave him a Ming the Merciless vibe. She shouldn't let any one of these guys near her, let alone surrender the keys to her car. "I think it's better if Callie and I handle it ourselves."

The muscle at the back of Jace's jaw twitched and his eyes darkened.

"I don't mean to sound ungrateful," Viv added. "I appreciate everyone jumping in to help. It's way more than you needed to do. I just don't know you guys. Have you watched the news lately?"

"That's fair." Trevor's focus was locked on Jace when he spoke, but then slid his gaze to Viv. "But this is my bar, your sister drank too much while she was in it, and hurt herself on the way out. It's in my best interest to make sure you make it home safe. Anything bad goes down between here and there, you could give me and my new business a whole lot of heartache I don't need, right?"

Trevor had a point.

"Give me the keys, sugar." Jace crooked the fingers on his outstretched hand. "You've done enough solo tonight."

She handed them over and Zeke stepped in, gently prodding the muscles along the back of her neck. "Any soreness?"

Viv shook her head as much as she could with Zeke's big hands wrapped around her throat.

Behind Zeke, Jace handed off the keys to Ivan. A second later, jogging boot heels rang against the asphalt followed by the chirp of a disengaging car alarm.

Zeke tested her movement side to side and front and back as he'd done for Callie and checked her pupils. "I doubt you'd feel it until tomorrow anyway. Probably wouldn't hurt to take a few ibuprofens before you go to bed." He jerked his head toward Callie, still swaying next to Trevor. "Same goes for her. You'll have a hard time keeping her awake and not puking with as much as she's had to drink, but if she starts to act confused, can't remember things, or complains of ringing in her ears, get her to an ER."

"You got anyone that can help you tonight?" Jace asked.

Trevor piped up. "I can ask one of the girls to stay with you if you want."

"No, I can handle it."

Zeke gave her a knowing look, pulled a card out of his billfold, and handed it over. "You need help, call. We'll get her where she needs to be."

As in to an ER, or a place that had a minimum thirty-day stay? God knew she'd begged her sister to at least try an AA meeting, but Callie and their dad had cornered all the stubborn genes for the fam~~ily~~.

Her hybrid hummed up beside them and Zeke stepped away. "Lay her down in the back, Trev."

The bouncer hopped out of the driver's seat and opened up the back door for Trevor, who'd given up steering Callie and opted for carrying her to the car.

Jace moved in close and lowered his voice. "She get like this a lot?"

The men situated her sister in the backseat.

"Yeah." God, she was tired of this routine. She'd give just about anything to surrender, curl up into a little ball and let someone else handle Callie's tricks for a day or two.

Jace splayed his hand along the small of her back and urged her forward as a big, mean-looking bike with even nastier-sounding pipes rolled up behind her car. "Danny's gonna follow you home and help you get Sleeping Beauty settled in for the night."

"I don't think—"

"If your sister passes out, can you get her in the house on your own?"

"No."

"Then stop thinking and let us handle this," Jace said. "Danny so much as breathes funny, you call the number on Zeke's card and we'll deal with it."

Another good point. After everything they'd done for her tonight, the odds of any of them having bad intentions were pretty slim. And her dog would leave even a big guy like Danny a heaping bloody mess if Viv so much as snapped a finger.

He opened the car door and she slid behind the

wheel, fastening her seat belt in a bit of a daze. "Thank you. For everything."

"Just doing what decent people do." He started to shut her door and stopped. Leaning slightly into her space, he seemed to listen for something, glanced at the stereo display, then eased back. He studied her car, Callie curled up in the backseat, then Viv. His gaze lingered on her hair and he ran a few fingers through the curly strands. "Like it better down. Kinda wild."

Her heart tripped, and the last bit of logic left in her brain poofed to nothing. She clenched the steering wheel and swallowed, grateful to find her mouth wasn't hanging open.

He winked and stepped back. "Take care, sugar."

The car door thumped shut, muting out everything but the quiet strains of Shinedown and Callie's muffled snore.

She put the car in drive and forced her eyes to aim straight ahead. She wouldn't look back. He might've nudged her long-dead sex drive out of a coma, but he was bad news. Everything about him screamed danger and headstrong alpha, and she'd sworn she wouldn't have that kind of life for herself. One look in the backseat showed where that landed a person.

Still, making a right turn onto Highway 75 for her town house in Uptown instead of circling the block for another peek was tempting as hell.

Buy ROUGH & TUMBLE by Rhenna Morgan now
Available wherever Carina Press ebooks are sold.
www.CarinaPress.com

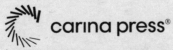

Don't miss the **For You** novella series from
New York Times and #1 ebook bestselling author

ALEXA RILEY

Available now wherever ebooks are sold.

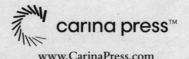

www.CarinaPress.com

Love.
Loyalty.
Meet the Men of Haven.

A self-made man with his fingers in a variety of successful businesses, Jace Kennedy lives for the challenge. From the start, he sees Vivienne Moore's hidden wild side and knows she's his perfect match, if only he can break it free. Earning this woman's trust is a task unlike any he's faced so far, but Jace didn't get where he is by giving up.

Available now wherever books and ebooks are sold.

For those times when size does matter.

The Dirty Bits from Carina Press gives you
what you want, when you want it.
Designed to be read in an hour or two,
these sex-filled micro-romances are guaranteed
to pack a punch and deliver a happily-ever-after.

Grab your copies today!

www.CarinaPress.com

Get 4 **FREE REWARDS!**

We'll send you 2 FREE Books
<u>plus</u> 2 FREE Mystery Gifts.

Harlequin® Romance Larger-Print books feature uplifting escapes that will warm your heart with the ultimate feel-good tales.

FREE
Value Over
$20

31901062681772